DENIAL OF MURDER

Peter Turnbull

severn
House

This first world edition published 2014
in Great Britain and the USA by
SEVERN HOUSE PUBLISHERS LTD of
19 Cedar Road, Sutton, Surrey, England, SM2 5DA

Turnbull, Peter, 1950-
  Denial of murder. – (A Harry Vicary mystery; 4)
  1. Vicary, Harry (Fictitious character)–Fiction.
  2. Murder–Investigation–Fiction. 3. Police–England–
  London–Fiction. 4. Detective and mystery stories.
  I. Title II. Series
  823.9'2-dc23

ISBN-13: 978-0-7278-8297-4 (cased)
ISBN-13: 978-1-84751-507-0 (trade paper)

All Severn House titles are printed on acid-free paper.

Severn House Publishers support the Forest Stewardship Council™ [FSC™],
the leading international forest certification organisation. All our titles that
are printed on FSC certified paper carry the FSC logo.

MIX
Paper from
responsible sources
FSC   FSC® C013056
www.fsc.org

Typeset by Palimpsest [
Falkirk, Stirlingshire, S
Printed and bound in G
TJ International, Padsto

Monday

ONE

Geoff 'the milk' Driscoll found the lifeless-looking body of Gordon Cogan very early one Monday morning in mid-July.

It was, as he would later inform the police, just as the dawn was breaking that Geoff Driscoll turned his battery-powered, cream-coloured, red-lettered milk float into Lingfield Road, Wimbledon, SW19, once again feeling uplifted by the wealth of lush foliage that met his eye. Driscoll was, an observer would note, a man of lithe and sinewy physique, who had been a milkman for in excess of thirty years and, for the greater part of those thirty years, had delivered milk in SW19. Only snow, he found, ever made his round difficult, and that rarely fell in London, but rain and cold and the dark winter mornings he could easily cope with – once he was on his float. On those mornings he ensured that he was always well protected by the waterproof clothing and thermal underwear which he had purchased out of his own pocket, being far superior to the rainwear which was provided by the Merton and South London Dairies, Ltd. There had, occasionally, been those years when Friday, collection day, had fallen on Christmas Eve, thus obliging him and all other milk delivery men in the United Kingdom to work from 5.00 a.m. until approximately 8.00 p.m., when the fatigue forced him to stop collecting for the day. He would then return to the depot, cash in, plug his float into the power supply to recharge the batteries and then travel wearily home, usually arriving too exhausted to do anything but fall into a deep sleep, often in his clothing, and often in an armchair, with the welcoming cup of tea provided for him by his wife – or in later years, by one of his daughters – remaining untouched. It was days like that particular day in July, though, in the middle of the summer in the suburbs of south London, that always made his job seem worthwhile. For here, he found, was south

London at its most well-set, being an area of prestigious housing, which he, as a tenant of a council-owned high-rise flat, could only covet, but he nonetheless enjoyed the calm and settled atmosphere, the mature gardens, the frequent glimpse of suburban wildlife: numerous foxes – too numerous, he felt – and, very occasionally, a badger. Both species, worryingly, thought Driscoll, becoming scavengers rather than the predators which nature had intended them to be, and both species, equally worrying to Driscoll, clearly losing their fear of humans. The wildlife made his round interesting but it was the customers who were the particular source of his enjoyment. They could be reserved at times and also aloof, but they always seemed to appreciate the effort which he put into his job, and always, *always* paid their milk bill, and did so promptly. When Geoff Driscoll had first joined the Dairies he had, as the 'last in', been given the least popular of the rounds, that being the delivery of milk on one of the 'sink' estates where he found the residents unnecessarily surly, and where they frequently avoided paying their milk bill, thus obliging Driscoll to feel that he was harassing them for the outstanding money. He would also often encounter evidence of the previous night's violence on the estate: the burnt-out cars, the broken windows in people's flats, the kicked-in front doors and the pools of dried blood on the concrete. It was also on the sink estate where Driscoll felt that he could not turn his back on the milk float without some person, male or female, pensioner or child, dashing from dark cover to steal a bottle of milk before darting back into the shadows. The cost of stolen milk was deducted from his pay, that being one of the clearly spelled-out conditions of his employment. Turning from the main road into the dull, grey, slab-sided concrete mess that was the housing estate on a cold winter's morning never failed to sink his spirits. Indeed, the very thought of having to drive to the Clifton Towers estate to deliver milk often depressed him to the point that he had to force himself to rise from his bed, especially on the dark mornings when rain was lashing against the windowpanes. Geoff Driscoll felt himself to be trapped because he was the sort of man, not infrequently met, who might be described, and might feel himself to be 'not a people person'. In his life, Driscoll had never known universal popularity. He was, on that particular day, approaching state retirement age and had always felt himself to be the classic square peg in a round hole, never fitting in, always on the edge if not on the outside of any group of colleagues. He was a man who marginalized his life. Any employment which had involved teamwork had proved unsuitable for him and so he found himself pursuing solitary occupations. He was unhappy being a bus driver because the one-man operation involved too much interaction with the public and the frequent traffic jams caused him distress. A postman's job with its very favourable conditions of service would have been ideal for him had it not been for a back injury which prevented him from carrying heavy bags of mail. He had thus gravitated to a job as a milkman with Merton and South London Dairies and started at the 'bottom' delivering to one of the sink estates. He had doggedly stayed at the round, given five years of good service, and his present round had been his reward. That had been some twenty-five years earlier. In that time he had stopped being simply 'the milkman', and had become 'Geoff the milk', being valued by the residents as much as 'Pete the postie' was valued. Here, in 'the village', as it was known, in winter and summer, but especially in the summer, his spirits were lifted each morning by civil humanity combined with nature's bounty. In 'the village' no one stole milk from his float, nor did he ever encounter evidence of any violent act perpetrated during the previous night.

Until that fair Monday morning in mid-July.

The strange, even the oddest thing about the grim discovery, Geoff Driscoll would often, in later weeks and months, recall when telling and re-telling the tale, was that he saw the shoe before he saw the body, even though the latter was in plain sight. The finding of shoes and other items of clothing, even underclothing lying in the roadways or parking bays, or on the pavements was not at all unusual for Driscoll when he delivered milk in Clifton Towers, but finding clothing in the street in Wimbledon Village was, in his experience, utterly unheard of. That morning he had turned into Lingfield Road from the

Ridgeway and the parade of shops, relishing the fresh morning
air and the blue, almost cloudless sky. He'd driven onwards,
leaning forward, resting both his elbows on the steering wheel
as the float whirred slowly along the road under the overhanging
branches when he saw, some one hundred feet ahead of him,
a man's shoe, lying on its side, brown against the dark grey of
the road surface. The shoe lay on 'his' side of the road opposite
a line of parked motor vehicles. Driscoll eyed the shoe with
growing curiosity and slowed the float as he approached it. On
the Clifton Towers estate the shoe would not have merited a
second glance but here, in Wimbledon Village, it was, he
thought, unusual, and one of his late father's often-used expressions, 'The hairs on my old wooden leg tell me something is
amiss', surfaced in Driscoll's mind.

Then he saw the body.

Focusing on the shoe, as he had been, it was thus a few
seconds before he noticed the body lying to the left of it, half
in and half out of the gutter, looking, he thought, like a crumpled pile of unwanted clothing. Geoff Driscoll brought the
float slowly to a halt just in front of the shoe, and nimbly
stepped out on to the road. He approached the body slowly,
with awe and caution. It was, he saw, that of a male – probably, Driscoll guessed, in his late thirties or early forties. The
man, he noted, was in a very bloody mess, particularly about
the head. The body showed no signs of life that Driscoll could
detect. Being of the age he was Driscoll did not, and often
thought himself to be the only person in the Western world
who did not, possess a mobile phone. As a consequence he
ran up the driveway to the front door of the nearest house,
which he saw was a rambling three-storey, late-Victorian
Gothic-style building with a highly complicated roof line and
elaborate turret windows. By then in a state of increasing
agitation, he took the stone steps up to the front door two at
a time, rang the doorbell and, for good measure, rapped the
metal doorknocker – repeatedly so – until he had succeeded
in raising one of the occupants of the house, who opened the
door and presented themselves in the form of a well-built man
with white hair, dressed in a blue Paisley-patterned dressing
gown. The man looked down at the small, gasping for breath

figure of Geoff Driscoll, pulling a facial expression which to Driscoll seemed to be a blend of curiosity and annoyance.

'Sorry, very sorry, sir,' Driscoll panted, 'but I must use your phone . . . or if you could phone . . . the police . . . and an ambulance . . . emergency . . . three nines . . . to come here . . . in the street outside this house . . . right outside your house, sir, if you please . . . Damn me if there hasn't been a murder.'

The householder resolutely remained calm. He was clearly not going to allow himself to be influenced by Driscoll's panic. 'I'll phone the authorities,' he said softly. 'You had better go and stand by whatever it is that you have found, and you'd also better not touch anything.' He then shut the door of his house, closing it with a gentle *click*. It was, Driscoll thought, as he turned to return to the road, as if the man had simply gone to the manual and looked up what to do when someone knocks on your door telling you that a murder had taken place outside your house. There was no anxiety. There was no alarm. There was no panic. Just note the information, close the door, make a phone call and, doubtless, return to bed. That was clearly the way of it in London, SW19.

Detective Inspector Harry Vicary, following Geoff Driscoll's route, turned his car from the Ridgeway into Lingfield Road and instantly saw the police activity ahead of him: the white police cars, with just one keeping its blue light relentlessly lapping; the black, windowless mortuary van; the blue and white police tape strung across the road, delineating the crime scene. Two uniformed constables stood on the outer sides of each tape and were firmly turning back any traffic which approached the area of police interest. One or two local residents, Vicary noted, stood at their windows looking out at the incident, but Wimbledon being Wimbledon, a curious crowd of wide-eyed onlookers had not gathered. The pedestrians, on their way to work, were, like the cars, turned away and, unprotesting, found alternative routes, while those who remained at home, for the most part, just got on with their daily routine. Vicary stopped his car close to the police tape. He walked towards it, and the constable lifted it for him as he drew close, half saluting as Vicary bent to get underneath it. Vicary saw two of his team, Frankie Brunnie and Tom Ainsclough, and he also noted the short, stocky figure of forensic pathologist John Shaftoe, all of whom stood close together, and all of whom turned reverentially to Vicary as he approached them.

'Good morning, sir.' Frankie Brunnie smiled and nodded deferentially to Vicary. Brunnie was senior to Ainsclough and so it was he who spoke. 'Quite a start to the day.' Brunnie was a large man, even for a police officer. He was broad shouldered, wore a neatly trimmed rich black beard and had black hair. 'Thank you for coming, sir. We thought you ought to be in on this, sir, right from the start.'

'All right, Frankie, thank you.' Vicary returned the brief smile. 'What have we got?'

'Deceased male, sir,' Brunnie replied, 'with what appears to be extensive head injuries.'

'Battered to death, if you ask me,' John Shaftoe offered. He was, thought Vicary, dressed in a strange combination of ill-fitting cream summer jacket and heavyweight brown corduroy trousers, which were, Vicary thought, more suited to digging an allotment in winter conditions. 'I can't determine any other injuries, but as you can see he is still clothed, and there may be other injuries as yet to be found. There are no defensive wounds to his hands . . . again, none which are immediately obvious, but the injuries to the head are extensive. I can feel his skull move in separate places and, by themselves, those blows would probably, in fact certainly would have been fatal. It seems that somebody really wanted this fella dead.' John Shaftoe bent down and lifted the heavy-duty plastic sheeting which covered the deceased and exposed the head and shoulders. 'Meet our friend, Mr Still-to-be-identified.'

Harry Vicary considered the deceased. He saw a man of small stature, with short, neatly cut hair, nominally clean-shaven, but then with a little stubble on his chin, seemingly as smartly dressed as a limited budget would permit and, like Geoff Driscoll, he too thought the deceased to be in his late thirties to mid-forties. Vicary also saw a large amount of dried blood matting the hair close to the man's scalp, and also staining his face and neck.

'The police surgeon pronounced life extinct at . . .' Shaftoe turned to Brunnie. 'What was the time again, please, Sergeant?'

'Zero seven sixteen hours.' Brunnie consulted his notepad. 'He, the police surgeon, was one Doctor Paul.'

'Thank you.' Shaftoe replaced the sheet and stood holding his lumbar region as he did so. 'I arrived at approximately eight thirty.'

'An early start for you, sir.' Vicary smiled.

'Yes . . . I had planned to come in early to commence a post-mortem which had been delayed. It's going to be further delayed now but that's the rule, as you know: recent corpses with clear suspicious circumstances come first; they get priority. The first twenty-four hours in any murder case and all that . . . the other PM is in respect of a corpse which was found washed up at Woolwich Reach. I've glanced at the body . . . he must have been in the river for at least a week . . . and so I think that he can afford to wait another few hours.'

'Indeed, sir,' Vicary mumbled. 'Indeed.'

'So . . . I assume that you will want to know the time of death?' Shaftoe grinned widely.

'If you have the information, sir,' Vicary also grinned, 'but I know what you're going to say . . . that's not really a pathologist's job despite the impression given on television police dramas.'

'Yes . . . that's the rule, but common sense tells us that he was still alive a few hours ago . . . it is a reasonably fresh corpse.'

'Who found it?' Vicary asked.

'The milkman, sir,' Brunnie replied. 'He has continued with his round but will be giving a statement later. I have his details. He is adamant that he saw nothing but the corpse . . . no other person or persons acting in a suspicious manner. He's getting on in years, close to retirement, but was really quite calm about it all; at least he was calm by the time I arrived.'

'All right.' Vicary absorbed the information.

'It's a fresh corpse, as you can see,' Shaftoe continued, 'so he was assaulted and murdered last night, sometime before dawn, and his body was then dumped here. There is a little hair growth on the upper lip and chin . . . two days' worth, perhaps . . . it seems to be much more than a five o'clock shadow, though, of course, some men have to shave more frequently than others. I would say that our friend here is normally clean-shaven but did not, or could not, shave for up to forty-eight hours before he was killed. But, of course, hair will continue to grow on a corpse until rigor sets in, so don't let that mislead you.'

'Dumped here?' Vicary queried. 'You don't think he was assaulted here and his body left where he was attacked?'

'Well . . .' Shaftoe paused and looked about him, 'that still has to be determined. Of course, this is very early days, but there is no sign of violence hereabouts . . . not that I can see, anyway . . . the hedgerows are clearly undisturbed, for instance. He must have bled profusely but there is no sign of blood splatter and, believe you me, blood would have splattered far and wide with this sort of injury . . . very far and very wide.'

'One of his shoes, sir,' Brunnie addressed Shaftoe, 'was found a short distance away from the body. In fact, the milkman remarked that he saw the shoe lying in the road before he saw the body in the gutter.' Brunnie then turned to Harry Vicary, 'The shoe is in an evidence bag, sir, but it matches the other shoe that is still on his foot.'

'I see,' Vicary replied, and then turned to Shaftoe for his comment.

'I still don't think he was attacked here,' Shaftoe insisted. 'The shoe could quite easily have fallen off or have been knocked off when the body was removed from whichever motor vehicle was used to transport it here. No . . . no . . . I am certain, the complete absence of blood splatter and lack of localized disturbance means that this site is where the body was dumped. The murder scene is elsewhere. I mean . . . no doubt you'll spray Luminol on the cars parked around here . . . and also on the pavement and the road surface . . . but as I said, my little naked eye cannot detect any blood spatter so I'm sure this is not the crime scene.'

'Fair enough.' Vicary looked about him, glancing up and

down the richly foliaged Lingfield Road, noting it to be long and straight. 'No CCTV,' he remarked. 'That's a shame.'

'The suburbs, sir,' Frankie Brunnie replied. 'It'll be quite a while before the suburbs are covered by CCTV as thoroughly as city centres are covered.'

'If ever,' Vicary growled, sourly, 'if ever. The professional middle-class citizenry won't take too kindly to their every move being monitored. And quite frankly, even as a copper I don't think I would much care for it.'

'Yes, sir.' Brunnie cleared his throat, 'Sir, with respect, I should notify you of another incident the police dealt with last night, also in this area.'

'Oh?' Vicary raised an eyebrow. 'Connected, do you think?'

'Quite probably, sir. It involves a car being set ablaze. Very non-Wimbledon, you might think . . .'

'As you say, Frankie,' Vicary nodded in agreement, 'very non-Wimbledon. Very, *very* non-Wimbledon indeed.'

'We will still have to determine whether the two incidents are connected but Wimbledon Police Station has been notified of the crime number for this incident and any information they might receive about the burnt-out car will be cross-referenced to the Murder and Serious Crime Squad.' Brunnie spoke confidently.

'Good man,' Vicary smiled. 'Where was it burned out? Far from here?'

'Two streets away, sir,' Brunnie advised. 'No CCTV there either, I'm afraid.'

'I see,' Vicary replied softly. 'So it seems that the villains of today are learning to avoid CCTV just as the villains of yesteryear learned to wear gloves when committing felonious acts . . . but . . .' Vicary turned to the immediate location. 'You see it's a very good place to dispose of a body – you've really got to hand it to them. They did a recce . . . they very definitely did a recce, and found a leafy suburb with plenty of foliage to conceal their activity in discarding the body from view – that is, all but the closest of views, at any rate. They placed it in the gutter; if the milkman hadn't found it, it would have been found by the first commuters later in the morning. So then, tell me, what do you do after you have dumped the body?' Vicary looked first at Brunnie, then at Ainsclough, and then at Brunnie again. 'What do you do? Well, I'll tell you what you do . . . you drive your car slowly away to avoid the sounds of a racing engine and squealing tyres. You drive leisurely to a location just two streets away to avoid bringing the police straight to the body, then you torch the vehicle . . . then . . . then what you do is hide in the shrubs of someone's front garden . . . not too close to the burning car . . . make sure you are a few streets away. Then you wait until daybreak and calmly walk away towards the bus station or the Tube station . . . which is?' Vicary turned to Brunnie.

'Wimbledon terminus,' Brunnie replied. 'A very easy walk from here.'

'All right, so he or they then wait until folk start walking to the Tube station or the bus stops, mingling with them, and by their dress they ensure that they are not looking too unusual or too out of place.'

'That's certainly what I would do,' Brunnie growled in the same sour manner in which Vicary had growled a few moments earlier.

'And me,' Tom Ainsclough added. 'That's exactly what I would have done.'

'Likewise myself.' Vicary paused, as if in thought, and then he said, 'You know, gentlemen, I think that it would take at least two people to put this body into a car and then remove it and dump it at the side of the road like this. Possibly one person might be able to do it but, frankly, I would put money on two people doing the deed; at least two persons. I would also say that after torching the car they would have separated and, at dawn at this time of year . . . say about six a.m. and later, when the first commuters emerge, they would have made their own separate ways to the public transport system. Do we know if the police helicopter attended the burning car?'

'We don't, sir,' Brunnie replied, 'but I can easily check.'

'Yes, if you could, Frankie, if you could,' Vicary replied with a warm smile. 'I was thinking that the helicopter's infrared camera might have picked up body heat from someone skulking in the shrubs in the locality and, if so, the local police might have investigated and taken a name, at least a name, and if they did they would have recorded it and told us. So I think we can safely assume the helicopter did not attend. But please check anyway.' Vicary paused. 'We'll have to trawl through the CCTV on the nearest streets, on the buses and on the Tube trains and stations. Tom . . .'

'Yes, sir,' Tom Ainsclough responded eagerly, promptly.

'Can you organize a house-to-house inquiry, please? If someone saw something of relevance I am sure that they would have come forward by now, but a house-to-house will still have to be done, nonetheless.'

'Of course, sir,' Tom Ainsclough replied. 'I'll get on to that right now.' He turned and walked away.

'Good man . . .' Vicary called after the withdrawing figure of Tom Ainsclough. He then addressed Brunnie. 'Any ID?' he asked.

'No wallet has been found, sir,' Brunnie replied. 'But we still have to do a thorough search of his clothing. Some other form of ID may be concealed therein.'

'Very good. So, the post-mortem.' Vicary glanced at John Shaftoe. 'When can it be conducted, sir?'

'I'll do it directly,' Shaftoe replied. 'I have completed my examination at the scene . . . if you've taken all the photographs you need to take . . .?'

'All done,' Brunnie advised, 'black and white and colour, long distance, close-ups from every angle . . . all done . . . all done and dusted.'

'Very well,' Shaftoe rubbed the palms of his hands on his jacket, 'I'll arrange for the body to be immediately removed to the Royal London. Will you be attending for the police, Mr Vicary?'

'Yes,' Vicary replied with finality and nodding his head as he spoke, 'I will be there for the police. For my sins, I will be in attendance.'

John Shaftoe reached up leisurely for the anglepoise arm which was bolted into the ceiling above the stainless steel dissecting table. The corpse of the as yet to be identified male who had, that morning, been found lying in the gutter in a street in a

leafy well-set south London suburb was lying face up on the
table with a starched white towel covering his genitals. Shaftoe
pulled the anglepoise arm downwards until the tip which held
the microphone was level with his mouth. 'Dykk,' Shaftoe
mumbled with undisguised annoyance, 'damn and blast the
wretched man.' Shaftoe turned to Vicary. 'Do you know that
he fought tooth and nail against my appointment here at the
Royal London . . . tooth and nail.'

'Really?' Vicary raised his eyebrows. 'No, sir . . . in fact I
didn't know that,' he replied diplomatically, rather than giving
the truthful answer of 'yes, you've told me many times'. Vicary
stood against the wall of the pathology laboratory in the Royal
London Hospital, Whitechapel and, like Shaftoe and Billy
Button, the mortuary assistant, he was also dressed in green
paper disposable coveralls with a matching hat and slippers,
also disposable after being used once.

'Well, he did but he was jolly well overruled and, being the
grossly immature half-wit he is, he took it personally and has
resented me since the day that I arrived. This is one of his
little games . . . one of his tiny-minded little games. He's quite
a tall man, you see, and I am short, and he likes to push the
microphone up out of my reach.' Shaftoe paused. 'You see,
he . . . the good professor, doesn't think that the sons of
Yorkshire miners, that is when the UK had a coal industry
. . . he doesn't think that the sons of colliers who had modest
local authority educations should be permitted to enter the
elevated ranks of doctors. He is a pain. He is poison. He is
the bane of my life.' Shaftoe paused again, drew breath, and
then continued. 'So . . . a case file number and today's date,
please, Helen.' Shaftoe spoke into the microphone for the
evident benefit of the typist who would, later that day, be
typing up Shaftoe's report on her computer. 'The corpse is
that of a person of the male sex who is Northern European or
Caucasian in respect of his racial extraction.' Shaftoe laid both
of his fleshy hands with their stubby fingers on the edge of
the table and studied the corpse. Vicary noticed with satisfaction that the fingertips of the corpse were blackened with ink,
clearly indicating that the scene of crime officers had already
visited the hospital and taken the fingerprints. He knew it

meant that, if the deceased was previously known to the police, then the man's criminal record would at that moment be on its way to his desk at New Scotland Yard. Vicary further pondered that if the man was not known to the police, he would certainly be known to someone. The trim figure, the usually clean-shaven face, the neat haircut; this man was no socially isolated down-and-out. Somebody would already be missing him; somebody somewhere would soon be walking into a police station and making a missing person's report. If indeed, Vicary pondered, they have not already done so.

'Immediately obvious is extremely severe head trauma to the deceased.' Shaftoe continued to speak into the microphone in a soft yet authoritative voice with a clear Yorkshire accent. 'The head injury caused massive blood loss and was probably the cause of death. It is certainly sufficient to be fatal. No other injuries are in evidence on the anterior aspect and the body overall appears to be well nourished and hydrated.' Shaftoe turned to his left and glanced across the laboratory towards Vicary. 'He didn't experience hunger or thirst before he died . . . at least not for a long time beforehand.'

'Noted,' Harry Vicary replied. 'Thank you.' Vicary then looked across to where Billy Button stood. Vicary had grown to despise him, always finding Button to be a nervous, whimpering wreck of a human being, living in a state of permanent terror of his own death yet strangely, Vicary had always thought, working as a laboratory assistant in a pathology laboratory, rather than, as Vicary had further thought, pushing a lawnmower for whichever London borough he lived in.

'Billy,' John Shaftoe, whom Vicary had observed was always much more accommodating of the timid Button than he could ever be, smiled at the awkward man and asked, 'could you take the feet, please?' Shaftoe then moved to the head of the corpse and took hold of the shoulders. 'Clockwise from your aspect as usual, Billy,' he said, then he counted 'one . . . two . . . three,' and the corpse was turned to lie upon its stomach in a single, clearly well-practised manoeuvre. 'No injuries are noted on the posterior aspect.' Shaftoe spoke into the microphone. 'So back again, please, Billy, one . . . two . . . three,' and together he and Button rotated the corpse once more so that it rested face up on the stainless steel table. Button stooped unasked to pick up the towel which had fallen on the floor during the first rotation and replaced it neatly over the middle of the corpse.

'I have a little problem here, Mr Vicary.' Shaftoe turned to Vicary whilst once again resting both hands on the edge of the table. 'I have to remove the scalp so as to enable me to examine the head injuries . . . That might cause the face to sag . . . and that is going to be a problem if the identification is to be done by relatives viewing using the old mark one eyeball method.'

'We could always use familial DNA,' Vicary suggested. 'I think that destroying the man's appearance is a risk we will have to take if we are going to establish the cause of death. It seems to me that it's unavoidable,' Vicary added as he noticed Billy Button wring his thin wrists, clearly nervous at the prospect of having to watch flesh being peeled back from the skull of the deceased.

'Don't you worry, Billy,' Shaftoe winked mischievously at Button and grinned, 'he won't feel a thing. I promise. Scalpel, please.'

Billy Button, thin of face, forced a meek smile by means of reply as he handed Shaftoe the requested instrument, placing it firmly, handle first, in Shaftoe's palm. Shaftoe took it and confidently drew it around the head of the deceased, just above the level of the ears. He placed the scalpel in a stainless steel tray of disinfectant and then, using both hands, peeled the scalp backwards, causing a slight tearing sound as he separated the scalp from the bone of the skull. 'Ah . . . neater than I thought,' he said to himself. Then, speaking into the microphone, he commented, 'Two linear fractures are noted, both of which caused significant and indeed life-threatening injuries. Would you care to have a look, Mr Vicary?'

Harry Vicary stepped forward, padding silently across the brown industrial-grade linoleum in his paper slippers. He approached the dissecting table and stood next to Shaftoe.

'See this here . . .?' Shaftoe pointed to the skull and with his fingertips traced the line of a fracture which ran around the right side of the skull of the deceased. Shaftoe turned the head. 'Rigor is establishing,' he observed. 'That will help approximate the time of death. I would estimate that he was probably assaulted about six to eight hours ago . . . so say no earlier than about two or three a.m. today but that,' he added with a smile, 'is very unofficial.'

'Yes, sir.' Vicary also smiled. 'Understood. Clear as daylight.'

'Good man. This line was the first blow to be struck,' Shaftoe continued. 'As you can see, it caused a very serious fracture which runs round all the way to the back of the skull, from the side above the ear completely round to the back of the head of the deceased. Then he was struck a second time on the top of the head . . . this fracture just here . . .' Shaftoe put his fingertip close to the second fracture, which Vicary noted ran from the middle of the top of the skull to the back of the skull where it terminated at the line of the first fracture. 'You see how it does not go beyond the fracture line which runs round the back of the skull?'

'Yes, sir,' Vicary replied promptly.

'Well, thanks to this we can tell the order in which the blows were struck because a fracture line will stop if it meets an existing fracture. So the first blow he sustained was this one, running around the side to the back of the skull, then he was struck again on the top of the head, causing a fracture line which then ran down the back of his skull and stopped when it met the first, pre-existing fracture. Both caused extensive bleeding and either could have been fatal.' Shaftoe paused. 'All right . . . so we continue . . . let's look inside the mouth. You know your average gob is invariably a veritable gold mine of information.'

'The gob . . .' Vicary grinned. 'Haven't heard that word for a long time.'

'Yorkshire for mouth.' Shaftoe also grinned.

'Yes, I know,' Vicary replied. 'It's such a lovely word.'

Shaftoe peered into the mouth of the deceased, having prized open the jaws which gave with a soft *crack*. 'Well, I can tell you that he's home grown . . . he's one of us all right, a true Brit . . . or at least a long-term resident of our right little, tight little island. I note British dentistry, so he is not from North America or Continental Europe, or anywhere further afield like Australia or New Zealand. He's a Brit. Or, as I said, a

long-term, very long-term resident here and because of the
British dental work we can use his dental records to establish
his ID, they being just as unique as his fingerprints. I think I
might have preserved the face and so if a relative does come
forward they can view the deceased, identify him and obtain
some measure of closure for themselves, but if a name is
suggested then we can always use dental records . . . Nothing
else of note is in his mouth. There is no food caught in his
teeth so he doesn't appear to have eaten just prior to being
murdered.' Shaftoe paused. 'Speaking of food, let's see what
he had for his last meal.' Shaftoe asked Button to hand him
a scalpel as he patted the stomach of the deceased. 'There has
not been much gas build up as would be in keeping with such
a recently deceased corpse and so there is no need to take a
deep breath.' Shaftoe placed the scalpel at the throat of the
deceased and drove an incision down over the chest to the
bottom of the rib cage. From that point he drove the scalpel
to each of the man's hips, thus creating an inverted 'Y' figure
on the anterior aspect. 'I am making a standard midline incision.' Shaftoe spoke authoritatively to the microphone as he
skilfully manipulated the scalpel. He then peeled back the
folds of flesh revealing the ribs, stomach and other internal
organs. 'The stomach is not distended.' Shaftoe spoke again
for the benefit of the tape. He then punctured the stomach
wall, and as he did so Vicary heard a slight *hiss* as what
stomach gases had built up escaped but, as Shaftoe had
predicted, the pathology laboratory did not fill with sufficient
malodorous air to dislodge the heavy scent of formaldehyde,
as Vicary knew would be the case if a corpse of about seven
days old or older were being dissected.

'Oh . . .' Shaftoe groaned with evident dismay, 'he must
have been quite hungry when he died. I can detect no remnants
of food at all . . . none whatsoever. Yet I still stand by my
earlier observation that he appears to be well nourished. Hunger
and food scarcity was not a constant experience in his life,
but for the last forty-eight hours of it, possibly the last seventy-
two hours, he ate nothing at all. He would have been quite
hungry, even very hungry, but far from starvation. It takes
three weeks for an adult human to starve to death, though

hunger strikers in hospital conditions where no exertion is required of their bodies have lasted nearly thrice that length of time . . . but a man trying to walk to safety out of a wilderness with no shelter can expect to live for three weeks without food and our friend here is far from that point. I can also detect fat deposits . . . and they would be the first to be gobbled up as hunger really sets in, so . . . no food for the last two or three days of his life.' Shaftoe paused. 'I will take a blood sample and use it to test for toxins as well as to extract his DNA, but I am pretty certain that I have found the cause of death . . . blunt force trauma to the head . . . two blows with a linear instrument. The first to the side of the head and the second to the crown or top of his head, both delivered with great force. As I said, either could have been fatal. So one to do the job and a second one to make sure.' He turned to Vicary. 'I will have my completed report faxed to you at New Scotland Yard later today, Mr Vicary.'

'That would be much appreciated. Thank you, sir.' Harry Vicary left the pathology laboratory and walked silently to the changing room where he placed the coveralls in the waste bin provided and then re-dressed in his outer clothing. He left the Royal London Hospital and walked casually to Aldgate East Underground Station where he took the Tube to St James's, and from there walked the short distance to New Scotland Yard. As he had hoped, and indeed as he had half expected, a file on the deceased, having already been identified by his fingerprints, had been placed in his in-tray for his attention.

TWO

The slender file on Gordon Henry Claude Cogan so far made, Harry Vicary found, interesting but not wholly surprising reading. In Vicary's experience, victims whose skulls are splintered and who are then left lying half in and half out of the gutter to await discovery by the first luckless member of the public, in this case the milkman, to chance upon them are usually people with enemies who are also invariably known to the police. Gordon Cogan was no exception. Cogan was, according to the date of birth in his file, forty years old when he was murdered. He had one conviction for the abduction and rape of a minor, and a second conviction for murder. Any other crime(s) that Cogan had committed had either not been solved or not been reported, and there had to be other crimes, Vicary reasoned, because felons who abduct, rape and murder tend to 'graduate' from less serious crimes. What did cause Harry Vicary eyebrow-raising and jaw-dropping astonishment was the seemingly unduly lenient sentence of just six months imprisonment for the offence of abduction and rape of a minor, which was committed when Cogan was in his early twenties. Vicary continued to read the file and he found that very shortly upon his release from prison for that offence he was then convicted of the murder of a young woman and served fifteen years of the mandatory life sentence. He had been released from that term of imprisonment just a few weeks before he was murdered. 'Not a wholesome individual,' Vicary murmured to himself as he reached slowly forward for his mug of tea which stood on his desktop, next to his telephone. He drained the tea, which was by then lukewarm, then stood and carried the file on Gordon Cogan to the detective constables' room where he found Detective Constables Penny Yewdall and Tom Ainsclough both sitting at their desks, reviewing paperwork. 'Busy, I see,' he commented warmly. 'That is a pleasing sight. Most pleasing.'

'Last month's statistics for me, sir,' Yewdall replied, equally warmly, glancing up at Vicary.

'Writing up the results of the house-to-house on Lingfield Road here, sir.' Ainsclough tapped the paper in front of him. 'And I can tell you now that it won't be taking very long . . . there has been nothing to report. The good citizenry of Wimbledon saw or heard nothing of note.'

'Frankly, I didn't think they would.' Vicary sighed. 'As I said at the time, but that the job had to be done.'

'Oh . . . yes, of course, sir,' Ainsclough replied, 'I realize that. Fully realize it.'

'Good . . . look . . . I'd like you two to do a visit, please.' Vicary held up the file on Gordon Cogan.

'Yes, sir.' Yewdall put her pen down.

'It is in respect of the Wimbledon Village murder, doubtless Tom here has told you about it?' Vicary glanced out of the DCs' window which, like the view from his own, offered a vista of Westminster Bridge, the river and the solid buildings on the South Bank, all at that moment bathed and glinting in a strong sun.

'Yes, he has, sir.' Yewdall glanced at Ainsclough. 'It sounded like an interesting start to the day. Quite intriguing . . . that sort of thing does not happen in Wimbledon. At least not in the Wimbledon that I know.'

'It was, and we are still in the most important twenty-four hours so, as you know, it takes priority.' Vicary continued to look warmly and approvingly on the two detective constables, who were both still in their twenties and both of whom, Vicary had constantly found, always worked very well together. Very well indeed. 'The visit in question is in connection with the murder. The victim has now been identified and is known to us, as I suspected he might be given the kind of injuries he sustained, but his next of kin have still to be notified. They may also wish to view the body. I attended the post-mortem this morning and Mr Shaftoe believed he might have been able to save the face of the deceased, so the body may be viewed if the next of kin request it . . . but you had better check with the Royal London first. Frankie and Victor are to visit his release address later today.'

'Yes, sir,' Ainsclough replied. 'Understood.'

'You will have to read the file before you visit, of course.' Vicary laid it on the edge of Yewdall's desk. 'He . . . the victim, was not, it seems, the most pleasant of individuals, but no matter what you might feel about him getting what was coming to him, if that was the case, remember that he is also a murder victim and that he deserves justice. Fair enough?'

'Understood, sir,' Penny Yewdall answered for both she and Tom Ainsclough.

'His next of kin,' Vicary continued, 'are the only contacts we have. As you'll see from the file, the box for "criminal associates" is marked "none known", and so he appears to have been a bit of a lone wolf, as indeed are the great majority of sex offenders.'

'Sex offender?' Yewdall commented. 'Really?'

'As you will read. As, in fact, both of you will read. So . . . break the news as gently as you can . . . it's never easy . . . then play it by ear. See what you see,' Vicary requested, 'find out what you find out . . . you know the drill. You've both been there before.'

The Cogans invited Yewdall and Ainsclough into their home, cautiously so and with apparent wariness, upon seeing the officers' warrant cards. The Cogans' home revealed itself to be a modest but neatly kept terraced house in the cul-de-sac of Evelyn Road in Richmond upon Thames. Standing in the shaded downstairs room to the rear of the house, Yewdall broke the news of the death of Gordon Cogan as gently and sensitively as she could, she being the only person to speak in the hushed silence which had by then descended upon the household. The man, who had viewed the officers' ID cards and then identified himself as being one Derek Cogan, and who was clearly in his early middle years, nodded slightly and kept his lips firmly together. Then he spoke in a soft whisper, saying, 'Thank you for telling us.'

The woman who had said, 'I am Mrs Cogan,' was, noted the officers, frail, elderly and slightly built, and fought to contain her tears. Eventually she was able to say, also in a whisper, 'Please excuse me.' And then she turned, left the room and was heard running up the stairs – a demonstration of great agility for one of her years which surprised and impressed both Ainsclough and Yewdall.

'Mother never likes anyone to see her cry,' Derek Cogan explained, somewhat apologetically. 'She belongs to a different era, you see. Values were different when she was young, and she has retained them.'

'I quite understand, sir. There's no need to apologise.' Penny Yewdall 'read' the room. She saw that it was cluttered but in an everything-has-its-place way, and had a tasteful number of furnishings, so she thought. Photographs in heavy metal frames stood on the mantelpiece; the furniture was old and solid and, like Mrs Cogan, seemed to be of an earlier era. The curtains, somewhat strangely, she felt, were left half open; a single uncovered window looked out on to a small garden enclosed by three brick walls about six feet high and painted white, with the topmost curved coping stones painted black. A green painted door was set in the wall at the bottom of the garden, which Yewdall assumed opened into a back alley which would run parallel to the line of houses. The garden itself was, Yewdall noted, a little untidy but it was by no means overgrown, as if the householder was content to keep the vegetation in check but sought nothing neater. The room in which they stood was, she thought, a little musty and Yewdall felt it could benefit from the opening of a window. Overall, though, Yewdall was satisfied that the house seemed to be age and standard of living appropriate for the occupants and it seemed to blend well with the neighbourhood in which it stood. She saw nothing to arouse her suspicions. It was, she thought, all very SW20.

'So, what happened?' Derek Cogan asked. 'What happened to my younger brother?' He remained standing and did not ask Yewdall and Ainsclough if they'd like to sit down, as if he was still absorbing the news of his brother's death.

'I'm afraid that he was attacked,' Tom Ainsclough explained. 'He was a victim of a violent crime.'

'Murdered!' Derek Cogan gasped. 'You mean to say that he was murdered!'

'Yes,' Ainsclough continued, 'he was quite severely battered about the head, I'm afraid to say.'

'When?' Derek Cogan gasped. 'When did it happen?'

'During the night,' Ainsclough replied. 'His body was discovered lying in the street very early this morning.'

'Mugged?' Derek Cogan asked insistently. 'Or was it a random attack? What is the story?'

'As yet I'm afraid we have no clues as to the motive but we did not find a wallet on his person,' Ainsclough advised, 'so robbery may have been a motive.' He paused. 'He was identified by his fingerprints, and his police record lists this address for his next of kin. Hence our arrival.'

'Yes . . .' Derek Cogan lowered his head. 'Gordon . . . yes . . . he was a little ill-advised once . . . he was in fact a little silly. In fact, he was once very, very silly. A very silly boy indeed.'

Penny Yewdall felt that describing the abduction and rape of a child as a 'silly' act was a little overgenerous, even allowing for family loyalty, but she diplomatically kept her own counsel.

'Can I see his body?' Derek Cogan asked. 'Would that be possible? I am sure it is him if the fingerprints have identified him, but . . . but for myself, I won't be able to accept his passing unless I see the body, and mother will want to know that I have seen him. She won't accept the news unless I can tell her I have seen him.'

'Yes . . . yes, you can.' Ainsclough smiled slightly and nodded his head. 'His body is at the Royal London Hospital. We can take you there now.'

The journey across London to the Royal London Hospital from Richmond upon Thames was passed in near total silence. In the mortuary of the hospital Yewdall, Ainsclough and Derek Cogan were shown into a room of richly polished, dark-stained wooden panelling which covered three of the four walls. The fourth wall was covered with a thick velvet curtain coloured a deep shade of purple. The floor was covered with a dark brown deep pile carpet. There was no sound. The three of them waited patiently without speaking. After they had been waiting for approximately a minute or so, Yewdall estimated, a door set in the wall adjacent to the curtain opened silently on well-oiled hinges and a nurse entered the room, closing the door equally silently behind her. She was, thought Ainsclough, in her mid-forties and wore a manner which seemed appropriately sombre. The nurse glanced at Ainsclough, who nodded once, and then, using both hands alternately, pulled on a cord and thus wound the curtain open. The opening of the curtains exposed a large pane of glass, and beyond the glass was the body of Gordon Cogan. It had been tightly wrapped in white bandages and blankets, leaving only his face visible, and by some ingenious trick of lighting and shading, he seemed to be floating in space. Nothing but ink-black darkness surrounded the body.

Derek Cogan took a deep breath and then said softly, 'Yes . . . yes . . . that is my brother. That is Gordon . . . Gordon Cogan. Thank you. I needed to see him.' Derek Cogan then turned to the sombre nurse. 'Thank you for taking care of him.' He then moved away as the nurse pulled on the cord again; hand over hand, quietly closing the curtains. She then left the room.

'It is very sensitive,' Derek Cogan commented. 'That arrangement, I mean . . . very sensitive . . . how it's done. I was expecting him to be in a metal drawer and banks of drawers each with a body in them . . . the drawer pulled out and a sheet lifted from his face . . . like you see on television and films.'

'That used to be the way of it,' Ainsclough replied, 'but not these days, not any more, as you have just seen . . . and yes, it is preferable this way . . . much better by far.'

Derek Cogan took another deep breath. 'It's going to be a good way to remember him . . . as if he is floating at peace . . . floating so peacefully. But all for his wallet? There'd be nothing in it anyway – he was unemployed, you see, he was surviving on benefits. I mean, who would want to mug a doley? It makes no sense . . . it makes no sense at all.'

'We were surprised at the severity of his injuries,' Ainsclough commented as he and Yewdall and Cogan left the viewing room. 'They were quite extensive, more severe than would normally be the case in a mugging. It was as if someone had a personal grudge against your late brother. Can I ask . . . did he have any enemies that you know of?'

'My late brother,' Cogan echoed the expression and gave Ainsclough a deeply pained look. 'I suppose I will have to get used to that term now. Once I had a brother . . . now I have a late brother. But no . . . no particular enemies that I knew of. We saw each other infrequently so I knew little of his day-to-day life. In fact, I knew nothing of it . . . but of course he might have had enemies. You must make enemies in prison and he was not long released, as you know. Where was he found?'

'In a suburban street in Wimbledon,' Ainsclough informed.

'Wimbledon!' Derek Cogan gasped and his chest tilted forward as if he had been punched in the stomach. 'But he lived in a dingy bedsit in Kentish Town – what on earth was he doing in Wimbledon? I mean, Wimbledon of all places . . .'

'We might never know,' Ainsclough replied. 'But there is . . . there was an indication that he was attacked somewhere else and that his body was left in Wimbledon to be found by a member of the public.'

'Oh . . .' Cogan groaned deeply, 'that doesn't sound like a mugging. I'm not a police officer but what mugger carries his victim's body away?'

'Which were and still are our thoughts exactly.' Ainsclough and Derek Cogan fell into step as they walked down the long, narrow corridor in the basement of the Royal London Hospital. 'Hence our question about your late brother having any enemies . . . enemies who would want to kill him.' Ainsclough paused. 'It does seem to us to be much more than a random attack, or a mugging gone badly wrong. It seems to be more in the manner of some person or persons, as yet unknown, targeting your brother, as though someone had a reason for wanting to kill him.'

'We have limited contact, as I said. Or, we had limited contact,' Derek Cogan explained, 'and I mean very, very limited contact. But we knew where he was, of course. We're family, and once or twice I would visit him, and mother and I pushed him some money now and again. Not much, we're not wealthy but we gave him what we could afford. He was ashamed of what he did, you see . . . he was consumed with guilt . . . he felt that he had let the family down . . . his convictions, you see.'

'Abduction and rape of a minor, and then a conviction for murder,' Penny Yewdall, walking behind the two men, replied coldly. 'Yes, we know about his convictions. We know all about them.'

'I detect hostility in your voice.' Derek Cogan turned and looked at Penny Yewdall but instead of replying with the scowl Yewdall had expected she saw that he wore a knowing smile. 'Your hostility is understandable,' Cogan turned away and again looked to his front, 'but it's not as bad as it sounds. Is there somewhere we can go for a quiet chat?'

Ainsclough turned and he and Yewdall glanced at each other. Yewdall said, 'There's a pub across the road; it ought to be quiet at this time of day.'

The public house which Yewdall had in mind was the Blind Beggar and it was in fact a few hundred yards to the east 'across the road', but it was quiet, as she had expected it to be, with just a few patrons drinking in isolation when Yewdall and Ainsclough and Cogan entered.

'You know I've always had a desire to visit this pub,' Derek Cogan sat in a corner seat, 'but I have never been able to pluck up the courage to enter it.'

'Why not? It's just a normal pub, like any other East End pub.' Yewdall sat adjacent to Derek Cogan.

'Yes . . . but it's a pub with a history. What was his name . . . the gangster, George Cornell, he was shot in this pub by Ronnie Kray . . . a pub full of witnesses and no one saw anything. Do you know where Cornell was sitting?' Cogan looked curiously around the pub. 'I have to lose my brother in order to get in here and fulfil an ambition. It's a funny old world.'

'Before my time,' Yewdall replied offhandedly. 'I wasn't even alive then . . . and the pub will have been refurbished since the mid-sixties when that accident occured, probably many times over, in fact.'

'Yes . . . I suppose.' Cogan continued to look around him at the high ceilings, the solid furniture. 'On a healthier note, do you know that this pub was where the Salvation Army was born?'

'Inside a pub!' Yewdall forced a grin though she still felt uneasy with Derek Cogan. 'That's rich. But no, I didn't know that.'

'Well, outside actually.' Derek Cogan nodded to the window. 'John Booth preached his first sermon right outside this pub, out there on Whitechapel Road. The paving flags will be the same. They won't have changed.'

'You live and learn.' Yewdall sat back as Tom Ainsclough placed a tray of drinks on the table: a mineral water for Yewdall, an orange juice for himself and a whisky for Derek Cogan.

'Gordon was a teacher,' Derek Cogan explained as he sipped his whisky. 'He was a bright boy, he was the bright spark of the family, he was just brilliant . . . our Gordon took school in his stride, got his degree when he was twenty, his MA at twenty-one and his BEd at twenty-two – three degrees and still just twenty-two years old. All in the bag at that age. Imagine.'

'Not bad.' Ainsclough sat opposite Yewdall with his back to the window. He drank his orange juice, savouring the vitamin C which he imagined coursing through his veins and then resolved to eat more fruit, reasoning that if he was sensitive to the vitamin C then it must mean that he was suffering from some degree of deficiency in it. 'Not bad,' he repeated, 'not bad at all.'

'Yes. It was very impressive. We were very proud of him.' Derek Cogan spoke softly. 'He was set to fly high in the world of education, an early head of department, possibly an early headship. He was a linguist. All set for a glittering career but it all came at a dreadful price. I wouldn't go so far as to say Gordon was a savant . . . but equally there was an immaturity about him. So . . . a lovely future lay ahead of him, and then he had an affair with one of his pupils.'

'Oh . . .' Yewdall groaned, 'so he lost everything. Is that what you are saying?'

'Yes.' Derek Cogan put his hand to his forehead, 'Yes, that is it exactly. That's what I am saying. She . . . the pupil, the girl in question, was fifteen, he was twenty-three . . . just an eight-year age gap . . . nothing much in adults but in the eyes of the law she was a minor and he was an adult and they didn't keep it discreet, just the opposite, in fact. They ran away together. Would you believe it? In mid-term as well. It made quite a splash in the media. It was widely covered by the newspapers and the television channels. The authorities were fearful for the girl's welfare, you see, so they made sure that the press and the television and the radio people were all over the story like an army of driver ants.' Derek Cogan took another deep breath. 'It was so embarrassing. I can still feel the shame. It nearly destroyed mother; fortunately her apparent frailty hides an inner strength . . . But that was Gordon . . . it was Gordon all over . . . He was my younger brother – very brainy but that came at a price, like I said, because he was also so very immature. He and that girl were very well-suited because they were both on the same emotional level. They were both fifteen-year-olds . . . in a sense.'

'I see,' Yewdall murmured. 'I was assuming a much younger girl had been taken against her will.'

'Yes . . . you see, it's not quite the situation that his conviction for abduction and rape would suggest.' Derek Cogan sipped his whisky and then continued, 'Anyway, they ran away to Ireland and they lived in a guest house in Galway for a few days, until the owner of the guest house recognized them from the television and newspaper reports and alerted the Garda. The Garda arrested Gordon and handed the girl over to the Irish social services. They were both returned to England. Gordon was put under arrest and remanded in custody while the girl was placed in the care of the local authority for a brief period before returning to her parents. The English social workers had to make sure that it was safe for her to return home, you see.'

'Of course,' Yewdall replied.

'It clearly was safe because she went back home quite quickly. Gordon was held on remand, as I said . . . no going home for him, and he was eventually put on trial. Fortunately for Gordon he went in front of Mr Justice Easter, who has subsequently died. I read his obituary in *The Times* – 'the lenient judge' as he was described, probably befitting a man whose surname was that of a Christian feast. He was certainly very lenient with Gordon; in fact, he could not have been more lenient. He said before sentencing Gordon that he knew he had a reputation for leniency and that he was going to add to that reputation in Gordon's case.' Derek Cogan took another sip of his whisky. 'The judge, Mr Justice Easter, explained that he had taken into account the crime was driven by passion on both sides, and that he was also taking into account Gordon's very sensible plea of "guilty" which meant that his "victim" was saved from being cross-examined by an aggressive defence barrister, which would have been very difficult for her and might have risked causing her great emotional damage. Mr Justice Easter also explained that no prison sentence he could pass would cause Gordon more damage than the damage he had already brought upon himself: the glittering, safe career that had been ahead of him, the early head of department, the early headship . . . he had lost it all. No more employment in teaching, or any profession for that matter, not with such serious-sounding criminal offences against his name, and also because he was, by then, a registered sex offender. Mr Justice Easter had thusly allowed for the fact that Gordon's future was, by then, a bleak one. Any employment he might be able to obtain would be low grade, very low grade indeed, with poor conditions of service, no job security, no pension at the end of it all . . . nothing.' Derek Cogan took yet another deep breath before continuing. 'And you know, the really annoying thing is that the girl was only a few weeks short of her sixteenth birthday. For the sake of not waiting for a few short weeks – a couple of months at most – Gordon's life was in ruins. It was over. If only . . . if only . . . if only they had been more discreet . . . if only they had kept their love affair hidden from the world until after she turned sixteen, then what they did would not have been illegal. Gordon would have lost his job, he would be finished in teaching because having a sexual relationship with a pupil, even if she is over the age of consent, is still a sackable offence, but he could have carved out a good career as a linguist because he would not have criminalized himself. He was just very emotionally immature . . . he could not see beyond the end of his silly, stupid nose . . . and they were both consumed with passion . . . as in the old Romeo and Juliet number . . . what is that phrase?'

'A pair of star-crossed lovers?' Yewdall suggested. 'Is that the phrase you are thinking of?'

'Yes,' Derek Cogan smiled briefly, 'that's the phrase. That's it exactly. Driven by emotion and they, particularly Gordon, who should have been in control, did not think logically . . . it was all very impulsive. So kindly old Mr Justice Easter took all that into account and sentenced Gordon to six months in prison, backdated to the date of his arrest, which meant he walked out of the court that day, having been arrested and remanded more than six months previously. It all happened back to front for him; he served his sentence, then was put on trial, then released from custody. But his life to all intents and purposes was over by then. His real sentence was just beginning.'

'I see,' Yewdall replied, allowing a little more warmth to enter her voice. 'I can see what you mean now when you described your late brother as being "silly". His record, as I said, suggests something much more unpleasant.'

'Oh, yes, don't I know it.' Derek Cogan took another sip of his whisky. 'His convictions conjure dreadful images of a young girl being taken against her will and bundled into the back of a car and all the sordid rest of it. So yes, I know how badly it all reads but, as I said, it was the actions of an immature young man and soon-to-be sixteen-year-old schoolgirl who were both hopelessly head over heels in love with each other. In fact, they were actually arrested whilst they were strolling up Shantalla Road in Galway, holding hands.'

'That's a precise location you mention,' Ainsclough commented. 'It's very interesting in its precision.'

'Ah . . . yes . . . yes . . . perhaps I should explain.' Derek Cogan nodded gently. 'I'd better explain. You see, our parents did not use the annual holidays to introduce their children, Gordon and I, to different parts of the UK – you know, Cornwall one year, Devon the next, Scotland the next . . . then the Isle of Man . . . the Isle of Wight. No . . . we went to Galway every summer, without fail, because that's where our parents had spent their honeymoon. So year after year, summer after summer it was two weeks in Galway for us. Gordon and I got to know the town and the surrounding area well, very well indeed. And Gordon might have got three university degrees but they were all taken at the University of London so for Gordon, Galway was the only other place he knew outside

London. Where else to take his girlfriend when they ran away together but to Galway and, I believe, there was in fact, by coincidence, an Irish connection for the girl. Her parents came from that part of Ireland, and she had also visited Galway often, so she was apparently very happy to be taken there. It was something that they had in common – Galway was a home from home for them both.' Again Derek Cogan paused. 'So . . . to continue . . . anyway, when Gordon was sentenced there was total uproar in the court. I mean total pandemonium. Her father was there and her extended family . . . a whole team of them: men with rings in their ears and their hair tied back in ponytails, but I mean in a very manly fashion . . . they were real bruisers, you understand, really heavy-looking, beefy, brawny guys and all with that pinched face of a criminal. Geezers that you would not want to meet up and mess with, geezers who are used to people stepping out of their way when they walk down the street. And the women of the family . . . my God, the women . . . thin with cold eyes and hard faces, really spiteful-looking females, and all of them shouting in protest against the lenient sentence, saying things like, "We'll be out there looking for you, Cogan", and "There's nowhere for you to hide, Cogan", you know . . . threats like that, but it was all for show at the time – nothing but hot air.'

'That's interesting,' Yewdall commented. 'So nobody attacked him when he was released from custody?'

'No, but he very sensibly made himself scarce. He at least had enough common sense to do that. He moved into a bedsit in Acton Town, well away from where he used to live and well away from the school he used to teach at. Then, just a few weeks later, he was arrested for the murder of a young heroin addict who lived in the same building.' Derek Cogan looked to his left, then to his right and said, 'Now . . . now I tell you that did not, and it still does not, make any sense at all. The affair with one of his pupils, well, yes, all right, that was the sort of ridiculously stupid thing that Gordon would do, he would indeed do a stupid thing like that, an action borne out of his emotional immaturity . . . but murder? Prison didn't harden him up all that much, not in just six months, and during those six months he was kept in the vulnerable prisoners unit, among all the paedophiles – the real paedophiles – so he never mixed with the hard men who would have toughened him up somewhat. You know, nothing added up about the murder. Nothing added up at all.'

'Why do you say that?' Tom Ainsclough asked. 'You seem to be wholly sure of what you are saying.'

'Because it just didn't and it still doesn't add up and deliver. It just . . . just does not add up and deliver.' Derek Cogan drained his glass and put it down heavily on the table top. 'It makes no sense. It makes not the slightest sense at all.'

'Would you like another whisky?' Ainsclough pointed to Cogan's empty glass. 'I sense you need one. I sense you are about to tell us a story.'

'Oh . . . oh . . . I shouldn't, I really shouldn't, but it's been quite a day,' Cogan smiled in a resigning manner, 'so yes, yes I would like another whisky . . . thank you . . . it will help me to explain things.'

As Tom Ainsclough walked leisurely across the floor of the Blind Beggar towards the bar, Penny Yewdall asked Derek Cogan what he did for a living.

'Nothing.' Cogan beamed his reply. 'I'm retired.'

Yewdall saw a thin-faced man, balding, bespectacled, tall yet thin-framed, almost skeleton-like. 'I was a teacher like Gordon but whereas he went to the university and taught high-ability pupils in a private day school, I taught remedial classes in a large inner-city comprehensive, having only attended teacher training college. Like I said, Gordon had all the brains in our family. It was like he had my share on top of his fair share. In the school I taught at we had children who arrived at the age of eleven and still could not read or write or do elementary arithmetic. It meant that I was really a primary school teacher with teenage pupils . . . and their handwriting . . . you had to see it to believe how awful it could be. It was as though they were writing using matchboxes dipped in mud, but we teachers in the remedial group always derived a great deal of satisfaction in ensuring that very, very few pupils left our school without basic literacy or numeracy. It was a very rewarding part of our job. Ours was a large comprehensive school where the brightest pupils went on to university and

the less bright into some form of gainful employment . . . and
. . . regrettably not a few became known to you people . . .
mostly for petty crime but I am pleased to say that I don't
think we ever produced a career criminal. Oh . . . thank you,'
Derek Cogan reclined as Tom Ainsclough set his whisky down
on the table in front of him. 'This really has to be my last.'

'So . . . Derek,' Ainsclough prompted, 'not adding up and
delivering, you were saying.'

'Yes.' Derek Cogan sipped the whisky. 'So after he was
released from custody, Gordon went to live in a grubby little
bedsit in Acton Town. It was not easy for him but he was
courageously trying to rescue what little he could from the mess
he'd made of his life. He was able to obtain a little translating
work now and again but nothing ever became permanent. The
convictions, you see, worked against him as the judge had
said they would, so mostly he was on the dole and getting a
little cash-in-hand work. In the early days he worked damned
hard to keep away from the drink and he began to attend a
non-conformist church which accepted him as a repentant
sinner. You know, the old hallelujah handshake foxtrot, and
he went along each Sunday for the human company more than
anything else, you know the sketch, someone to have a chat
with over coffee after the service. I would visit and write to
him and let him have twenty pounds now and again, plus
whatever mother could let him have out of her state pension
. . . it was all we could afford. You don't enter teaching for
the money, that's for sure, but the main thing was that Gordon
was living cleanly and not sinking into crime. He also seemed
to be avoiding the bottle.'

'Good for him.' Yewdall raised her mineral water to her
lips. 'Was there any contact between him and his girlfriend?
His ex-pupil?'

'Not that I know of,' Derek Cogan replied, 'but I would not
be surprised if there had been some form of contact between
them. I mean, they were utterly committed to each other, and
he was on remand for just six months and so they could have
picked things up upon his release and done so quite easily.'

'What was her name?' Yewdall took her pen and notebook
from her bag.

'Lysandra Smith.' Cogan smiled. 'Smith's a bit of a common name, though not Lysandra . . . but you'll most likely be easily able to trace her despite her common surname.'

'Really?' Yewdall raised her eyebrows. 'We will?'

'Yes . . . she will be in her early thirties now and along the way she has acquired a criminal record.'

'Oh . . .' Yewdall smiled. 'That will help us greatly. We will need to chat to her.'

'I thought it might.' Derek Cogan held his glass but didn't lift it from the table top. 'Yes, once, a few years ago now, I read a small filler in the evening paper about a woman of that name and of the age she would have been, acquiring a conviction for shoplifting.'

'We can check that easily enough.' Penny Yewdall wrote the name on her notepad. 'Conviction might be spent but nothing is erased from the Police National Computer. Any and every conviction remains on record.'

'So I believe. Anyway, things settled down for Gordon,' Derek Cogan continued, 'bedsit living, dole, a few jobs, hand-outs from the family but eventually the drink became a failing with him. This stuff.' Derek Cogan tapped the side of his glass. 'I mean the heavy bevvy, not just a few beers in the evening but drinking bottles of spirits at home, and he hid the problem by drinking vodka . . .'

'Hid it?' Yewdall queried.

'From himself,' Cogan explained. 'I mean he hid it from himself. Vodka has so few impurities you can demolish a full bottle of it in the evening and wake up the next morning without a hangover.'

'Yes.' Yewdall nodded. 'I am aware that that is the case with vodka.'

'As opposed to drinking a bottle of this stuff,' again Derek Cogan tapped the side of his glass, 'or a bottle or two of red wine which will cause you to wake up feeling like your head is being crushed by a steamroller . . . there is just no aversion therapy at all to be had with vodka. So Gordon would buy a bottle when he had the money and he'd drink it at home. It was in the midst of that lifestyle that he was arrested for murder.' Cogan paused. 'That was a bolt from the blue, I can tell you . . . a real bolt from the blue, and his victim was a seventeen-year-old heroin addict who had had a flat in the same building. In fact, her flat was just across the hall from Gordon's room. I saw her once during one of my visits, a pale, sickly-looking waif of a girl. She could pose no threat to anyone, yet he allegedly strangled her, and he was no Mr Universe.'

'Allegedly?' Tom Ainsclough echoed. 'You say allegedly?'

'Yes . . . yes . . . I do,' Derek Cogan repeated, 'he allegedly strangled her. I say again, he *allegedly* strangled her. Allegedly.' Derek Cogan sipped his drink. 'Gordon always claimed that he was innocent and he was a truthful man by nature. He was also an unlikely sort of person to strangle someone. He was slightly built, mild mannered, bookish, living quietly, trying to rescue something of his life. All right, he was also drinking by then but drink just made him sleepy, not violent, and he would not readily associate with a rough street girl who injected herself with narcotics. I mean, if someone strangles someone else . . . I would have thought that that suggests passion, which suggests a relationship. It didn't make any sense. It still doesn't make any sense. No sense at all.'

'But he was convicted,' Yewdall pointed out. 'There must have been solid evidence against him, for him to be convicted of murder.'

'Yes, there was,' Cogan advised, 'they found Gordon's DNA on her body, especially around her throat . . . and all over her room.'

'Good enough,' Tom Ainsclough commented. 'That sounds good enough to me.'

'So the police thought, but despite that Gordon pleaded not guilty and he did so against legal advice.' Derek Cogan sipped his drink once more. 'Again, you see, that is Gordon. He pleaded guilty to the abduction and rape of a fifteen-year-old because he was guilty and he had an integrity about him, and he would only plead not guilty if he believed that he was not guilty. He was my brother, I knew him well, but DNA does not lie and unsurprisingly the jury found against him. He collected his mandatory life sentence, but he consistently refused to accept his guilt and was classified as an IDOM. "In denial of murder".'

'Yes . . . thank you . . .' Yewdall replied coldly, 'we know what IDOM stands for.'

'Sorry . . . of course you do. Sorry. Sorry.' Derek Cogan held up his hand and then continued. 'I was so proud of him sticking to his guns like that, and not admitting guilt, so as to be able to work towards his parole. He was a man of integrity . . . and in fact you do read of DNA results being compromised which will invalidate them, so they can lie in a sense. Because of that we began to think that was what had happened and we planned for him to appeal against his conviction.' Cogan looked as if he was mustering strength. 'Then, talk about another bolt from the blue, he damn well changed his plea to "guilty". He did ten years as IDOM and then changes his plea. I was devastated. I couldn't – I freely confess that I still can't believe that our Gordon could kill someone, not the younger brother that I knew, but there he was, as large as life, putting his hand up to it. I was . . . well, as I said, I was devastated. I did not visit him for a long, long time after that. I just could not bring myself to face him. Then I went from being disappointed to being annoyed with him. In fact, I was furious. Livid. Why on earth would he want to murder a seventeen-year-old drug addict? What on earth was his motivation? What had been the nature of their relationship? But anyway, he became a model prisoner, and he eventually got re-categorized down to a Category B and then Category C prison, and was in time released on licence five years after he changed his plea.' Derek Cogan took a deep breath. 'He kept himself well away from mother and I, but we would receive the occasional postcard, now and again, usually letting us know of a change of address. He was last living in a bedsit in Kentish Town. So that was his life. That was the life of Gordon Cogan. Newly out of university as a highly qualified teacher, kept on remand for six months and then released, his life in tatters, then arrested for murder a few weeks after his release, inside for fifteen years, released again and a matter of weeks after his second release he was murdered. It was as if someone really wanted him dead. As I said, nothing adds up and delivers.' Derek Cogan drained his glass. 'I don't think I can tell you anything else. I must get back to Richmond now. Poor mother . . . she won't accept the news until I tell her that I have seen poor Gordon's body. God rest him.'

Inkerman Road in Kentish Town was, as Swannell and Brunnie discovered, a straight, narrow road lined with three-storey, flat-roofed, mid-Victorian terraced housing. The houses were painted in sombre whites and greys and blacks, and the street enjoyed one or two trees growing from the pavement along its length and at either side of the road. Gordon Cogan's prison release address was on this street, close to the junction with Alma Road.

Inside the house, Gordon Cogan's room revealed itself to be neat and cleanly kept, though, Brunnie thought, perhaps a little threadbare and spartan. Nonetheless, it read correctly for a man on limited income who had very recently been released from fifteen years in prison. The bed was made correctly with the prescribed 'hospital corners' and all items were neatly in their place. It was evidently the room of an institutionalized man.

'He hasn't been here very long. He was very recently transferred from another hostel,' the warden of the bail hostel was a softly spoken Asian man of medium build, 'but he was not ever any bother at all. He was always quiet and always sober.'

'When did you last see him?' Swannell casually opened a drawer at random and saw that it contained a few items of inexpensive and well-worn clothing, all neatly folded.

'Friday. He signed out after breakfast on Friday morning. He always seemed to be a man about a mission.' The warden held on to the handle of the opened door. 'He once told me that he was looking for someone, but not in a threatening way, you understand. He said that he believed that the person he was looking for could help him, and that he would return mid-evening, have a meal and then stay in his room until the next morning. I reported him to the police as being in breach of his licence conditions when he had not returned by eleven p.m. on Friday, as I am obliged to do. But . . . deceased, you say?'

'Yes.' Brunnie nodded. 'I reckon you can notify the probation and aftercare service that you have a vacant room.'

'I suppose so.' The warden spoke solemnly. 'I'll parcel up his belongings. Does he have any family?'

'Yes, though we understand that they thought that he was living independently in a bedsit, not in a probation service hostel,' Swannell replied. 'They'll be in touch about his things.'

'Very good.'

'Did he say anything about the person he was looking for,' Brunnie asked, 'in the non-threatening sense?'

'Only that she was a woman.' The warden glanced round the room. 'He said, "She can help me".'

'She?' Brunnie repeated. 'She?'

'Yes,' the warden replied, 'I'm certain he said, "She can help me".'

The phone on Harry Vicary's desk warbled. He let it ring twice before making a leisurely long arm and lifting the handset up to his ear. 'Detective Inspector Vicary, Murder and Serious Crime Squad.' He spoke in a calm yet authoritative manner.

'Good afternoon, sir,' the voice on the other end of the line was male, equally calm and also with a certain warmth. It had, Vicary believed, a strong echo of the West Country about it: most probably Devon, he thought, not Somerset, possibly east Cornwall, but most likely Devon. 'Detective Constable Trelawney here, Wimbledon Police Station. About the motor vehicle that was burnt out in our patch last night or early this morning . . .'

'Ah, yes . . . any luck?' Vicary changed the phone from his left to his right ear.

'I am afraid not, sir. I have no news to report. We have traced the owner, who lives in north London and hadn't even realized that his car had been stolen. He seems quite genuine . . . a young lawyer . . . he is not a criminal type at all.'

'I see,' Vicary replied. 'I had expected that sort of result, but it had to be checked out anyway.'

'Of course, sir.' Trelawney took the phone from his ear, enabling Vicary to hear the background noise of the interior of Wimbledon Police Station as Trelawney coughed. 'Excuse me, sir,' he said, 'wretched summer cold.'

'No worries,' Vicary replied patiently.

'The car might, but only might, be connected to the murder in Lingfield Road,' Trelawney continued. 'We have trawled through all the CCTV footage we could muster which covers the immediate area and have picked up the car turning from the Ridgeway into Lingfield Road at three fourteen a.m., from where we lose sight of it.'

'But it did turn into Lingfield Road?' Vicary asked. 'You are certain of that?'

'Yes, sir.'

'It has to be the car that was used to transport the body,' Vicary mused.

'My thoughts also, sir,' Trelawney replied. 'The car was burned out in Parkside Gardens, which is just beyond Lingfield Road as you drive from the Ridgeway. We have enhanced the footage of the car and observed two male-looking figures wearing hoods, and the driver was wearing gloves.'

'Those will be our suspects,' Vicary growled. 'Hoods. Gloves. Hiding themselves like that.'

'Again, our thoughts also, sir.' Trelawney coughed again but courteously away from, not into the phone. 'We then trawled through the footage of folk leaving the area later that morning, the commuters, but we could not see any likely candidates.'

'That doesn't surprise me either,' Vicary growled again. 'As we thought at the time, they would most likely have hidden in someone's front garden and emerged when the first commuters began to walk past them, and they would also have taken off their hooded jackets and replaced them with sports jackets or some similar garment. They might even have had business suits under the hooded jackets, and pushed their hooded jackets into briefcases . . . really looking the part. I also think that they would have left the area separately, each using a different route as well as walking separately. Did you see any indication of race?'

'None, sir. The driver wore gloves as I said and the front-seat passenger kept his hands out of sight,' Trelawney explained. 'They were definitely aware of CCTV.'

'Very well, thank you for telling me,' Vicary replied. 'I'll record this information or non-information in the file, but you'll be faxing me a written report anyway?'

'Of course, sir,' Trelawney confirmed. 'It'll be with you later today.'

'Thank you . . . Oh, Mr Trelawney,' Vicary caught Trelawney just before he hung up, 'it's just an interest of mine . . . but your accent, mild as it is . . .'

'Cornwall, my handsome,' Trelawney replied with good humour and in an exaggerated accent. 'Padstow, to be exact.'

'Ah . . . I thought Devon or east Cornwall.' Vicary allowed his smile to be 'heard' down the phone line.

'Well, you were almost correct there, my handsome – north-east Cornwall. But I'll write this up asap and fax it to you directly.'

'Appreciated. Thank you.' Vicary replaced the handset gently. He had very much enjoyed the brief conversation with DC Trelawney from Padstow, and he felt greatly uplifted by it.

The man ambled slowly out of the side door of the building and stepped on to Turner Street. He wore corduroy trousers, rolled up at the bottom in the form of rough turn-ups, brown shoes, a lightweight summer jacket and a flat white golfing cap. He had an ex-military khaki canvas knapsack slung over his left shoulder. The man turned right towards Whitechapel Road and when he got there turned left and kept close to the line of buildings as much out of the way of the other foot passengers as he could. He did not particularly enjoy the view of the Gherkin as he walked. He felt it was a monstrous building, very symbolic of the plethora of new buildings which he felt were ruining London, making the lovely old city slowly vanish. He once again noticed how that part of London in which he was walking had now been strongly given over to the influence of Islam: there were huge Mosques, for example, and many buildings that were originally public houses were occupied by businesses selling Asian clothing or halal meat. As the man approached Aldgate East Underground Station he crossed Whitechapel Road and walked into the White Hart, one of the few remaining public houses along the road. In the cool and calm interior of the pub he ordered a beer and chose to remain at the bar rather than sitting down. The man would cut a modest figure to the casual observer, with a barrel-chested upper body, short legs and standing just five feet six inches tall. As was his wont, the man kept himself to himself and avoided eye contact with other patrons. He was a man minding his own business and he clearly expected other people to mind theirs. He attracted little attention from the patrons, most of whom just glanced at him once and then forgot him, thinking as any observer would be forgiven for thinking, that he was just an ordinary 'geezer', having a beer or two at the end of the working day, on his way home to the 'trouble and strife', middle-aged, scratching pennies, but still able to afford to eat and still able to afford a few beers. The man the other patrons were in fact glancing at once and then forgetting was John Shaftoe, MD, MCRP, FRCPath, Home Office registered forensic pathologist.

John Shaftoe remained in the White Hart until approximately 6.30 p.m., at which time he reasoned that the rush hour, which he often referred to as the 'crush hour', would have largely subsided. He walked back across Whitechapel Road to Aldgate East Underground Station and took the Metropolitan Line to King's Cross, from where he took the mainline service to Brookmans Park. From Brookmans Park Railway Station he walked in a slow, ambling manner over the footbridge and into the centre of the village, then arrived at a gentle incline that was Brookmans Lane, observing, as he always did, the well-set detached houses on either side of the road, some with single driveways while other properties had U-shaped 'in and out' drive-ways. Shaftoe felt, once again, particularly envious of the owners of houses on the northern side of the road whose properties backed on to the golf course and which would never be built on. Not in his lifetime, anyway. He walked on, up to nearly the very top of the lane and then turned right down a single driveway and let himself into the house. His wife greeted him warmly and helped him out of his summer jacket as he hung his knapsack on a clothes peg. 'Good day, pet?' she asked warmly.

'So, so, pet,' Shaftoe replied, sitting down on a wooden chair in the hallway and tugging at his shoelaces. 'I went in early, as you know, to look at a decayed corpse which had been pulled out of the river and, in the event, got called out to attend a recent corpse.'

'Oh, my . . .' His wife sighed.

'Yes. He was quite a young bloke; forty . . . he'd been

battered over the head. I was able to wrap that up before lunch, and then I addressed the decayed corpse which I had intended to do first thing. Unlike the first corpse, I couldn't determine the cause of death. He had no identification and no distinguishing features. They'll give him a name and bury him in a pauper's grave.'

'I always find that upsetting.' Linda Shaftoe shook her head slowly. 'Dying . . . nobody misses you . . . nobody knows who you are . . . nobody cares . . . Just given a name and buried, and forgotten.'

'It happens, pet.' Shaftoe slid his feet into an old and very comfortable pair of slippers and stood up. 'It happens . . . especially in large cities. Folk come from all over to live in the cities looking for anonymity, and they find it. They find it all right.' He smiled at his wife. 'Do you feel like touching base, pet?'

'Oh aye . . . let's do that,' Linda Shaftoe replied enthusiastically. 'We have not done that for a while.'

'Right, I'll make a point of coming home early one day this week and we'll go out somewhere for the night.' Shaftoe beamed at his wife, pronouncing 'right' as 'reet' and night as 'neet'. 'I'll leave before the crush hour – so long as I miss it, that's the important thing. What's for supper?'

'Cottage pie.' Linda Shaftoe turned and walked to the kitchen. 'I know it's summer, but I also know how much you like your cottage pie.'

'Champion, pet,' Shaftoe smiled at her, 'just champion.' Linda Shaftoe was the same age as him, also from Thurnscoe and also the child of a coal miner whose father had hoped his only daughter would marry a 'lad with a trade': a fitter, an electrician or a plumber – anything but a coal miner. He was subsequently a man who could not contain his glee when he found that his beloved daughter had 'pulled' a doctor, and not just a doctor but an 'ologist'. Not only that, the 'ologist' in question was not 'stuck up' with a posh accent but a 'right good lad from the next street'. So 'our Linda had done herself proud'. Perfect. Just perfect.

Early that same evening, Harry and Kathleen Vicary strolled

contentedly arm in arm from their terraced house in Hartley Road, Leytonstone to the Assembly Rooms in the town centre. They sat near the back of the six rows of seated persons as the guest speaker was introduced. After being introduced the speaker said, 'Hello, my name is Felicity and I am an alcoholic,' upon which the Vicarys and all other persons in the room, save the person who had introduced her, replied, 'Hello, Felicity', and then listened as Felicity, a slight figure in a scarlet dress, recounted her journey from the gutter to her divorce, then to becoming a 'dry' alcoholic who was by then in full control of her life. After the talk Harry and Kathleen Vicary joined others for a coffee and a biscuit and a chat.

Upon leaving the Assembly Rooms the Vicarys went to the Wagon and Horses pub and joined the quiz team to which they belonged, drinking tonic water while the other members of their team drank beer. Their team was eventually placed fourth out of eight teams when the results were announced, but Harry Vicary felt that fourth was perfectly respectable. It was not the winning that mattered anyway, so he believed, but the taking part. It was also the small items of knowledge he never failed to pick up on each and every quiz night which added to the enjoyment. As he and his wife walked slowly back home through a balmy summer's evening, Vicary pondered that he had, that evening, learned that a 'Fletcher' was an arrow-maker in Medieval times, and during the round on the Great Fire of London in 1666, he had learned that Samuel Pepys had buried a Parmesan cheese in his garden to preserve it from the flames. Interestingly, he had also learned that the fire was sometimes known as 'the food fire' because it had started in Pudding Lane and had eventually died out in Pie Lane.

Tuesday

THREE

G eoff 'the milk' Driscoll hummed a catchy tune to himself as he turned his milk float off the Ridgeway and into Lingfield Road. The first thing he did as he straightened the float was to check the road surface ahead of him for any footwear lying upon it. He smiled gently as he saw that the road surface was clear of any debris, although the remnants of the blue and white police tape which had enclosed the area where, twenty-four hours earlier, he had found the corpse of the man, still hung from the shrubs, utterly motionless in the morning air. His discovery of the body had caused a stir in the dairy and that morning, as he was loading up the float, he had enjoyed much attention from his fellow rounds men who had pressed him for details.

Driscoll proceeded up Lingfield Road and then slowed the float to a halt as he saw the body. It was lying precisely where he had found the other body of the man but between two cars which had been parked closed to each other, thus concealing it from view until Driscoll was almost alongside it. A pair of red shoes lay on the ground nearby. Unlike the body he had found the previous day this one was female and, also unlike the body he had found the previous day, this body was Afro-Caribbean.

'This,' Driscoll murmured softly to himself, 'just cannot be happening to me.'

He applied the handbrake of the float, stepped out of the vehicle and walked, calmly this time, up the steps he had run up the previous morning. Once again he knocked at the door of the large Gothic Victorian house with its complicated roof line and turret windows, and once again the door was opened, casually so, by the same, tall, well-built man who wore the same blue paisley patterned dressing gown. 'Sorry, Squire,' Driscoll said, employing a familiarity of address he had not used the previous morning, 'but you are just not going to believe what I have found on the road outside your house.'

Once again the householder remained utterly calm, then he nodded slowly and said, 'I will call the police,' before shutting his door on Driscoll.

It was, once again, the dawn which woke Tom Ainsclough, as it so often did because of his wont to sleep with the curtains of his bedroom open. He rose slowly, feeling utterly refreshed after a solid eight hours of deep sleep, and sat on the edge of his bed. He half turned, placed his palm on the other side and found that it was still warm from Sara, who had quietly left the house without waking him, having lain there. Ainsclough stood at the window and looked out across the suburban garden to Lambeth Hospital where Sara would be, by then, working as a staff sister. Ainsclough washed, dressed and breakfasted. He then left the upper portion of the house, taking the stairs down to the common hallway he and his wife shared with the Watsons, who were the mortgagees of the lower conversion of the house. The Watsons were also a young and childless couple, who had proved good neighbours. The wife of the union was, like Sara Ainsclough, also employed as a nurse at Lambeth Hospital.

Ainsclough departed the house, turned left and walked up the Victorian terraced development that was Hargwyne Road, intending, as usual, to take the Underground from Clapham North into central London and to New Scotland Yard. As he walked he thought, once again, that he and Sara working shifts, sometimes arriving as the other was departing, was what kept their marriage healthy, in that they saw just sufficient of each other to maintain a sense of mutual intrigue.

Harry Vicary smiled warmly and leaned back in his chair. 'Well,' he said, glancing briefly to his left out of his office window at the River Thames and the buildings opposite before returning his attention to his assembled team of officers, 'the two murders are either connected, or somebody has got it in for poor old, sunny old, leafy old Wimbledon. Any suggestions? What does the team think?'

'They're both connected, sir.' Frankie Brunnie returned the smile. 'They have to be.'

'Of course they are.' Vicary leaned forward and rested his elbows and forearms on his desktop. 'And the car, also burned out in the same place that the car was burned out the previous evening.'

'The same two streets,' Penny Yewdall confirmed. 'That's more than a coincidence.'

'We can also consider the possibility that someone is sending us a message,' Tom Ainsclough offered.

'Either that,' Victor Swannell also leaned forward in his chair, 'or it is just plain sloppy on the part of the felons. That would be my guess. They might have realized that that part of Wimbledon is a good place to get in and out of without being picked up by CCTV cameras, they know the routes in and out, and they have discovered all those overgrown front gardens to hide in. They did it successfully one night, and so they decided to dump the second body and torch the second car in the same two locations but, by doing so, they have invited us to link the victims. Quite a serious mistake on their part.'

'Or someone is sending us a message, as Tom suggests,' Penny Yewdall added.

Vicary sipped his tea. 'Sadly, I have to report that the police helicopter wasn't available last evening; it had a pressing errand involving the chase of a high performance car . . . a stolen high performance car, the driver of which was intending to carve up all the traffic on the North Circular. It couldn't be diverted to search for infra-red images of people playing hide and seek in suburban front gardens south of the river. So, if there is a connection between Gordon Cogan and last night's victim, we must find it ourselves.' Vicary paused. 'Tom and Penny . . . I want you two to stay teamed up.'

'Yes, sir,' Yewdall and Ainsclough replied in unison as they glanced approvingly at each other.

'I want you two to look at last night's victim, attend the post-mortem . . . you're particularly looking for a connection with Gordon Cogan. If it's there you'll find it.'

'Yes, sir,' Yewdall answered for herself and Ainsclough.

'Victor and Frankie.'

'Yes, boss,' Brunnie replied enthusiastically.

'I'd like you two to go back and look at the murder for which Cogan was convicted. Penny and Tom talked to Gordon Cogan's brother yesterday after he viewed and identified the body of Gordon Cogan at the Royal London Hospital. They have recorded their findings in the file. You'll read it, of course, but in a nutshell Gordon Cogan pleaded not guilty despite compelling DNA evidence, and according to his brother he did not seem to be a man in denial. He had put up his hand to an earlier offence because he was guilty of that, and so he seemed to have been a man who possessed a powerful sense of integrity. He was also a highly educated man – three university degrees, no less – and thusly was someone who, one would think, would know the compelling weight DNA evidence carries. Yet he offered no defence at all. He just pleaded not guilty. It seems to have been the case that his attitude was, "Yes, I know all about DNA and its importance as evidence, but I didn't do it". And then, after ten years of being IDOM he suddenly changes his plea. It's as if there is a story there, and it's a story which he did not share with his elder brother. So that's what I want you two blokes to do . . . go back into that murder, talk to any interested parties, find out, if you can, exactly what Gordon Cogan's story was. As I said . . . if you can.'

'Yes, boss.' Frankie Brunnie spoke confidently. 'Leave it with us.'

Harry Vicary leaned backwards and paused as if in thought, then he leaned forward. 'You know, it doesn't take two to observe the post-mortem for the police . . . so . . . Tom . . . if you could do that, please . . . if you could observe the post-mortem, then that will free you up, Penny, to go and visit Gordon Cogan's victim-cum-pupil . . . or rather, I should say, his pupil-cum-victim. She's in her thirties now and is known to us, as Derek Cogan said that she would be. Just petty stuff, but she's known.'

'Yes, sir,' Yewdall replied with prompt alertness.

'Go and talk to her . . . that's a one-hander, I think. Are you happy to visit her alone?'

'Very happy, sir.' Yewdall nodded. 'It's a one-hander, as you say, woman to woman.'

'Good, then after you have visited her, team up with Tom to look at the background of last night's victim. Look for a connection with Gordon Cogan.'

'Yes, sir,' Penny Yewdall replied with enthusiasm.

'Good.' Vicary leaned backwards. 'So we all know what we are doing? If any of you should stray into another task, then let me know.' He patted his phone. 'I must know where each of you is at all times.'

'Yes, sir. Understood.' Frankie Brunnie replied for the team as the officers stood.

'There was just nothing, nothing at all happening in his life.' Lysandra Smith revealed herself to be a small woman, slight to the point of being borderline anorexic, Yewdall guessed, who lived in a high-rise council flat on an estate of sixties 'Brutalism' design in Stepney. She had, Yewdall noted, grown from a love-struck schoolgirl into a woman with a hard face and steel-cold eyes, who had a worn and used look about her. Yewdall felt she had 'sex-trade worker' written all the way through her like a stick of seaside rock, either retired, semi-retired or still fully active, Yewdall couldn't tell, but she intuitively knew that Lysandra Smith could tell more than a few stories of the street. Yewdall read the living room in which she and Lysandra sat. She noted that the room, and probably the rest of the flat, was kept in an untidy and cluttered manner. It was furnished with inexpensive items and had a musty smell. A tabloid newspaper was strewn on the plastic cover of the settee while a packet of cheap cigarettes and a yellow disposable cigarette lighter stood on an inexpensive and flimsy-looking coffee table, the surface of which was heavily stained with circular rings caused by the base of hot coffee and tea mugs being placed directly on to it, rather than on coasters. Lysandra Smith wore brightly coloured plastic bangles on both wrists but no jewellery at all and certainly no wedding band. The woman wore faded blue denims, a loose-fitting red T-shirt and was without footwear. She sat hunched forward in an armchair which stood next to an old portable television set. Penny Yewdall began to feel itchy as she sat opposite Lysandra Smith in an identical armchair. 'That's it . . . that was it,'

Lysandra Smith looked downwards at the matted carpet and seemed to Yewdall to avoid any eye contact with her, 'nothing was happening in his life. He was a ruined man struggling to make ends meet . . . like I tell you . . . the gospel truth is . . . his Sunday lunch was a tin of spaghetti hoops and sometimes not even that. He had lost everything. And I mean everything. He tried to stay off the booze but when he did get some cash he'd be off round the "offie" for a bottle of vodka which he'd take home and demolish. Once or twice he'd go on a two- or three-day bender but that wasn't often. He never had that sort of money. Hardly ever, anyway.'

'So you kept close to him?' Yewdall asked.

'Not so close,' Lysandra Smith replied with a certain sadness in her voice. 'We were lovers and I visited when I could get away, but it wasn't easy. Then I got pregnant and that certainly didn't help my situation any.' She reached for the packet of cigarettes, opened it and offered one to Penny Yewdall, who shook her head briefly, smiling her thanks as she did so. Lysandra Smith put the cigarette to her lips and lit it with the disposable lighter. She then tossed the lighter back on to the coffee table top with a clatter. Yewdall watched as Lysandra Smith inhaled deeply and then exhaled the smoke through her nostrils with a sense of gratitude about her, as if the nicotine was clearly reaching her. 'We had to keep it on the old Q.T., didn't we? I mean, like very Q.T. We couldn't breathe a word to no one, could we?'

'I don't know, couldn't you?' Yewdall continued to 'read' the room which began to say 'retired brass, now on the dole'. She sensed that Lysandra Smith had finally left the street behind her . . . perhaps not fully . . . but definitely 'retired from the game'; otherwise, Yewdall reasoned, there would be indications of a greater degree of spending power around her flat.

'No, we couldn't say a word. Not a dicky bird.' Lysandra flicked the ash from the end of her cigarette on to the knee of her jeans and rubbed it into the weave of the denim. 'It was my old man, wasn't it? He was not well impressed with me seeing Gordon, not impressed at all. But despite that we'd still manage to meet up from time to time. There was a pay phone in the hall of the home where he had a bedsit. I'd phone him when I could get away, and that wasn't often, and we'd arrange to meet up and we'd go and sit for an evening in some dingy battle cruiser or other. We had no money to speak of, and so we'd make the drinks last as long as we could. We'd sit there until the landlord started to glare at us, then we'd walk out into the night.' Lysandra Smith inhaled and then exhaled through her mouth as she continued speaking, so that the cigarette smoke egressed in small, disjointed clouds. 'Then one night he said that he'd been thinking and he'd decided that we should stop seeing each other. He said that he had no income or future to speak of. He couldn't support no one . . . he couldn't support a family. He said that he was finished before he was started. Gordon said that we should stop seeing each other and that I should find someone else; that I should get married and have a life.'

'How did you feel about that?' Yewdall asked.

'I wasn't happy about it but I saw the sense in it. By then I was pregnant but I wasn't showing so Gordon didn't know.'

'He wasn't the father?' Yewdall pressed.

Lysandra Smith shook her head firmly. She leaned forward and this time the recipient of the ash from her cigarette was a badly chipped green porcelain ashtray with Bass Charrington embossed on the side in gold lettering, clearly taken from a pub by some person, or persons unknown, some years previously and which had, by some circuitous route, eventually ended up in the flat of Lysandra Smith in Stepney. 'So all in all, I thought he was right.' Smith inhaled more smoke. 'He was a broken man, young but broken, like Humpty Dumpty . . . no one was going to put Gordon Cogan together again . . . The man I had that schoolgirl crush on was clean and neatly turned out, very well-spoken, well educated, looking so . . . so . . . awesome in his university gown, not a confident teacher but finding his feet, a man we still looked up to despite his nervousness. Then a few months later he was smelly, unshaven, unwashed, wearing drab clothing with hot, searing breath, and unable to make a living. All right, so I was part of his fall from grace, I was part of that, his downfall . . . but he just wasn't the geezer I had gone to Ireland with. So yes, in the end I thought he was right, there was no future for us, none at all, and it also meant that I wouldn't be at risk from my old man anymore.'

'At risk?' Yewdall probed. 'What do you mean?'

'Yeah . . . my old man was a bit . . . physical. He can still be a bit violent.' Lysandra Smith's voice trailed off. 'I mean, when I came back from Ireland he gave me a dreadful hiding, a real leathering he gave me, so he did.'

'Social services had ensured that you were safe, so we were told,' Yewdall observed.

'Well, yes,' Lysandra looked up at the ceiling, 'they visited my old man and my old woman before I was returned and got an assurance that I'd be safe, but my old man's words don't mean nothing. They visited again once I'd been home for a few days and found that all was OK. It was when my old man realized that they wouldn't be calling on us no more that he took his belt off and half an hour later he put it back on again. He waited for ten days before he did it. He was clever like that. He knew the value of not showing his hand too early on.'

'I am sorry,' Yewdall said softly. 'You were not to blame . . . your parents should have known that.'

'My old man didn't see it like that, did he? He . . .' Lysandra's Smith's voice faded as they heard a sound of shuffling from the room above the living room. 'Oh, he's up early today; he doesn't usually stir until well gone midday.'

'He?' Yewdall asked.

.'Pancras,' Lysandra Smith explained. 'My son, Pancras.'

'Lovely name.' Yewdall smiled.

'He hates it,' Lysandra Smith looked sideways, 'but his father gave it to him. He said it would toughen him up at school. His father said that the other children would ridicule him and so he'd learn from that to stick up for himself and that's what's happened . . . it's hardened him up all right and he's taken after my old man. He's very violent – it'll be his downfall.'

'Oh . . .' Penny Yewdall allowed a note of disappointment to enter her voice. 'I am sorry to hear that.'

'His father is in Parkhurst. He's doing twenty years for armed robbery and keeps throwing away any hope of parole with his bad attitude. He's just anti-authority . . . got involved in a prison riot once and got five more years added to his sentence for that. He was sent down when Pancras was three years old and the only male influence in Pancras's life since then has been my old man. I reckon Pancras will be up and coming downstairs now because he'll have heard your voice; he'll be wanting to know who you are. He's very . . . what's the word? Territorial. He wants to know about everything that goes on in this house.'

'Why . . . how old is he?' Yewdall asked.

'Fifteen.' Lysandra Smith replied in a matter-of-fact manner.

'Fifteen . . .' Yewdall gasped.

'Yes. He's well used to hearing daytime television but a visitor . . . that will have got him out of bed. But me . . . little me.' Lysandra Smith shrugged. 'Think of it . . . Gordon Cogan, then Elliot Reiss, an armed robber . . . I mean, tell me, am I a magnate for losers or am I a magnet for losers?'

Yewdall could only smile a sympathetic smile in reply.

'He's already known to you.' Lysandra Smith dragged heavily on the cigarette.

'Pancras? Your son? He's known to the police?'

'Yes, he is. He wants to be like his father . . . his old man. I did my little old best but with a father like he's got and him also being away for all but the first three years of Pancras's life . . .' Lysandra Smith shrugged for a second time, '. . . what chance has he got? He's been in youth custody for acts of violence. He was suspended from school for attacking a teacher with a knife when he was seven years old, but things like that just give him street cred . . . and that is all he wants. Street cred. He lives and breathes street cred. He hangs around the estate making contacts in the underworld he wants to be part of. He's already a gofer for a local firm of villains; it's a step on the ladder he wants to climb.'

'He should be at school,' Yewdall protested. 'He's still just fifteen . . .'

'I know, I mean don't I know that, but he's a persistent refuser. He'll soon be sixteen and the authorities and I have given up all hope of ever getting him back into the classroom. So he's well on his way to becoming a career criminal like his old man.'

'You're still Lysandra Smith?' Yewdall clarified. 'Not Lysandra Reiss?'

'Yes. Still Smith. I was born Lysandra Smith and I reckon I'll shuffle as Lysandra Smith. You see, me and Elliot have a common-law marriage and because of that Pancras has my name . . . but he wants to be Pancras Reiss. He is known as Pancras Reiss, but Smith is on his birth certificate.'

'I see.' Yewdall made a mental note to check Pancras Reiss's criminal record.

'He's up to some serious felony though,' Lysandra Smith continued. 'He has a source of income and he spends each night in the boozer.'

'He's fifteen!' Yewdall protested.

'He's a big lad, you'll see for yourself any minute now. He passes for eighteen or nineteen and he does so without difficulty. The publicans round here know he's part of the local villainy and the rule of the game is that any villain who gets refused service for anything other than being drunk and out of order . . . well, he then has words in the right ear and the pub gets smashed up . . . maybe even torched. So Pancras gets his beer and comes home and sleeps till gone noon.' Lysandra Smith dogged her cigarette in the ashtray. 'The wonder of nature . . . who would have thought that little old me could produce a rugby full back . . . all six foot of him?'

A heavy footfall was heard descending the stairs and Pancras Smith entered the living room. He was, Yewdall saw, just as he had been described: tall and muscular, though slender rather than broad-chested, with short hair and a shadow on his chin, but he appeared to be normally clean-shaven. He wore a green T-shirt, loose-fitting red jogging bottoms and white and blue sports shoes. Yewdall had to concede that he would pass for nineteen, and that he would have no difficulty in being served alcohol in any public house. Pancras Smith eyed Yewdall with undisguised hostility, clearly recognizing her as a police officer. Yewdall held his stare.

'A rozzer!' Pancras Smith snarled. 'A filthy rozzer! In this house!'

'Don't go doing no bother, now, Pancras,' Lysandra Smith appealed to her son as he towered over both her and Penny

Yewdall. 'No one's in any trouble. This young lady is just asking me about someone I knew a long, long time ago.'

Penny Yewdall observed that Pancras Smith, aka Reiss, had already developed the hard-looking, cold-eyed, humourless face of the criminal. He had piercing blue eyes and a long scar on his cheek which he seemed to wear with pride, as if it were a medal. She saw a hard-hearted young man comfortably on his way to a life of crime and prison . . . and more crime . . . and more prison.

'So what does she want?' Pancras Smith demanded of his mother in a raised voice while not moving his gaze from Yewdall.

'I told you . . . just a bit of information. We're just having a chat. There's no need to get moody, Pancras. We're just having some quiet verbals . . . that's all.' Lysandra Smith attempted to placate her son and Yewdall saw that she was clearly in some fear of him. 'Quiet verbals . . . just some quiet verbals. It's only about someone I knew before you were born.'

'Who? That old teacher geezer you ran off with to Ireland?' Pancras Smith demanded in an aggressive manner. 'Is it about him . . . about that geezer?'

'Yes. Yes it is,' Lysandra Smith replied calmly. 'If you must know. You see, no one's in trouble. You needn't get worried.'

'But why?' Pancras Smith snarled. 'Why does she want to come here and talk about that slimy toe-rag? That's all blood under the railway tracks, isn't it?'

'Because he's brown bread,' Lysandra Smith explained with a patience which impressed Yewdall. 'This lady just wants to know a little bit about him, but I can't tell her much 'cos I don't know much.'

'Good. I'm glad he's dead.' Pancras Smith strode out of the living room and into the kitchen where he could be heard banging pots about, showing no more interest in Penny Yewdall.

'His grandfather, my old man,' Lysandra Smith spoke in a hushed tone, 'turned Pancras against Gordon Cogan.'

'I quite understand.' Yewdall smiled. 'Let's pick things up again. So you used to visit Gordon in the bedsit in Acton?'

'Yes . . . a few times . . . not often. It was quite an old ride on the Tube from my old man's drum up in Southgate . . . didn't have to change . . . but twenty-plus stations . . . that's a long ride on the Tube.'

'It was in that house that Gordon Cogan murdered that girl,' Yewdall said, 'so we understand.'

'Yes . . . yes it was. The house of horror . . . Alfred Road, Acton . . . number one hundred and ninety-six. It must have been a lovely old house in its day . . . four storey, Victorian terrace house . . . it had a basement, a ground floor, first floor, second floor and attic space but no one went up to the attic, not when I was visiting Gordon. Gordon had a room on the first floor. There were two other flats on that floor. Gordon had the big room at the front of the house and Janet Frost, the girl he murdered, well, she had the little box room which was above the front door next to Gordon's room.' Lysandra Smith glanced up at the ceiling. 'It must have been lovely in its day . . . the house, I mean . . . back in the day. It wasn't up to much when Gordon was there . . . damp, smelly, over-crowded . . . but once it must have been a lovely house.'

'It must have come as quite a shock to you when you heard that Gordon had murdered someone?' Yewdall asked, bringing the conversation back into focus.

'A shock,' Lysandra Smith looked at Yewdall, 'that's putting it mildly! I followed the trial in the newspapers and on the television. The DNA evidence was . . . so strong . . . but I still couldn't believe that Gordon was a killer. Even when he was half cut, and we all do and say stupid things under the influence of alcohol, I still couldn't believe he could strangle someone. He just didn't have that sort of bottle. It takes a lot of bottle to off someone with your bare hands and Gordon just didn't have it. I knew he'd been drinking at the time . . . or so I heard, and I saw bottles of voddy on the floor of his room . . . I mean, empty bottles. But that's drink – it can turn calm men into complete monsters, although voddy just made Gordon want to close his eyes and sleep. And he wasn't a big man either . . . though she wasn't a big girl, mind, his victim, Janet Frost. She was quite small, like me.'

'You knew her?' Yewdall asked.

'No . . . no . . . I didn't know her.' Lysandra Smith shook

her head. 'I met her a couple of times but just in passing . . .
poor girl. No chance at all. She was seventeen years old and
already a totally wasted smack head. Seventeen and she looked
like she was in her thirties . . . pale skin, like she'd been bled,
white and yellow eye sockets. Looking at her face was like
looking at urine holes in the snow – yellow holes surrounded
by white. She was shooting up like there was no tomorrow
which, in her old case, wasn't too far from the truth . . . I tell
you, by the Ancient of Days, she was a mess.'

'That's an interesting turn of phrase,' Yewdall smiled. 'The
Ancient of Days. I've never heard it used before.'

'Yes, it means God . . . from the hymn "Immortal, Invisible".
You must know it? "Most blessed, most glorious, the Ancient
of Days, Almighty, victorious, thy great name we praise."'

'Yes, I know it, I remember it,' Yewdall replied. '"Thy
justice like mountains high soaring above, thy clouds which
are fountains of goodness and love". Yes, it's very uplifting.'

'Well,' Lysandra Smith explained, 'we had a teacher at
school, the formidable Miss Armstrong, a Scottish woman
who formed her words at the back of her throat, not the roof
of her mouth, so even when she thought she was talking she
was actually shouting, and she tended to use that expression,
"By the Ancient of Days, unless I see some improvement in
your work, girl, I will write to your father suggesting he
takes you out of this school because he is wasting his money
sending you here. Would you like that? Would you like to go
to a comprehensive school among the rough and smelly children?" That's what she often would say, to me and one or two
other "feet draggers" as she used to call the poorly performing
pupils . . . "the feet draggers of this form". Actually, I would
have loved it but I kept silent, and I also didn't remind her
that my father's house was in Southgate and the children in
the comprehensives up in Southgate were anything but rough
and smelly. And where do I fetch up? In a split-level flat on
a high-rise estate in Stepney among the rough and the smelly.
But when she was not angry, which was very infrequently,
she explained that she used that expression because she thought
it sounded less blasphemous than saying "by God", even
though it meant the same. Anyway, she retired and Gordon

took her place as the French teacher. All the French I remember from school is from Miss Armstrong's "I take no prisoners" approach and nothing from Gordon's "let's be friends" approach . . . but our eyes met early on in Gordon's time at the school, and the rest, as they say, is history.' Lysandra Smith glanced down at the threadbare carpet at her feet. 'But that girl, Janet Frost . . . a mess . . . like she had real craters in her forearms where she had jabbed the needle. You could see the layers of her skin . . . that's no exaggeration.'

'I know.' Penny Yewdall nodded her head. 'Believe me, I have seen the like.'

'Yes . . . I imagine you have in your line of work.' Lysandra Smith looked at the packet of cigarettes. 'Shall I have another one? Shall I have a fag? What's another coffin nail? I'm trying to cut down . . . no . . . I'd best not, not yet anyway. Each minute I can resist a fag is a victory.' She took a deep breath. 'There was no flesh on her, Janet Frost; like she had an eating disorder . . . what is it? Anor . . .?'

'Anorexia nervosa?' Yewdall suggested.

'Yes, that's the name.' Lysandra Smith nodded her head. 'She had that in a bad way. Honestly, she was like something out of a Nazi death camp but Gordon was very kind to her, you know. When he had a bit of money he bought her food and encouraged her to eat it . . . food she could digest . . . like soup. And then he strangles her? I don't think so.' Lysandra Smith shook her head. 'He strangles her and then goes back to his room to sleep the drink off? But they . . . the Old Bill . . . you lot . . . The Bill finds his DHSS signing-on card in her room and bits of her underwear in his room . . . and they found his DNA on her body . . . so they said at his trial . . . and as he had no defence other than, "I don't remember doing it" . . . no defence at all, down he went . . . life, but at least the judge didn't set a minimum term . . . and that was the last I heard of Gordon Cogan until you showed up at my door telling me that he is brown bread. Poor soul.'

Pancras Smith emerged from the kitchen, scowled at Penny Yewdall and walked out of the flat without a word to, or a glance at, his mother.

'That'll be him until well past midnight,' Lysandra Smith

explained apologetically. 'He'll roam far and wide like a hungry animal.'

'Really?' Yewdall replied. 'You have no control over him at all?'

'None.' Lysandra Smith sighed. 'He just runs with the wolves on the estate and he claims he has a shooter.'

'A gun!' Yewdall gasped. 'That sounds like serious stuff he's mixed up in.'

'Yes, so he claims and I believe him. I've never known him make an empty boast. Never.' Lysandra Smith looked hungrily at the packet of cigarettes.

'Here? In this house? In his room?' Penny Yewdall pointed to the ceiling. 'He keeps it here?'

'No, he says he has it stashed somewhere on the outside,' Smith replied. 'I believe him on that as well. But he seems to see the shooter as a good way to get into the big league. He wants some gaol time under his belt. Youth custody won't cut it. He needs adult gaol time to be accepted as a serious player. He's practically sixteen now so all I can do is sit back and watch. He stopped listening to me a long time ago.'

'If he's got a gun at his age . . . well . . .' Yewdall said, 'I can tell you that he's fast-tracking his way to prison.'

'I told you, that's what he wants!' Lysandra Smith succumbed to temptation, took another cigarette from the packet and lit it with the yellow lighter. 'That's exactly his plan.'

'Are you on the dole, Lysandra?' Yewdall asked as she watched her inhale deeply. 'You don't mind if I call you "Lysandra"?'

'Don't mind at all, darling – I don't mind one little bit. And yes, I am on the dole . . . I've been on the dole all my life. Never been employed. Not once. I don't know what a wage packet looks like.' Lysandra Smith exhaled as she spoke. 'I do a little shoplifting; you can't get by without that. I am a little old for the game now so hardly do that anymore, but I can still stand on a street corner if push comes to shove and if the geezer is drunk enough or if he doesn't look too closely, then, in that case, I can earn twenty quid. I hate doing it but a girl has to eat and with him . . .' Lysandra Smith jabbed the cigarette in the air in the direction of the front door, 'he's just like a bottomless pit when it comes to food, totally bottomless. You've seen his size . . . Well, I can tell you that he's got the stomach to match. I come downstairs in the mornings and open the fridge and it's like it's been raided by locusts . . . totally stripped bare. But if Pancras or Elliot find out that I sometimes stand on street corners then it's the end of me, and no mistake.'

Penny Yewdall instinctively took her purse from her handbag and from it extracted a ten-pound note which she laid on the surface of the coffee table. 'That's all I can spare,' she said apologetically.

'Oh, thanks, Duchess.' Lysandra Smith swept up the note with the practised ease and skill of a hungry ghetto dweller. 'It's just that I got no food at all, not right now, and I don't get my old Giro until tomorrow.'

'No worries, it'll tide you over.' Penny Yewdall replaced her purse inside her handbag and stood, preparing to leave the flat.

'It was such a good school I went to as well.' Lysandra Smith also stood up. 'I was so well-spoken, not just grammatically perfect but with a plummy accent. I had to lose the accent to survive here. If you put on the dog on this estate you get your windows panned in . . . even with Pancras to look after me . . . and the grammar, well, that just evaporated. If you put a well-spoken person and a poorly spoken person together and keep them together, the poorly spoken person will bring the well-spoken person down to their level of speech, not the other way round.'

'You think so?' Penny Yewdall slung her handbag over her shoulder.

'Happens all the time. Believe me; well-spoken people have got to keep in each other's company if they want to remain well-spoken.' Lysandra Smith shrugged. 'A lot of girls from my school went on to university and this is where I fetched up. I married into crime . . . and so this is my house. You know, I lay down each night and if I can't sleep I think . . . I think what could have happened to me if I'd gone to university. What would I have been now? A doctor, a lawyer . . . if not one then married to one . . . but I was expelled when I returned from Ireland with Gordon Cogan and I didn't sit my exams. I never completed my education. I met Elliot Reiss in a bar when I was all tarted up and we moved in together soon afterwards.'

'Doesn't your father help you out . . . I mean, financially speaking? He can't still be angry with you for running away with Gordon Cogan,' Yewdall queried. 'If he lives in Southgate, if he sent you to a fee-paying school, he must be quite a wealthy man?'

'No, he doesn't help and I don't want his help,' Lysandra Smith retorted with an anger that surprised Yewdall. 'I don't want his help at all. In fact, I haven't seen him since Pancras was born. But Pancras and my old man get on like a house on fire. In fact, he sends for Pancras quite frequently.'

'Sends for him?' Yewdall repeated with no little astonishment. 'You mean that he summons him?'

'No . . . I mean he sends a car to pick him up. It takes him to Southgate and brings him back again later that day,' Lysandra Smith explained. 'It's been that way for years.'

'Well, doesn't your father make any attempt to turn Pancras away from crime if they have that sort of relationship?'

'No,' Lysandra Smith smiled, 'not my father . . . you know my father. You know Pancras, you know me and you know my father.'

'We do?' Yewdall replied. 'We know your father?'

'Yes, very well. He's Tony Smith,' Lysandra Smith spoke matter of factly, 'you know . . . *the* Tony Smith, Tony "the Pestilence" Smith. Sometimes "Pestilence Smith". Sometimes just plain old "Pestilence".'

Yewdall felt her jaw sag. '"Pestilence Smith" is your father?'

'Yes.' Lysandra Smith smiled. 'That's why Pancras dotes on him. What better grandfather could a fifteen-year-old boy who wants to be a gangster have? But thanks for the ten sovs, Duchess. Promise I'll buy grub with it, not smokes. Promise.'

FOUR

'It really was an open and shut case.' Detective Sergeant Darwish clasped his hands behind his head and leaned backwards as he sat at his desk. The man was, Frankie Brunnie noted, a large man, even for a police officer, with a massively broad chest, a large, bald head and huge, bear-like paws for hands. He had a warm, affable manner, at least towards fellow police officers. He seemed to Swannell and Brunnie to be a team player, a rugby fullback, playing hard but enjoying conviviality at the clubhouse after the game. 'It was, I tell you plain,' he continued, 'the open-ist and shuttest case you ever did see. It was no sooner opened than it was shut, all in a single day. There was nothing at all that we needed to turn to New Scotland Yard for; it had no depth, no intrigue. It was just the old, old story of two lowlifes living in the same damp, overcrowded rental building, separate bedsits but just across the landing from each other. One was an alcoholic kiddie snatcher and underage sex fiend, the other a totally wasted smack head. She was just seventeen years old but she looked older than my grandmother; both were no-hopers and one snuffs out the other. It's most often the way of it with murder.'

'You reckon?' Victor Swannell, sitting beside Frankie Brunnie, cast his eyes around DS Darwish's office. He saw it to be neat, functional and cold, with a police mutual calendar as the only decoration.

'Well, I'd say so,' Darwish replied cheerfully. 'Most murders are handled locally – there are very few that require the expertise of you gentlemen from New Scotland Yard. In fact, we had one such murder last week. It was all wrapped up in half an hour.'

'Half an hour?' Brunnie gasped. 'That was quick. I must say that you didn't mess around there.'

'It was all the time it needed.' Darwish smiled. 'Picture it, if you will. Two derelicts living in a bedsit, sharing a room plus cooking facilities in a house which was falling apart around them with wet rot and dry rot and subsidence and everything else that can make a house crumble into dust. It was, quite frankly, astounding that the building was still standing upright. It looked like a gentle breeze would knock it over. Anyway, it was condemned by the local authority and about to be demolished. The council had found alternative accommodation for those two old geezers. They were in their fifties and were to be rehoused separately. So they started to divide up the flat but they argued as to who should take the television and the argument escalated into a fight. One pulled a blade . . . quite a serious shiv . . . an old military bayonet, in fact . . . and it did the job it was designed for all right. One was dead and the other collects a life sentence, all over a battered old television, an old black and white set. It had no value at all. Even a charity shop would not accept it as a donation. I dare say it was all a matter of pride and principle rather than the value of the television as an item of property . . . but that is your average murder. Here, in Acton, all over the rest of London, all over the rest of the country, all over the rest of the world, in fact, and it was the nature of the murder of Janet Frost, pale little waif and stray that she was. She was the victim of Gordon Cogan and all he could say was, "I don't remember doing it". You know, I often wish real murders had the mystery and the richness of quality of the murders featured on TV dramas – that would make our job so much more interesting. But it's always . . . nearly always, grubby, cheap and impulsive; humanity at its lowest, at its worst.'

'Such was the murder of Janet Frost, you say,' Brunnie replied. 'I am so pleased you said "nearly" by the way.'

'All right, I dare say that you need the occasional murder of quality,' Darwish grinned, 'but yes, that was the way of the murder of Janet Frost. It was just like that. Just as I have described. They lived on top of each other in a house full of lowlifes, alkies, smack heads and cheap brasses; it was a real den of thieves. The perpetrator, Gordon Cogan, had been a schoolteacher until he ran away with one of his pupils – took her to the west coast of Ireland. He was lifted by the Irish boys and when his case came to court he went in front of Mr Justice Father Christmas who says Cogan's lost everything so no prison sentence is needed, and sends him down for six months backdated to the date of his arrest so he walks out of court that very day. Would you credit it?' Darwish shook his head. 'Raping and abducting a schoolgirl – he should have got a ten-year stretch for that at least. At the very minimum he should have collected a full decade. So he fetches up in a dosshouse in Acton Town and, lo and behold, who's across the corridor but another little girl, so he goes into her drum and chokes the life out of her, doesn't he? You see, that's what lenient sentencing gets you – it gives out the wrong message, let's 'em think they can do it and get away with it.'

'You reckon?' Victor Swannell said for the second time.

'Yes, of course . . . I mean, if that little toe-rag Cogan had got the ten-year stretch he should have got, Janet Frost would still be alive . . . or then again maybe not given the way she was putting away the heroin, but she would have lived a bit longer anyway.' Darwish leaned forward and rested his elbows on his desktop, clasping his huge hands together. He wore a light blue shirt with the sleeves neatly rolled up cuff over cuff and an expensive-looking watch around his left wrist. He beamed at Swannell and Brunnie. 'I hope Mr Justice Father Christmas re-assessed his sentencing values after that murder. He would have read about it. He let the little pervert out for abducting and raping a schoolgirl because he's done six months on remand and within a matter of weeks he's strangled another young girl. There was no clear motive, just theft, and a little passion possibly, when he was under the influence. He was no great shakes as an example of British manhood, he was a weedy little non-descript of a man, but despite that, Janet Frost was no match for him.'

'A small girl?' Brunnie asked.

'About the size of your average twelve-year-old.' Darwish held eye contact with Brunnie. 'His DNA was all over her body and also all over her room: on her shelves, in her drawers, her cupboards, everywhere. And I mean everywhere. He'd rifled her room, plundered it, ransacked it, really gone to town and there she was in the middle of it, a little naked body with a massively bruised neck and his DNA all over her . . . not just round her neck but all over her . . . No indication of sex, though, but he went all over her room. Robbery when under the influence, or so we assumed, but she had nothing of value so he took a pair of her thongs back into his room . . . filthy little pervert . . . he runs off with a schoolgirl, then he murders a seventeen-year-old for a single item of her underwear.' Darwish grinned and shrugged his shoulders, 'Like I said. Open and shut.'

'What did he say had happened?' Brunnie asked.

'He claimed he had no recollection, like I said,' Darwish replied. 'I slapped him around a bit but he still said he couldn't remember anything.'

'You did that?' Swannell raised an eyebrow. 'That could have backfired on you.'

'Yes, I did,' Darwish replied. 'I mean, within these four walls, of course, I mean between you and me and the gatepost.'

'Dangerous confession,' Swannell growled. 'It could still get you into bother.'

'Come on, he got what was coming to him and it was a long time coming if you ask me . . . a very long time coming . . . the rape of a schoolgirl . . . then he murders a teenager for her underwear . . . and all he could bleat was, "I don't remember, I don't remember". But it was a solid conviction, and so we were well happy. Why all the interest in the little toe-rag? Is he under suspicion for another felony?'

'No, nothing like that,' Brunnie replied coldly. 'He's dead. He's been murdered.'

'Has he now?' Darwish smiled a broad smile and once more put his hands behind his head. 'Well, there's justice for you, as my old Welsh grandfather would have said.' Darwish's smile was broad enough to reveal a gold-capped molar.

'Yesterday,' Swannell added, deadpan. 'The body was found in the street in Wimbledon.'

'That was Cogan?' Darwish slapped one of his mighty palms on his desktop. 'I heard about that on the radio. No name was mentioned, just that a body had been found . . . police appealing for witnesses, et cetera. Well, that's a turn-up for the books and no mistake . . . and Wimbledon . . . Acton to Wimbledon, that is quite a social climb. Didn't he go up in the world?'

'Hardly,' Brunnie replied, 'he was living in a bail hostel in

Kentish Town when he was iced. We believe his body was dumped in Wimbledon after he was murdered elsewhere.'

'I see,' Darwish replied.

'There were no CCTV cameras where his body was dumped,' Swannell explained. 'Somebody knew what they were doing – someone was CCTV savvy.'

'So . . .' Darwish pursed his lips, 'someone didn't like him. That I can well understand. But yes, I gave him a right pasting in the cells when he came back from the Magistrates Court after his solicitor had left.' Darwish paused, noting the expressions on Swannell and Brunnie's faces. 'Well, he was getting away with too much, wasn't he? Abducting and raping a schoolgirl . . . then he strangles a tiny little seventeen-year-old. She could have turned her life around, or she'd be dead within a year anyway . . . we'll never know . . . but the point is that time was on her side, it could still all have been ahead of her. With treatment and rehab she could have had a life. Cogan got money for a bottle and when he's tanked up and gets a bit angry about this and that and forces his way into her room, very usefully for us he drops his DHSS signing-on card on her carpet, chokes the life out of her and steals her undies. His DNA is all over the shop . . . I mean, everywhere, like I said . . . and would you credit it, does he even try to help himself? No . . . the stupid oaf pleads not guilty. Anyway, he was found guilty, goes up before Mr Justice Very Sensible this time and collects a life sentence. He changes his plea once inside, works the system and gets parole after fifteen years. Me, I would have thrown the key into Old Father Thames and left him to rot. That's the sort of justice that I understand.'

'Yes,' Brunnie replied sourly, 'I think that you would have done just that. I can quite easily see you doing just that.'

'The fact is, gentlemen,' Darwish snarled, and in doing so revealed an alarming side to his personality, 'that you know and I know that there are just some people who should not be let out on to the street, and Gordon Cogan is . . . *was* one of them. So he's been topped – why am I not surprised? Why am I not very, very, very upset? What happened to the little pillock?'

'We don't know yet,' Brunnie replied, 'but he was filled

in with great determination. Someone made a right jigsaw puzzle of his skull.'

'Right now we are just gathering as much information as we can,' Swannell explained calmly. 'We're looking for a motive . . . getting some background information . . . you know the score.'

'It was probably a bit of good old-fashioned street justice,' Darwish offered. 'A guy like that will upset a lot of people; he will make a lot of enemies. All those girls . . . all those angry relatives . . .'

'All what girls?' Brunnie asked. 'He had other victims?'

'Well, on the basis that we only ever get to hear of about ten per cent of what goes on, it's highly likely that Cogan had other victims,' Darwish explained, 'and each victim would have had a father or an older brother . . .'

'I see,' Brunnie replied. 'But speaking of victims, what can you recall about his victim in the bedsit, Janet Frost? Apart from the fact she was very small and that she was a heroin addict?'

'Not much else.' Darwish picked up the handset of the phone on his desk. 'Just a moment, please . . .' He pressed a four-figure number and when his call was answered he said, 'Hello, DS Darwish here. Can you send up the file on the Janet Frost murder? It will be dated about fifteen years ago. A geezer called Cogan was convicted, so it will be filed under his name, C.O.G.A.N. OK. Great, thanks muchos, me old china, muchos.' He replaced the handset and informed Brunnie and Swannell that the file was being sent up from the collator's office.

'Just DNA?' Brunnie asked.

'Sorry?' Darwish clasped his meaty hands together on his desktop. 'What do you mean, just DNA?'

'I mean was it the DNA evidence alone which convicted Cogan of the murder?' Brunnie clarified.

'And his signing-on card in her room, and her clothing in his room and his previous convictions, the whole snowball effect . . . but yes, mainly the DNA evidence was used to obtain the conviction,' Darwish advised. 'Why do you ask?'

'Were his fingerprints found in her room?' Brunnie pressed.

'I don't think we dusted for them, come to think of it,' Darwish replied. 'They were not produced in evidence.'

'You didn't dust for his prints?' Swannell could not contain his surprise. 'I would have thought that that was an elementary step.'

'Hey . . .' Darwish held up his hand, 'don't shoot the messenger, squire. Don't shoot the messenger. I was only a junior detective constable at the time; in fact, I was only very recently promoted from uniform. I was not the officer in charge of the investigation . . . he is long retired . . . but as I recall we broke in after a tip-off. Found him hung-over . . . barely with us, and her knickers on his bedroom floor. We found her body in the next room. The white coats found his DNA everywhere, like I said, and his DNA was on the database because of his previous offences. So it was like game, set and match. No need for fingerprint evidence . . . no need for independent witnesses.'

'That conviction wouldn't stand today,' Brunnie said calmly. 'All you really had was the DNA and that by itself isn't sufficient for a conviction. Not these days, not in the UK.'

'It was all that was needed fifteen years ago,' Darwish replied in a defensive manner. 'We were well happy with the result. Very well happy. And he changed his plea to guilty anyway, so fingerprints or no fingerprints, it was a good result. It was a result we can live with.'

There was a soft, referential tap on Darwish's office door, in response to which Darwish shouted, 'Come in!' The door opened and a tall, Nordic-featured young policewoman, dressed in a white shirt and a black skirt entered the room carrying a manila folder. 'The file you asked for, sir.' She spoke in a strong, Irish accent as she handed the file to Darwish.

'Thanks, Clodagh.' Darwish took the file from the hand of the policewoman who turned and left the office quietly, shutting the door behind her. Darwish pointed with relish to the closed door and said, 'That's the fittest bit of skirt in this nick . . . lovely . . . I like 'em like that.' He held up the file. 'And I like files like this. See how thin this file is? Open and shut. You often get a file on a murder case as thin as this because murders are the easiest of crimes to solve. It's . . . it's lovely, that's what it is . . . lovely . . . a thing of beauty . . . like Irish Clodagh there . . . a thing of beauty. So we put a nasty away for life, then he comes over all guilty and repents, wins parole, out to rape and murder again except some good citizen tops him.' Darwish laid the file on his desktop and opened it. 'Yes, here we are . . . victim . . . Janet Frost, seventeen . . . next of kin out in Dagenham.' Darwish turned the file round and handed it to Brunnie. 'You think her family had it in for Cogan?'

'Don't know.' Brunnie took the file and copied the address of Janet Frost's next of kin into his notebook. 'But . . . well, such is not unknown . . . as you have suggested . . . such has happened before. We can't jump to any conclusions, largely because there was a development during the night, which has complicated things somewhat.'

'Or clarified them,' Swannell added, 'depending on how you look at it.'

'Oh?' Darwish queried. 'A development?'

'Yes . . .' Brunnie handed the file back to Darwish, 'a woman's body was found in the same place . . . the exact same location that Gordon Cogan's body was found . . . the exact spot . . . and a motor vehicle was found burned out at exactly the same place where the vehicle which we believed was used to transport Gordon Cogan's body was abandoned and set on fire.'

'Oh . . .' Darwish leaned back in his chair. 'Now that is most interesting. I see your point, gentlemen.' Once again he cupped his hands behind his head. 'I see what you mean, that is a bit iffy, very iffy indeed. It suggests a link between the two bodies . . . it suggests a very strong link indeed.'

'Exactly our thinking,' Brunnie added as he stood up, 'but we can't afford to overlook the possibility that the Frost family took their revenge and we'll be paying a call on them. We are keeping an open mind.'

'Thanks for the background information and the details of Janet Frost's relatives.' Swannell smiled as he also stood. 'It's much appreciated.'

John Shaftoe pondered the corpse which lay face up on the stainless steel table. He saw a particularly dark-skinned, large-boned Afro-Caribbean woman in her middle years. He glanced at Tom Ainsclough who, as had been requested, was observing the post-mortem for the police.

'She was found in the very same place that the body of
Gordon Cogan was found,' Ainsclough said.

'Yes . . . yes,' Shaftoe turned his attention back to the corpse,
'I noticed that when I attended the scene this morning. I assume
that the police are linking the two incidents?'

'We have to assume a link until we know otherwise, sir.'
Ainsclough turned his head as he choked briefly on the
formaldehyde-laden air in the pathology laboratory, 'but a link
seems extremely likely.'

'Yes . . . yes . . . I would think that that would be the sensible
thing. It seems far too coincidental otherwise.' Shaftoe continued
to look at the corpse. 'Do we have any identification yet?'

'Yes, sir.' Ainsclough nodded. 'We took her fingerprints this
morning at the scene . . . well, that is to say at the location
where she was found. She is quite well known to us. She is
one Cherry Quoshie, aged thirty-seven years.'

'How are you spelling that?' Shaftoe asked. 'It's an unusual
name.'

Ainsclough told him.

'OK, the deceased is one Cherry Quoshie . . . that's
Q.U.O.S.H.I.E.,' Shaftoe spoke into the microphone,
'pronounced 'Kwoshie. So the name, the next case number
and today's date, if you please, Helen . . . she is thirty-seven
years of age.'

'She has a lot of previous for being in possession of a
controlled substance and for soliciting, and also for a string
of petty offences like shoplifting,' Ainsclough advised.

'The controlled substance in question would be heroin,'
Shaftoe observed. Then he added solemnly, 'Just thirty-seven,
I would have thought her to be older. She looks an awful lot
older but that's what heroin does to a person.'

'I'm afraid I don't know the details,' Ainsclough stammered.
'I had a quick glance at the computer printout before leaving
Scotland Yard to attend the post-mortem.'

'Well, she has plenty of track marks up and down her forearms
. . .' Shaftoe ran his latex gloved hands along the arms of the
deceased. 'Really quite a lot, in fact. This suggests she was a
long-term, heavy user. Quite a few puncture points are noted . . .
but this here is interesting. Come and have a look at this, if you

would.' Shaftoe pointed to a red, circular area, about three inches in diameter, on the inside of the lower left leg of the deceased, close to the ankle. He then turned to Billy Button. 'Can you photograph this thermal injury here, please, Billy?'

Tom Ainsclough stepped silently forward, dressed in the required green paper disposable coveralls, and stood reverentially beside Shaftoe.

'That,' Shaftoe spoke quietly, addressing Ainsclough, 'is a thermal injury. Extreme heat caused that injury. Something metal, heated until it was red hot, was pressed against her leg.'

Ainsclough winced as he noted the angry-looking red circle on the leg of the deceased.

Billy Button gingerly approached the table holding a thirty-five millimetre camera with a flash attachment. Shaftoe and Ainsclough stepped aside to allow the trembling pathology laboratory assistant access to the body. Button made a low wailing sound as he placed a metal ruler by the side of the injury so as to give the photograph scale.

'Calm down, Billy,' Shaftoe spoke reassuringly. 'I've told you many times that our patients, like this lady here, are not feeling anything.'

'Yes, Mr Shaftoe,' Billy Button murmured meekly, 'but . . . but the pain of it when she was alive . . .'

'Just take the photograph, Billy.' Shaftoe spoke softly but firmly. 'Just take the photograph.'

Billy Button mustered sufficient self-control to hold the camera steady for a few seconds while he activated the shutter. The camera flashed and Button then retired speedily to the edge of the post-mortem laboratory and stood beside the instrument trolley.

'The thermal injury is perimortem, and is undoubtedly indicative of torture,' Shaftoe pronounced, 'especially as it is on the inside of the leg. This lady did not accidentally brush up against something very hot, or fall against something very hot which might have been the case had this injury been on the outside of her leg. This injury was deliberately occasioned to her.' Shaftoe turned to Ainsclough. 'Do you know if she has any known next of kin?'

'None that we know of, sir,' Ainsclough replied. 'It seems

that the wretched woman lived alone and that she was alone in the world. She served time in Holloway Prison and on the prison records, which have been copied into the police file, the next-of-kin box has been marked "none given".'

'That . . .' Shaftoe remarked, 'is quite shameful. Quite, quite shameful. But so many are like our friend here, people who have no relatives at all, and many end up here.' He tapped the stainless steel table. 'They are found in derelict buildings or washed up on the riverbank at low tide, often in a state of decomposition. They have died and have not been missed.'

'Indeed, sir,' Ainsclough replied. He too felt the tragedy that was the apparent life of Cherry Quoshie. 'She had had a hard life, going by her file. She grew up in a series of foster homes and care homes. She was listed as a chronic truant and she grew to be a juvenile offender. She has been known to the police since she was thirteen years of age and went on to commit a series of recordable offences . . . notably serious assault and possession of a controlled substance with intent to supply.'

'Ah . . . so you'll have her DNA on file?' Shaftoe smiled.

'Yes, sir.'

'Good. I'll extract a blood sample so that we can determine her DNA profile just to belt and bracer her identity,' Shaftoe announced. 'But the fingerprints have clinched it.' He looked at the corpse, 'So . . . Cherry Quoshie . . . what can you tell us about your life and, more importantly, what can you tell us about your horrible and untimely death?'

'There is a photograph of her in the file, sir,' Ainsclough added. 'It's her all right . . . and her dental records are also in the file. But the fingerprints have determined her identity, as you say.'

'I see.' Shaftoe paused. 'You know, I think that that makes it worse somehow, that she's all alone in the world, yet from the outset there is no doubt as to her identity.'

'Yes,' Ainsclough mumbled, 'that does seem to make it a bit worse, as you say. Somehow.'

'But we mustn't let her situation reach us on an emotional level. We have, of course, to remain detached,' Shaftoe advised. 'We couldn't do the job otherwise.' He forced open the mouth of the deceased. 'Rigor is beginning to establish itself,' he announced. 'Summer of the year,' he glanced at his watch, 'one thirty p.m. Allowing for the chill of the laboratory, I would say that death most likely occurred sometime after midnight. But I won't be tied to that, it's not the job of the pathologist to determine the when of death, just the how of it. As I keep saying to your Mr Vicary, and doubtless will continue to say it, quite frankly the most accurate determination of the time of death is that it occurred sometime between when the person in question was last seen alive by a reliable witness, and the time that their body was found. There are just too many variables in the field of forensic pathology to enable us to be any more accurate.'

'Yes, sir,' Ainsclough responded.

'In the tropics, for example, a dead body will actually heat up for a few hours after death, so in such cases the rate of cooling is meaningless,' Shaftoe added. 'But as I said, I just cannot commit myself on paper as to the exact time of Ms Quoshie's death. But, off paper, I think she died sometime after midnight, in the early hours of this day. Really the issue of time of death is muddy waters and no pathologist – no self-respecting pathologist, anyway – will step into it . . . not on paper.'

'Understood, sir,' Ainsclough replied. He added with a grin, 'Not on paper, anyway.'

Shaftoe peered into the mouth of the deceased. 'Well, we have some dental work but nothing recent. It is likely that the dental work here dates from the time that she was a guest of Her Majesty but once at liberty it appears to me that she took no care of her teeth . . . no care at all.'

'She was last released from prison about five years ago, sir,' Ainsclough advised, 'so I read.'

'Yes, that would appear to tie in with the state of her teeth and the build-up of plaque . . . I would say that there is about five years' worth of the stuff here . . . and advanced gum disease. She would have had very bad breath. Halitosis just wouldn't be the word in her case. But she hasn't left us any gifts in her mouth. Let's see if she left us any presents anywhere else. There are, of course, two places where a man can leave something for us to find, but a woman has three.' Shaftoe took the starched white towel which had been draped over the genitalia of the deceased and placed it neatly at her feet. He then took hold of the right ankle and asked Billy Button to take hold of the left ankle. 'All right, gently does it, Billy . . . slowly pull the ankles apart . . . there will be some resistance due to rigor but rigor has not fully established itself . . . so as I said, gently, gently does it.'

Ainsclough watched as Shaftoe and Button gently pulled Cherry Quoshie's ankles apart, thus allowing Shaftoe to access Quoshie's genitalia.

'Yes,' Shaftoe announced matter of factly, 'I sensed that there might be something for us to find. The torture, you see, suggests that she was held at a remote place. She would most likely have suspected, or even known, that she was going to be killed and if she wasn't continually supervised, she would have found a way of leaving us a present . . . I just had the notion – intuition, if you like . . .' Shaftoe probed the vagina with two fingers and extracted a piece of paper which had been neatly folded. 'And here we are.' Shaftoe took the piece of paper and laid it carefully on the surface of the bench which ran along the side of the pathology laboratory. 'This is for the police, not for me,' he said. 'Would you like to have a look at it, Mr Ainsclough?'

Once again Ainsclough walked silently across the industrial-grade linoleum which covered the floor of the pathology laboratory and stood beside Shaftoe as he carefully unfolded the piece of paper.

'Now then,' Shaftoe said quietly as he looked at it, 'is that or is that not a very useful piece of paper? One very useful gift indeed?'

'It most certainly is,' Ainsclough agreed, staring at the eighty-pound gas bill.

'As I said, she must have known that she was going to be murdered and yet still had the presence of mind to leave you gentlemen something by which you would know where she was being held, probably Mr Cogan as well. I will need to investigate further, but from what I can tell so far there are no signs of any sexual violence.' Shaftoe read the gas bill.

'"Scythe Brook Cottage, Micheldever, Hampshire". Do you know where that is, Mr Ainsclough?'

'Can't say that I do, sir,' Ainsclough replied. 'It's a new one on me.'

'What about you, Billy?' Shaftoe turned warmly to Billy Button. 'Do you know where Micheldever is . . . apart from it being in Hampshire, that is?'

'Sorry, sir, I don't.' Billy Button shook his head apologetically. 'I don't really know England outside of London, sir. Me and Mrs Button, we are not really ones for travelling, you see. Two weeks in Ramsgate is enough for us. We like to stay at home, you see, sir.'

'All right, Billy,' Shaftoe replied. 'Thanks anyway.'

'My cousin Mabel is the traveller in our family,' Button added. 'She even went to Scotland once and then . . .'

'Yes. Thank you, Billy,' Shaftoe said firmly. 'If you would be good enough to put the towel back in place and then get a production bag, please.' He turned to Ainsclough as Button handed him the self-sealing cellophane production bag. 'The piece of paper has been folded up as you have seen and that might have preserved it from body fluids, which in turn might have preserved one or two useful fingerprints.'

'Yes, sir, I am sure the boys in the forensic laboratory will give it a damn good try,' Ainsclough replied as he took the production bag containing the gas bill from Shaftoe. 'But even if they can't isolate anything, the real gift is the address where she was being held against her will.'

'So . . .' Shaftoe commented, 'what is the betting that she met the same fate as Gordon Cogan? Bashed over the head a couple of times by someone using something long and heavy? What's the starting price . . .?'

'About evens, I'd say,' Tom Ainsclough replied with a gentle grin, 'though having said that, betting is not one of my vices.'

'Well, evens is about it,' Shaftoe muttered a few moments later after he had removed the scalp from the skull of the deceased, 'although in her case, she sustained three linear fractures rather than just two which were clearly thought sufficient to despatch the first victim. Two to the top of the skull and a third to the side of the skull, and each of sufficient force to cause death, as in the case of Mr Cogan. Somebody really wanted her dead.' Shaftoe once again turned to Ainsclough. 'That will be the finding of this post-mortem, Mr Ainsclough. Death was caused by a blow or blows to the skull by some person using a long, linear object, and I will draw attention to the thermal injury sustained on the lower inside left leg, which is powerfully indicative of torture. I will also refer to the fact that she may have given some indication of where she was being held against her will.'

Tom Ainsclough looked upon the corpse of Cherry Quoshie. 'And yet she seems to have been given so, so little in her life . . . a poor start, foster homes, institutional care . . . prison . . . heroin addiction . . . possibly racism . . . selling herself to eat and pay the rent. She was probably a very embittered and angry woman and yet, at the very end, she had the wherewithal to provide the police, whom she probably disliked, with a very useful bit of information to help us catch her murderers. She was clear-headed in a crisis. A lesser person would have panicked. Good for her, I say, good for her. I am going to attend her funeral.'

A silence descended upon the pathology laboratory as Shaftoe, Ainsclough and Button looked upon the corpse of Cherry Quoshie. It lasted for a few minutes, perhaps two, and was broken when Shaftoe remarked, 'No restraint marks.'

'Sir?' Ainsclough turned to Shaftoe. 'Restraint marks?'

'No restraint marks are in evidence,' Shaftoe observed. 'She wasn't restrained by a rope or chain.'

'There aren't, are there?' Ainsclough looked at the ankles and the wrists of Cherry Quoshie.

'Which suggests that if she was kept against her will then it would have been within a locked room or similar,' Shaftoe mused. 'She was a big woman and it would have taken an awful lot to overpower her, but once overpowered by at least two very large men, so I would have thought, she was kept in a room but not restrained or closely supervised, so she had ample time to move about and to pick up what she left for the police to find, and to leave it where she left it.'

'The observations are noted, sir,' Ainsclough replied. 'Thank you.'

'Good. Well, they'll be in my report anyway. So let's wrap this up by seeing what she ate for her last meal.' Shaftoe took a scalpel and drove it across the stomach of the deceased. 'I doubt that the stomach contents will have any bearing on the post-mortem findings but we'll look anyway, just for the sake of completeness.' Shaftoe took the scalpel and parted the flesh over the stomach, and then used the scalpel to pierce the stomach wall, turning his head to one side as he did so. Ainsclough heard a sharp hiss as the stomach gases escaped. 'Not bad,' Shaftoe commented as he drew breath. 'Oh . . .' he sighed.

'Something, sir?' Ainsclough asked.

'No . . .' Shaftoe replied quietly, 'nothing. And that's just it. Nothing. As with the previous victim, Mr Cogan, her stomach is quite empty. She had had no food for at least forty-eight hours before she was murdered, which is again some further indication of torture . . . denial of food, to weaken the will, then she was burned with something red hot. As you mentioned, Mr Ainsclough, she had been given nothing in life, but for some reason someone, or some persons, were prepared to torture her before murdering her. She evidently knew something. She had information that someone wanted and who wanted it badly. Now she'll be buried in a pauper's grave with two other coffins. You deserved more in life, Cherry,' Shaftoe addressed the corpse, 'and you deserve more in death than a shared plot without a headstone. God rest you and keep you, sweet child.'

'Janet . . . my Janet?' The woman glanced up anxiously at Swannell and Brunnie who stood in her living room. 'Police?' She then pointed to a framed photograph of a smiling young girl in a school uniform of a blue blazer and grey pleated skirt which stood prominently in a silver frame on the mantelpiece above the fireplace. 'That is Janet when she started the secondary school . . . we'd just bought her uniform . . . she was so proud . . . she was my daughter.'

'And my sister,' announced the younger woman who had let Swannell and Brunnie into the house after closely scrutinizing their warrant cards. The younger woman had a hard face, thought Swannell, and he was chilled by her cold, piercing green eyes, with which she glared at the older woman as she sat in the armchair opposite her.

'She went off the rails,' the older woman stated, 'poor girl.'

'Pushed off, more like,' the younger woman said sharply. 'She was pushed off.' She spoke in clear anger. 'She was pushed off and you know it.'

'So it was my fault!' The older woman leant forward towards her daughter and her response was equally angry. 'Like always.'

'Yes,' the younger woman replied, 'frankly, yes, it was your fault. All of it was your fault. You were to blame. You still are.'

'So go on, blame me for everything as usual.' The older woman sat back in her chair and looked indignantly away from her daughter. 'As usual, blame me . . . if it has to be someone's fault, it may as well be mine.'

'Ladies, ladies.' Victor Swannell held up his hand, pleading for calm, though he felt the urge to say 'Girls! Girls! Quiet or you'll both go to your rooms for the rest of the day'. The two women were mother and daughter but he thought that they were more in keeping with two sisters who were endlessly squabbling.

'I got married again,' the older woman explained after Swannell and Brunnie had accepted her belated invitation to take a seat, and then sat down side by side on the settee, which was covered with a fabric showing blue and red flowers with green stems and leaves against a cream background. The home itself, both officers noted, was neatly kept, and the room and entrance hall smelled strongly of a combination of air freshener and furniture polish.

'Yes, yes you did get married again . . . to a rat.' The younger woman spat the words towards her mother. 'Go on . . . tell the whole story . . . it's the police . . . tell them the whole story.'

'He was all right with me,' the mother replied defensively. 'He still is.'

'Maybe he is still all right with her but he wasn't all right with me and Janet. He did all he could to drive us out of the house. He succeeded with Janet.' The younger woman raised her voice to near screaming pitch. 'But not with me, I was too proud, wasn't I? If I was leaving home I was going to go on my own terms, not his . . . but Janet, my sister, she was always more sensitive . . . she was always more vulnerable. So she went to live in a squat in Acton, looking for peace, and what happened? She only got herself strangled. All she got was death at the age of seventeen. I dare say that that is a form of peace, but it wasn't exactly the sort of peace she had in mind; it was definitely not the sort of peace she was looking for.' The younger woman folded her arms and looked angrily at her mother. Both women were small, Brunnie observed, and very finely made.

'My first husband was killed crossing the Heathway,' the older woman explained after a period of silence had descended on the room. 'He worked for the Ford Motor Company, like an awful lot round here do. He was walking home one night when he was knocked down and run over, just opposite the Tube Station.'

'He was about halfway home,' the younger woman added, seeming to have calmed herself. The older woman nodded and for a brief moment the two women seemed to the officers to be on the same side. 'Hit and run. The driver didn't stop and the police never caught him.'

'More than halfway home,' the older woman added. 'He liked to walk home; he always used to say that it kept him fit.'

'We are sorry to hear that,' Swannell said softly. 'Such tragedies always leave a family permanently scarred, emotional scarring that never heals.'

'Yes, permanent scarring,' the older woman echoed, 'that's what it feels like . . . inside your head . . . a scar that won't heal.' She pointed to another photograph on the mantelpiece showing a soldier posing next to a tank. 'That was him when he was in the army. He was a good man. I made the right choice. He was good to us.'

'Our Janet made her room so cosy,' the daughter commented.

'You visited your sister in Acton?' Brunnie asked. 'Or do you mean her room here?'

'Her room in Acton,' the daughter clarified. 'She and I

shared a bedroom here. But yes . . . I visited her in Acton a
few times. It wasn't a squat; I don't know why I said it was
a squat. She rented it, her room, and she made it so cosy.' The
younger woman looked at Swannell and Brunnie. 'It was a
real eye-opener for me; I'd never been out of Dagenham before,
not really. The house, that house in Acton, it was full of rough
people, all young still but not going anywhere, none of them
. . . and there was Janet, my little sister, living among that lot
. . . but at least she was away from the mad Irishman.'

'The mad Irishman?' Swannell queried, as a brilliantly clean
red and white delivery van, glinting in the sun, drove slowly
past the women's house on Fanshawe Crescent, which had
revealed itself to be an angled rather than a curved crescent
of refurbished small two- or three-bedroomed terraced houses,
with small gardens to the front and also with small gardens
to the rear.

'Her second husband,' the younger woman explained with
clear indignation. 'The mad Irishman, that's her second
husband. My dad wasn't cold in his grave, and she brings him,
the mad Irishman, back from the pub one night.'

'That's a lie!' The older woman shouted. 'You bitch . . .
you lying little bitch, that's a cheap lie. Your father was in his
grave for a year – more than a year – before I met Sean, and
we met at the Cruse Club. Not down the boozer.'

'The Cruise Club,' Swannell asked, 'as in a sea cruise . . .
a sailing club?'

'C.R.U.S.E.,' the younger woman explained smugly, 'there's
no letter "i" in the name. It's a social club for widowed and
divorced people held in the church hall near here. I went once
just to see what was going on. It was just a set of desperate
old wrinklies trying to get off with each other. I tell you it
really made me want to puke. I wanted to vomit all the way
home.'

'You just wait till you lose your man,' the older woman
hissed. 'That's if you ever get one. You'll be there; you'll be
down the Cruse Club.'

'I won't!'

'Yes, you will,' the older woman snarled. 'Just you wait.
You'll be down there.'

'Won't. Won't. Won't,' the daughter chanted vehemently. 'Won't. Won't. Won't. Won't.'

'Ladies, ladies, please,' Swannell once again appealed for calm. Then he asked, 'You said you visited Janet in her bedsit in Acton? Sorry . . . Sylvia, is it?'

'Yes,' the younger woman stated, 'I'm Sylvia. That one's Vera . . . Vera Wood, and just as thick as a plank of wood, she is, like as thick as two short planks of wood.'

'That's enough! This is my house!' Vera Wood shouted. 'You don't talk to me like that, not in my house.'

'Not any more, it isn't. Not any more is it your house,' Sylvia Frost replied, still in anger. 'You signed it over to the mad Irishman when you met him.'

'When we married,' Vera Wood spoke defensively, 'I made him co-owner. Not full owner. Half is in my name.'

'As bad as.' Sylvia Frost once again turned away from her mother and addressed Swannell. 'My father worked hard to pay off the mortgage, to give his family some security, some start in life, a little financial leg up, and what does she do? She only gives half of it to Sean Wood, who's never done a stroke of work in his life.'

'He works hard,' Vera Wood protested. 'He's a grafter.'

'That's when he is in work, but most often he's on the dole. And when he's working he's only down some hole in the road.' Sylvia Frost turned to Swannell and Brunnie. 'My dad had a proper job – he was a Ford Motor Company foreman . . . and she buries him and marries a navvy, a penniless navvy, and she gives him half the house, the house my dad worked each day to buy.'

'Please, please . . .' This time it was Frankie Brunnie who tried to calm the household, although he conceded that he was finding the visit to the Frost/Wood home to be quite an interesting, though not particularly enjoyable, exposé of family dynamics. 'Your visits to Acton, Sylvia . . . to your sister's flat . . .?'

'Yes,' Sylvia Frost took a slow, deep, temper-calming breath, 'yes, I dare say you haven't come all the way to Dagenham to listen to me and her having a bitch session. So how can I help you?'

'Well . . . for a start,' Brunnie asked, 'how was your sister Janet when you last saw her?'

'You should be married now,' Vera Wood grumbled in a low voice.

'I'm thirty-two, I've still got time,' Sylvia Frost replied sourly.

'I was nineteen,' Vera Wood said proudly. 'Nineteen.'

'Please . . . ladies . . .' Brunnie pleaded. 'Sorry, Sylvia . . . you were saying your sister, when you last saw her . . . what was she like?'

'In a word,' Sylvia Frost looked at the carpet, 'in a word, she was a mess. She was a right mess. Her room which she had made all cosy had become a mess, a real tip . . . and she was a mess.' Sylvia Frost paused. 'She was a heroin addict by then, you see. You probably know that already . . . injecting herself with the stuff.'

'Yes, we do know,' Brunnie advised. 'We read the file.'

'Her eyes were shrunken and yellow round the edges, her skin was pale . . . deathly white. She wasn't eating, hardly anything at all, anyway. She was never a big girl, none of us in this family are, but when I last saw her she was so . . . so . . . frail . . . as thin as a rake. Her door was always open, I noticed that. She wasn't bothered about keeping it locked. Other people in the house would just wander in and out of her room at will; it was like she hadn't got the energy to defend her territory, but she hadn't got anything worth stealing anyway, not by then.' Sylvia Frost's tone of voice became resigned. 'She was my little sister and she ends up like that, at just seventeen years old.'

'Did you ever meet anyone else?' Brunnie asked. 'I mean . . . did you ever meet anyone else who lived in the house at the time?'

'I met the guy who strangled her. I remember him very well. He was quite nice, I thought, but he was sober when I met him. When he strangled our Janet he was on a bender.' Sylvia Frost paused as if in thought. 'I also met a real hard cow of a black girl . . . she was bad news – short and heavy. I remember I thought she had a personality as black as the Tower of London ravens. I'll tell you that girl would sell her own mother for a wrap of heroin. She was like that. Hard and cold, out for herself and only for herself.'

'Just like you would.' Vera Wood turned to her daughter. 'You'd sell me.'

'So we agree on something. I knew we would eventually. Of course I'd sell you, but who'd buy you?' Sylvia snarled in reply. 'I'd get more for something I wiped off the sole of my shoe.'

'Bitch!' Vera Wood screamed. 'Bitch. Bitch.'

'Bitch! Bitch! Bitch!' Sylvia screamed her reply. 'Cow. Bitch.'

'Girls!' Victor Swannell used the word without thinking and was surprised when both women responded by instantly falling silent but still continued to glare at each other. 'Just try to keep calm, will you? At least until we have gone. Please.'

'You know, at his trial,' Sylvia Frost turned to Swannell and Brunnie, thus breaking another brief period of silence which had fallen on the room, 'the boy who . . . the man who strangled our Janet pleaded not guilty and you know, a bit of me actually believed him.'

'I didn't,' Vera Wood snorted and looked into the empty fire grate.

'Well, you never met him, did you?' Sylvia Frost snapped. 'I did. He was really a nice boy, a gentle, well-spoken young man. He used to be a teacher, so he said. I don't know why he gave up a good job like that, don't know what his story was that he drops from teaching to live in a bedsit in a house like that . . . but anyway, our Janet and him palled up and Janet told me that they had even sank into the same pit once or twice.'

'They were lovers!' Swannell exclaimed. 'We didn't know that.'

'No . . . they were never that close but he was always looking out for our Janet, he was always very protective of her, and I think Janet was looking for a father figure – someone to protect her. At least I think that she was. She didn't want a drunken Irish navvy who shouted all the time, but someone like our dad who used to dote on his two little girls. Our dad was a good man.'

Vera Wood made a low growling sound but passed no comment.

'Well, he *was* a good man,' Sylvia Frost insisted. 'Anyway, our Janet told me that Gordon Cogan would stick up for her and that he would try to stop her taking heroin . . . but that wasn't easy . . . and they'd sometimes spend all night with each other, more just for company really, but it wasn't a full-on romance.'

'I see,' Swannell replied. 'I fully understand what you mean.'

'So . . .' Sylvia Frost continued, 'I was well surprised, really very well surprised when he was charged with her murder. I can tell you that that really was a bolt from the blue.' She paused. 'But if he was on a bender, like he was supposed to be . . . and when men get a drink in them they change . . . but then . . . even allowing for that, Gordon Cogan was so slightly built for a man . . . I mean that he was all brain . . . just the opposite of her husband.' Sylvia Frost pointed to her mother. 'Who now owns half this house, incidentally.'

'Bitch!'

'Cow!'

'All right, all right, ladies . . .' Frankie Brunnie appealed, 'let's still try to keep it calm, shall we?'

'Well, tell that cow!' Sylvia Frost shouted. 'Tell her to keep calm, needling me like that. She's got no cause to do that.'

The two women, mother and daughter, then both sat forward in their chairs and began to speak harshly at each other, both speaking at the same time, and both speaking incessantly. Brunnie glanced at Swannell, who nodded, and the two officers quietly stood and silently walked out of the room, during which time the two women did not stop shouting at each other. They were still shouting as Brunnie and Swannell walked down the narrow entrance hall, opened the door and softly let themselves out of the house. Brunnie thought it doubtful that the two women had even noticed the two officers taking their leave.

Driving slowly down Fanshawe Crescent, towards the junction with Parsloes Avenue, Brunnie commented, 'You know, Vic, it's visits like that that make me glad I am not married and have my own family.'

'It doesn't have to be like that back there. That was just awful, but I bet those two can't live apart from each other, despite what we've just seen.' Swannell glanced to his left at the row of modest but self-respecting terraced houses. 'But I know what you mean. The single life has its compensations, if not indeed its advantages, but that was a useful visit, nonetheless. Very useful. Our time was not wasted by doing that visit.'

'You think?' Brunnie queried.

'Well, I think it means we can safely shut down one line of enquiry. No one in that house has the means or the motive to murder Gordon Cogan. His killer is elsewhere other than the Frost/Wood household, despite his conviction for the murder of Janet Frost. Neither of those two women wants revenge.'

Brunnie drove the car on to Parsloes Avenue and then turned right towards Wood Lane. 'Interesting that you say "conviction",' he observed, 'not "the murder of". Are your thoughts perhaps turning to embrace the issue of a possible wrongful conviction?'

'Yes,' Swannell replied quietly, 'yes they are.'

Brunnie slowed the car to allow an elderly woman to cross the road. 'So are mine.'

Victor Swannell returned home to his house on Warren Road in Neasden, north London. He slowed his car and parked it on the concreted-over area in front of his house. Once it had been a small lawn surrounded by a privet hedge, but the narrowness of Warren Road had obliged all households on the road to give over their front garden to parking space. Swannell got out of his car and heard the hum of traffic on the North Circular road. The noise from it was incessant – always, always there. At night it abated somewhat but was still constant. It was something which he, his family, and all other residents of that part of Neasden had learned to live with.

He walked up the path beside his house and entered by the rear kitchen door. His wife stood at the sink and glanced at him as he entered, then returned her attention to the washing up. In the lounge his daughters were glued to an Australian soap opera being shown on the television and did not even look at him.

Later on he went out for a stroll, to take in the evening, and his mind turned to the Frost/Wood household in Dagenham. He did not envy their household but he had to concede that at least they had some form of family life.

It was more than he felt that he had.

Later that evening Frankie Brunnie sat opposite the long-necked, brown-eyed nurse in the Cross Keys. They had eaten late and had then decided to go out for a nightcap. They had found the pub to be pleasingly quiet, as it so often was mid-week, and had settled into a corner seat and talked in soft conversation. Towards the end of the evening the landlord walked jovially from table to table and laid small straw baskets containing pieces of roast chicken on each of the occupied tables. It was, thought Brunnie, a generous and a pleasingly hospitable act. He and the nurse thanked the landlord and began to help themselves to the chicken. Despite their late meal, Brunnie and the nurse ate all the contents of the basket, with Brunnie taking the greater proportion of the meat for himself.

'Well,' Brunnie took a napkin and gently wiped grease from the nurse's slender fingers, 'your next meal is never guaranteed, even here in the west.' He smiled. 'So if it's there, eat it.'

'Too right,' the nurse replied. 'Too right.'

Still later during that evening, upon returning from the Cross Keys, the nurse and Frankie Brunnie stood at the window in Brunnie's flat and looked out upon Walthamstow High Street, which lay to the left and right beneath them. During the day the high street was the location of the longest street market in London, but by night it was quiet, containing only a few people who strolled home along the whole pedestrianized length of the roadway.

'I love you.' Frankie Brunnie turned to the nurse and smiled, holding eye contact.

'And I love you.' The nurse returned the smile and slid his hand around Brunnie's waist. 'I love you so very much indeed.'

Wednesday

FIVE

'Well, we have had some extremely interesting developments.' Harry Vicary glanced to his left out of the window across the Thames to the buildings on the Surrey Bank, which were, at that moment, gleaming in the morning sun. He then turned and smiled at his team. 'Courtesy of Penny, we know now that Gordon Cogan's victim . . . his first victim, the schoolgirl, is the daughter of Tony "the Pestilence" Smith. The Metropolitan Police have been after him for years . . . we've been wanting to put him away since I was in uniform. We can dismiss any attempt at revenge on the part of Janet Frost's family, courtesy of Victor and Frankie's visit to their home. Also, Cherry Quoshie left an interesting present for us. I won't report where she left it for us to find, but Tom was there when it was discovered, though we still don't know how Cherry Quoshie and Gordon Cogan are connected, but connected they will be. Once we find that connection, once all the dots have been joined up, then the case will begin to crack open. One further development I have to notify you of is that we have received a letter from someone claiming to have information about the murder of Gordon Cogan.' Vicary held the letter in his hands. 'It's from one Philip Dawson . . . he gives an address in Poplar. He asks to be visited . . . he refuses to come to the police station.'

'Refuses?' Frankie Brunnie repeated. 'He refuses . . .?'

'Well, it suits us,' Victor Swannell commented. 'It means we have to visit him, so we'll see where he lives, and we'll collect more information about him that way. I can cope with that.'

'Can you please forgive my ignorance?' Penny Yewdall sat forward. 'I have, of course, heard of "Pestilence" Smith, but how did he acquire his name . . . his nickname, I mean.'

'He and his "family" or "firm" seem to spread a pestilence wherever they go but they have no particular manor to call their own, so their activity isn't localized,' Vicary explained. 'It's like he is, or they are, an airborne pestilence which covers London and the Home Counties with links to European firms and families. People will tell us about "the Pestilence" but no one will testify. It's as if, as I say, it is airborne and you can't escape it. Potential witnesses tend to disappear . . . and, like any pestilence, he gets everywhere. If it's illegal and if it's a good earner then Tony "the Pestilence" Smith is likely to have a hand in it.'

'I see. Thank you.' Penny Yewdall sat back in her chair. 'I'll read his file.'

'There's not much to read.' Harry Vicary also reclined in his chair. 'Like I said, he's got a few petty offences against his name which are useful only for his fingerprints and his DNA, but he is believed to be behind a lot of very heavy numbers and serious crimes which have gone down in this town over the years: Class A drug supply, contract killings, people smuggling, theft of high-end cars for export to the Middle East. But can we pin anything substantial on him? Can we ever? He's always in the background. We have three murders, the murder of Janet Frost, the murder of Gordon Cogan and the murder of Cherry Quoshie, all being mentioned in the same sentences, and now Tony Smith's pestilential breath is blowing over the case like a miasma, that's just him. "Pestilence" Smith.'

'I see.' Yewdall spoke softly.

'Like a bad odour in the background. Silent. Unseen. But there, and deadly,' Vicary further explained. 'Now he's in the mix. So read his file anyway, but as I say, it won't take you very long at all.'

'I will,' Penny Yewdall nodded gently, 'I definitely will.'

'Well . . .' Vicary placed his hands on his desk, 'at least now we know who we might be up against. If he's in the background then we will probably find that folk are unwilling to talk. It's therefore going to be an uphill struggle. So what's for action?'

Frankie Brunnie raised his hand by a few inches.

'Yes, Frankie?' Vicary addressed him.

'It's just something that Victor and I want to float. It may have no bearing on the investigation, and we left it out of our report . . .'

'Frankie,' Vicary's voice continued in a note of despair, 'Detective Sergeant, you know what I feel about anything being left out of reports . . . all observations, all suspicions . . . it all goes into the pot, all of it.'

'Yes, sir, but on this occasion we both felt we ought to be . . .' Brunnie's voice faltered.

'Circumspect,' Swannell offered. 'I think that's the word. We both felt that a little diplomacy was in order before we committed our thoughts to print. That was our thinking, boss.'

'Oh . . .' Vicary glanced at Swannell, and then at Brunnie, 'is this something we should be worried about?'

'Well,' Brunnie leaned forward and rested his elbows on his knees and clasped his hands together, 'in a nutshell, it transpires that Gordon Cogan was convicted of the murder of Janet Frost based solely on DNA evidence.'

'Nothing else?' Vicary asked, a note of surprise in his voice. 'Just DNA?'

'Just DNA, yes, sir. It was before the rules of evidence changed. He was convicted back in the day when people thought DNA was as safe as houses, before its shortcomings were known.'

'Oh . . .' Vicary groaned, 'I don't think I like where this is going.'

'No one who knew Gordon Cogan had said that he was capable of murder. We would expect to hear that sentiment from his family but yesterday even the sister of his victim, Janet Frost's sister, who met Gordon Cogan before the murder of her sister – even she said she thought him incapable of murder. She even went so far as to say that when she sat through the trial and Gordon Cogan pleaded "not guilty", a part of her believed him.'

'A wrongful conviction,' Vicary stated, bluntly, 'is that what you are saying?'

'Possibly, sir. Possibly a wrongful conviction, no evidence yet, but Gordon Cogan had no motivation to murder Janet Frost and the police in Acton didn't dust Janet Frost's room for his fingerprints,' Brunnie added.

'They didn't!' Vicary gasped.

'No, sir,' Swannell confirmed, 'they didn't. To them that house, that crime scene, was just a vipers' nest full of lowlifes. One left his DNA over the dead body of another when he murdered her whilst under the influence of vodka so that explained, they assumed, why he has no recollection of the incident. "Open and shut", they said proudly. Just how they like 'em. Apparently.'

'I see your reason for being diplomatic.' Harry Vicary breathed deeply. 'I am surprised that the Crown Prosecution Service ran with that.'

'Well, fifteen years ago, sir,' Swannell explained, 'DNA was the magic bullet, DNA can do no wrong, it can be used to prove anything. Now we know it really only comes into its own when used to eliminate suspects, and is deeply flawed when it is used to convict, as you are aware.'

'Yes . . . yes . . .' Vicary nodded, 'you were right not to record that. We will keep this to ourselves for the time being, but if we do get evidence of a wrongful conviction, then we expose it.'

'Yes, sir,' Swannell replied, smiling in agreement, as did Frankie Brunnie.

'But only if we get evidence.' Vicary paused. 'Right, so what is for action? Tom and Penny . . .'

'Yes, sir?'

'I want you two to stay teamed up,' Vicary announced.

'Yes, sir.'

'Find out what you can about Cherry Quoshie,' Vicary directed. 'Find out what you can about her and look for a link with Gordon Cogan.'

'Yes, sir,' Ainsclough replied.

'Then go and visit Philip Dawson, whoever he is, and see what he wants to tell us.'

'Yes, sir,' Ainsclough replied again.

'Frankie and Victor.'

'Yes, boss?' Brunnie smiled.

'It's a drive down to Hampshire for you two.' Vicary grinned. 'Lucky you two, you get to go out of the city and into the country, some nice, breathable country air for you both to enjoy.'

'Indeed, sir.'

'Then, upon your return, I want you to call on the man himself, Tony "the Pestilence" Smith. Apparently he lives up in Southgate. You know the form . . . just to say hello . . . does he know that the man who abducted and raped his daughter has been murdered? Just so he knows that we have made the connection. I think he can also know that we are connecting Gordon Cogan's murder with the murder of Cherry Quoshie because they were murdered in the same, identical manner, and because their bodies were dumped in the same place . . . twenty-four hours apart but at the same location . . . and you can let him know that we know about Scythe Brook Cottage in Micheldever. If he has any involvement, which my waters say he has, then that will unnerve him. It might cause him to trip himself up quite nicely.'

Brunnie and Swannell drove south-west out of London and into Hampshire. The two men spoke seldom during the journey and so for the most part the drive was passed in a contented and a relaxed silence generated by two men who respected each other and who seemed to know what each other was thinking. Swannell was happy to let Brunnie drive and he greatly enjoyed the journey from the passenger seat, glancing as much to his left as he did the road ahead. Swannell was able to escape London only on infrequent occasions and he found the gentle, lush green landscape they encountered once they were beyond Guildford to be uplifting. Brunnie joined the A33, and then, fifteen minutes later, following Swannell's clearly given directions whilst consulting the road atlas, turned right, off the A33 and on to Duke Street, towards Micheldever, Hants, SO12. Brunnie slowed the car and raised a finger, pointing to a hand-painted sign which had been nailed to a tree and which read 'Scythe Brook Cottage'.

Swannell grinned. 'Well spotted,' he said, slowing the car as he read the white on green sign, 'I would have missed that. So here we are with no need to enquire at the post office after all.'

'None, it seems.' Brunnie turned left and put the car at what revealed itself to be an unmettled track with wheel indentations either side of a grassy moraine which ran down its centre. Hawthorn hedgerows lined the track up to a height of approximately four feet, Brunnie estimated, though in places the level of the hedge undulated above and below the average height. After about a quarter of a mile a second sign which also read 'Scythe Brook Cottage' was noticed. The second sign pointed to the right and just beyond it the hedgerow stopped and was interrupted by a raised grass lawn, upon which stood a small detached house about fifty feet from the roadway. The house itself stood in generous grounds, mostly beyond the building as it was viewed from the road, and covered what Swannell guessed to be about one-third of an acre. A gravel drive ran from the track to the side of the cottage. The track itself continued on beyond the cottage and seemed, so far as the officers could tell, to lead to a line of cottages, about six in all, whose red roofs could be seen about half a mile distant. Both officers remained in the car and looked at Scythe Brook Cottage. It was made of brick, white painted, with a red tiled roof. At the end of the gravel drive stood a dull, grey-coloured two-car garage of a prefabricated design, and beyond the garage the stream could be followed by walking along a line of shrubs which grew thickly along both banks.

Swannell and Brunnie glanced at each other and without a word being spoken Brunnie drove the car off the track and down the gravel drive, coming to a halt when he was level with the cottage. He switched off the car's engine and he and Swannell opened their doors and stepped out of the vehicle. They breathed strong country air with great appreciation as they walked side by side up a stone-laid path to the front door of the cottage, which was enclosed by an evidently recently painted porch. On a shelf inside the porch, clearly visible, was a neatly written sign which read 'all enquiries re. this building to 127 Rook Lane, Micheldever'. Brunnie rapped heavily on the door of the porch but, although his knocking was heard to echo loudly within the cottage, he could raise no response.

'Dare say it would be too much to expect that there would be someone at home,' Brunnie growled.

Brunnie and Swannell turned away from the cottage and walked towards the garage. As they turned they noticed the remnants of a fire on the lawn beyond it. Brunnie nudged Swannell who said, 'Yes, I see it, but the garage first.' At the garage Swannell lifted the up and over door to reveal an empty building with just a work bench at the far end. Swannell closed the door and he and Brunnie walked across the lawn to the remnants of the fire. The scorched area was circular and surrounded by a series of stones.

'Someone has been a boy scout,' Brunnie remarked.

'Indeed.' Swannell looked down at the stone circle. 'That fire would have made my old skip well happy, contained by stones like it was and not near anything combustible.' He looked about him and noted tall trees surrounding the land in which the cottage stood. 'The fire can't be overlooked, hidden from the track as it is by the house . . . the nearest other houses are about half a mile away . . . a gag in Cherry Quoshie's mouth and yes, a very good place to torture someone – a little far out of London for some reason, but nevertheless a good place indeed as a location to extract information from someone. Very good indeed.'

'And the cottage will be a rented property, that is to say as in a holiday let,' Brunnie added.

'You think so?' Swannell glanced at him.

'Well, yes, don't you? No one at home, not even one car in a double garage, the note in the porch directing any caller to another address . . . there will be nothing here to link the people who murdered Gordon Cogan and Cherry Quoshie to this building. And the cottage would have been rented under an assumed name, of that you can be sure.'

'Reckon you're right there.' Swannell once again looked about him. 'Of course it would. I mean, we don't know for certain yet, but if we are dealing with "Pestilence" Smith, then he knows his stuff and his tracks will be well and truly covered. Very well and truly covered indeed. All right . . . to horse, to horse . . . so let's make some inquiries about this property.'

Frankie Brunnie turned the car around and drove back down the rutted track to Duke Street, then turned left towards Micheldever. They followed the narrow, high hedge which boarded Duke Street on either side and first encountered two white-painted, half-timbered houses, one on either side of the road, with thatched roofs, the timbers of which had been picked out in black gloss paint. The houses stood, thought Swannell, like two sentinels guarding the entrance to the village. Beyond the two black and white houses there was a break in the line of properties. Swannell noted open fields to the right leading out across a flat farmed landscape to a distant skyline, all under a blue sky with high clouds at, in RAF speak, three tenths. Brunnie drove slowly and carefully onwards and they seemed to enter the village itself, where they encountered an area of small houses on their left and a linear car park on their right. Beyond the car park was a row of small thatched cottages, once again painted white, and once again the timber frames were painted black, and each cottage possessed a small, neatly kept front garden. The officers drove past a small, brick bus shelter with a path leading from it up a grass bank towards a cluster of newly built houses. The war memorial with two benches beside it and one in front of it seemed, to Swannell, to be covered with an inordinately large number of names for a village so small and, by English standards, quite remote. Micheldever, he pondered, had clearly suffered the loss of many of its sons during the twentieth-century conflicts. Disproportionately so.

Brunnie slowed the car and asked an elderly lady in a white blouse and a heavy grey skirt, who was at that moment struggling with a knot which held up a banner advertising a fund-raising coffee morning, for the directions to Rook Lane. He received clear directions given in a warm and homely Hampshire accent and drove on, turning right, as directed, at a small roundabout in which a tree had been planted and surrounded by three, at that moment unoccupied, varnished wooden benches. The officers drove past the parish church, a low, pebble-dashed, brick-built building with a square tower which, Swannell thought, had most probably been built to replace an older building, and then entered a narrow lane of more white painted cottages which was Church Street. Rook Lane was right off Church Street and led to a collection of neatly kept houses. Number 127 revealed itself to be a brick-built house which blended into a row of similar houses. And that, thought Swannell with a wry smile as he and Brunnie got out of the car, is exactly the reason why one joins the police. It is not to fight crime and apprehend felons, nor is it to protect and serve the community, it is rather to visit, quite by chance, idyllic corners of rural England wherein one would not normally set foot. And get paid reasonably well for doing so. Not bad. Not a bad deal at all.

Brunnie and Swannell left the car parked in the narrow thoroughfare that was Rook Lane, Micheldever, and walked calmly up the concrete path to the door of number 127. Swannell knocked reverentially, not loudly, not aggressively, but nonetheless, Brunnie noted, still with a certain assertiveness and self-confidence. The knocking upon the door caused a large-sounding dog to bark from somewhere within the property and a few moments later a short, frail-looking woman in a red blouse and a white skirt opened the door, showing no sign of fear of the two large, strange men who had suddenly called upon her. 'Yes?' she said, speaking in a strong Hampshire accent. 'Can I help you, gentlemen?'

'Police,' Swannell said as he and Brunnie showed the woman their warrant cards.

'Oh, yes?' The woman's reaction seemed to both officers to be curious rather than alarmed or defensive. It was, they both felt, a reassuring sign.

'We are calling in connection with the property known as Scythe Brook Cottage,' Swannell explained. 'A note in the porch window directed us to this address.'

'Yes . . . yes,' the woman replied, 'I am the key holder and the caretaker, and I clean it now and again.'

'Can you tell us who owns the property?'

'No . . . no, I can't,' the woman informed the officers. 'For many years it belonged to the Naylors, yes it did. The Naylors lived here for generations, yes they did, there's Naylors everywhere in the cemetery and then the last Naylor died. Scythe Brook Cottage was sold but no one moved in on a permanent basis. It gets let out for weekends or a week sometimes, that sort of time period. It's very popular with birdwatchers who go birdwatching in Micheldever Wood. The cottage is rented through an agency in Croydon, up in London – Fairley and Fairley. They let me know when someone is renting it and I have the key ready for them, yes I do. I check it before the guests arrive because we ask the ones who rent it to leave it clean and tidy. "Please leave the cottage as you would want to find it", we say. There's a sign up in the cottage saying just that, "Leave as you would want to find it". But I check it anyway, yes I do, just to make certain and also to check for damage. I was about to go there this afternoon because the next people to rent it are arriving this evening. They're renting it until Monday, yes they are.'

'Not anymore they're not.' Brunnie smiled. 'Sorry, madam.'

'It's a crime scene,' Swannell explained, 'and it will remain a crime scene for a few days to come.'

'Oh my,' the woman gasped, 'oh my!'

'You'll have to contact Fairley and Fairley up in London, notify them and tell them to contact the next guests to stop them from travelling; otherwise they'll be turned away from the cottage,' Swannell said.

'They will have had a wasted journey,' Brunnie added.

'Yes, I'll do that, yes I will.' The woman nodded. 'Can I do that now? Excuse me.' She turned and walked hurriedly into the shady interior of her house.

Brunnie and Swannell waited in silence at the door of the house. Around them was rural Hampshire in full summer: heat, blue sky, bloom, rich foliage, birdsong and bees and other flying insects. Swannell particularly noticed the bees and was gratified to observe that they seemed healthy because the bees in London had been observed to be acting strangely as if beset by some illness, walking on pavements or just sitting motionless on brick walls, as if confused and disorientated, but here, in Micheldever, all seemed to be just as it should be with the bees flying with clear determination from flower to flower. The woman bustled rapidly back to the threshold of her house.

'You've managed to contact them?' Swannell asked.

'Yes. They were not happy, no they weren't, but I told them it couldn't be helped. I told them that the police have made the cottage a crime scene, yes I did, and that any old soul arriving will be turned away. So they're contacting the next guests. They can do that these days wherever they are because everyone has one of those handheld phones . . . annoying things they are. Who on earth wants to hear one side of someone else's conversation? I certainly don't.'

'Do you have the keys to the cottage?' Swannell asked.

'Oh, yes, I'll get them for you, yes I will. Just a tick.' Again the woman turned and stepped nimbly into the darkened interior of her home, and then returned shortly afterwards with a single, large mortis key which she pressed into Swannell's palm. 'Don't lose it,' she said, 'it's the only one there is, yes it is . . . the lock is about two hundred years old.'

'Just the lock?'

'Yes,' the woman smiled, 'the cottage was rebuilt in the thirties but they kept the original lock on the main door . . . and that . . .' she handed Swannell a smaller mortis key, 'is for the lock on the porch door.'

'We'll take good care of them.' Swannell smiled reassuringly. 'Thank you.'

'When,' Brunnie asked, 'was the cottage last rented?'

'Last weekend,' the woman replied. 'They stayed later than normal and didn't drop the keys back until late on Monday evening, well after dark. Usually guests leave about midday or later on the Sunday if it's a weekend rental so as to get back home in good time to sleep before work on the Monday morning, yes they do. So it was a bit strange to have the keys handed back at eleven o'clock on Monday evening.'

'Quite late indeed,' Brunnie agreed. 'That is quite late.'

'Yes. I was thinking that they had driven off with them – that's happened before, causes all sorts of bother, oh my . . .'

'Did you get the name of the people or person who rented it?' Brunnie asked.

'No.' The woman shook her head apologetically. 'I am so sorry. Fairley and Fairley phoned me and told me that the cottage was being let out. The people came as expected a few days later and I handed the keys over, yes I did.'

'When did they collect the keys?'

'On Friday,' the woman replied, 'they arrived at about seven o'clock in the evening, they did.'

'Can you describe them?' Brunnie inquired.

'Only the woman,' the caretaker replied. 'She was young and thin and she had a cold-hearted attitude. They weren't no birdwatchers, no they weren't. No birdwatchers at all . . . no ramblers either. They had rented the cottage for the weekend, probably for a bit of the old how's-your-father if you ask me, mind you that's their business. She was all dolled up in city clothes. Usually the guests come in green jackets and corduroy trousers and walking boots, but not her . . . no, no . . . not her. She was all tarted up like she was going to dine at a posh restaurant, all platinum-blonde hair and jewellery and an expensive-looking watch . . . and her two boyfriends . . . they were all dandified as well, yes they were.'

'She had two men with her?' Swannell asked. 'Are you sure of that?'

'Yes, I saw their legs, yes I did . . . office trousers and city shoes . . . two men and her in the cottage for a weekend. Well, why not? She was young, she was making the most of her youth. I wish I had done that. I did some old walking in the woods when I was young but not as much as I should have done . . . or could have done.' She added with a smile, 'I should have made more of my youth.'

'What sort of car was it?' Swannell asked. 'Do you know?'

'It wasn't,' the woman replied confidently, 'it was a van with sliding passenger doors, which is why I saw the legs of the two men friends she had. It was about the same size as the vans the Royal Mail use to collect the post from the letter boxes.'

'A fifteen hundred weight,' Brunnie mumbled.

'It was blue,' the woman added, 'yes, it was . . . blue . . . light blue.'

A blue fifteen hundred weight, Swannell said to himself. Then he asked, 'Did you see anything of them during the weekend?'

'No . . . no I didn't,' the caretaker once again replied confidently, 'and I didn't see them around the village either. They didn't come in to shop at the village stores, and no one mentioned seeing them in the pub on Saturday night. They stayed at the cottage, helping the girl make the most of her youth, I imagine. Well, why not? I wish I had done that.'

'Would you recognize her again?' Swannell asked.

'I might. She was short, taller than me, but still short, yes

she was, on the short side . . . platinum-blonde hair . . . quite
thin . . . hard face . . . cold eyes . . . hard edge to her voice.
I can't imagine that she smiled very much, not easily anyway.
Or possibly only a massive amount of money would make her
smile, but not a good joke and she wouldn't be the sort to
smile at someone else's good fortune, no she wouldn't. She
seemed that sort of character; she'd smile at a million pounds
but not at anything humorous . . . all that jewellery, that cloud
of perfume and layers of make-up. No, I tell you she wasn't
down here to go creeping about the woods in a green jacket
and a pair of binoculars round her neck, looking at rare birds
in old Micheldever Woods, no she wasn't. Mind you, they had
been here before though, I can tell you that for nothing, yes
I can.'

'You had seen her before?' Brunnie asked. 'Is that what
you mean?'

'No, never seen her before at all, not ever, but it was the
way they came straight here, like they knew which door to
knock on to ask for the keys rather than walking up and down
the lane looking at the house numbers. I heard them arrive,
yes I did. The van stops, and madam gets out with her high
heels . . . click, click, click . . . straight up to my door, collects
the keys, says "thanks", and then turns and walks back to the
van. First-time guests have to search for my door and first-
time guests always want directions to the cottage, so at least
one of them, her or one of the two men, had been here before,
yes they had. The cottage is signposted from Duke Street,'
the woman added, 'but you'll be surprised how many people
miss the sign. I dare say that they're too busy looking at the
birds up in the tree branches.'

Brunnie and Swannell laughed softly and they then thanked
the elderly caretaker for the keys and for her information.
They turned and walked back to their car, drove back to Scythe
Brook Cottage and viewed it again, set back from the road,
standing upon a modest eminence.

Victor Swannell unlocked the doors of the cottage whilst
Frankie Brunnie snapped on a pair of latex gloves. Swannell
pushed the doors open and he too then put on a similar pair
of gloves. The two officers, Swannell in the lead, then entered

the building. Inside they found it to be cool but musty. Brunnie quickly shut the door behind him so as to preserve the stale air. 'Thank goodness they haven't cleaned the cottage or left a window open,' he commented.

'They will have cleaned it before they left, we can be sure of that,' Swannell said. 'I mean, it looks clean. Just look about you, all the surfaces have been wiped down, but you're right, the mustiness will have helped to preserve anything they might have missed.' He paused. 'You know, we have to hope that Cherry Quoshie left us another present somewhere in the building. She had the presence of mind to leave us the gas bill, knowing we'd find it if we found her body, but it still doesn't put her or Gordon Cogan in the cottage.'

'It doesn't, does it?' Brunnie growled. 'There's still a gap in the chain of evidence.'

'It leads us to the cottage but doesn't put either of them in it – only a fingerprint or two will do that or their saliva with their DNA, or a nail pairing,' Swannell pondered, 'something like that. We must hope that Cherry Quoshie left her finger-prints or something with her DNA on it in an obscure place, a surface which might not have been wiped down.'

The cottage was, the officers found, small and cramped, with an 'L'-shaped floor plan. A seating area of old and much-used armchairs, a settee and a chest of drawers gave way to a small dining-area-cum-kitchen. Upstairs the cottage had two bedrooms and a bathroom. All, Brunnie and Swannell found, had been left in a dismayingly clean and very neat manner. There were, they discovered, four bunk beds in each room, thus allowing the cottage to accommodate eight persons, though with eight people the building would, Swannell pondered, become horribly overcrowded.

'Just bunk beds.' Brunnie smiled. 'Difficult to see anyone making the most of their youth with these sleeping facilities. I wonder what the lady caretaker actually had in mind?'

'I wonder,' Swannell replied with a grin. 'I wonder indeed.'

The two officers returned downstairs and went out into the garden, shutting the doors behind them.

'We'd better get a SOCO team here.' Brunnie fished his mobile from his jacket pocket. 'It's too damn neat; it's been sanitized but, as you say, Cherry Quoshie might have managed to put a paw print or something similar in an obscure place and if she managed to persuade Gordon Cogan to do the same, then . . . then that will be very useful. Very useful indeed.'

'We'll tell them that . . .' Swannell looked about him and allowed himself to enjoy the rural tranquillity, the foliage, the blue sky, 'we'll ask them to go over the scene with a particularly fine-tooth comb.'

'Yes, I'll also ask Harry if he wants to come down as well; he might want to see this.' Swannell pressed a number.

'Good idea.' Brunnie fell silent as Victor Swannell spoke into his mobile phone. Like Swannell, he found it deeply pleasant to be out of the city and he found himself pondering the joy of being a constable in the Hampshire Constabulary and working in an environment such as this: the fields, the woodlands, nature's bounty, the wide, blue sky.

Swannell stopped talking and put his phone in his pocket. 'They reckon it will take them two to two and a half hours to get here, as getting out of London will take a lot of time . . . and Harry wants to come. So, do you want to wait or do you want to walk?'

'I'll wait,' Brunnie replied without hesitation.

'Thank you.' Swannell smiled his reply. 'I rather thought you'd say that. I'll take the car, though; those houses might be further than they look.'

'Fair enough. I'll make sure the cottage doesn't go anywhere.'

'It's a hard job you've talked yourself into,' Swannell grinned as he turned away and walked towards the car. 'Try not to let the pressure get you down.'

Swannell drove the car slowly and carefully away from Scythe Brook Cottage down the track towards the row of houses which could be seen in the distance. He halted the car upon approaching the houses and got out of the vehicle, leaving the driver's-side window wound down so as to enable the car to 'breathe' in his absence. He walked towards the line of houses, six in all, which stood in a terrace; each, he noticed, had a small plot of land in the front and a larger, much larger parcel of land in the rear. They were built of red brick with roof tiles in a darker shade of red. The date 1887 was set in stone above the door of the first cottage in the terrace. Swannell walked up to the door and politely and reverentially knocked on it using the metal knocker provided. It was opened by an elderly man who blinked curiously at Swannell.

'Good day, sir.' Swannell held eye contact with the man. 'Police.' He showed the elderly homeowner his warrant card. 'It's nothing to be worried about – I'm just making inquiries.'

The man remained silent. He made no response at all.

'The cottage . . . back there,' Swannell pointed from where he had come, 'Scythe Brook Cottage. Can you tell me if you saw or heard anything unusual there in the last few days, particularly over the last weekend?'

Still the man did not reply. He merely stood there in old, crumpled clothing, blinking absentmindedly at Victor Swannell.

'Anything at all?' Swannell pressed. He brushed a persistent fly from his face.

Again, no response.

'Any unusual sounds or movements that you might have noticed, especially over the last weekend?'

The elderly man continued to blink and look vacantly at Swannell for a few moments and then shut the door.

'Well, thank you anyway, sir,' Swannell said to the door, 'your public spirited cooperation is deeply appreciated.' He walked to the next house in the terrace, knocked upon the door but could not raise any response from within. At the third house, upon his knocking, the door was opened by a man who seemed to Swannell to be in his early middle years. He was dressed in white, summer lightweight trousers and a green T-shirt. He had a neatly trimmed beard and light framed spectacles.

'Don't mind Eric,' the man said affably.

'Eric?' Swannell replied.

'The old boy in the first house.' The man examined Swannell's identity card. 'Metropolitan police,' he remarked, 'how interesting. Yes, Eric, he's lost it,' the man tapped the side of his head, 'up here. Poor old soul. It's all gone . . . all of it . . . but he's very placid.'

'Yes, I got that impression.' Swannell put his ID back inside his pocket.

'Yes, the old boy, lovely old soul he is. We keep an eye on him and the welfare people call and he gets meals on wheels delivered . . . all that sort of thing . . . you know, the care-in-the-community package or whatever it's called. So how can I help the Met?'

'It is in connection with Scythe Brook Cottage . . . half a mile or so behind me.'

'Yes, yes, I know it; in fact, you can't get to these houses without driving past it. If you glance at the map you'll see that the stream which runs at the side of the cottage seems to form the shape of a scythe, a straight handle and then a wide curve for the blade. The cottage is next to the "handle" of the scythe.'

'I did wonder at the source of the name,' Swannell replied. 'Thank you.'

'It's been rebuilt, but the original cottage pre-dates these houses by a hundred years or more . . . and these cottages are all that remain of a country estate. The "big house" was a fine old Victorian mansion which was demolished and the land sold off to neighbouring farmers. These houses were built to home the estate workers and were sold at auction when the big house was pulled down. The "big house" was a lovely old building, but the owner didn't maintain it properly . . . or he couldn't afford to . . . in the end it was so full of rot that it had to be pulled down before it fell apart . . . so it was demolished and the land sold off. It was the only thing he, the last owner, could do.'

'I see . . . but the cottage,' Swannell pressed, 'did you see or hear anything unusual at the cottage over the last few days, particularly over this last weekend?'

'It was rented out,' the man replied, 'I can tell you that. It's not unusual, especially during this time of the year. They stayed after the weekend, stayed until Monday . . . that's not usual . . . but not really very unusual either. It seems most renters want the cottage for a weekend. The last lot of renters had a coal fire on Monday evening.'

'Monday?' Swannell confirmed. 'Are you sure it was on the Monday?'

'Yes, definitely the Monday evening. I do recall that – coal smoke has a very distinctive smell, you know. I only got a whiff of it by the time it got here, but it was coal,' the home owner said. 'I manage a toy shop, by the way, and this is my day off.'

'I'm sorry?' Swannell replied. He was taken by surprise at the man's sudden disclosure.

'Just in case you were wondering what I do for a living and why I am at home during office hours in the middle of the week,' the man explained, 'I manage a toy shop and this is my day off. Harris is the name.'

'I see,' Swannell smiled, 'thank you, Mr Harris, but I really am only interested in the goings on at Scythe Brook Cottage over the last few days.'

'All right . . . A bit naughty of them,' Harris continued, 'it was a bit naughty.'

'Naughty?' Swannell queried. 'What do you mean?'

'To burn coal,' the man explained, 'this being a smokeless zone. Coal has a distinctive smell.'

'Yes, I know,' Swannell replied, 'I know what coal smoke smells like.'

'Nobody was going to report them, not all the way out here in the country,' Harris continued. 'I just stood on my doorstep . . . just here, and enjoyed the smell.'

'You enjoyed it?' Swannell queried.

'I think it smells lovely. Coal smoke smells divine.' Harris spoke with clear fondness. 'I always think it smells very homely . . . but they must have brought it with them; there is nowhere round these parts that any old soul can buy coal.'

'I see,' Swannell replied. 'And that was on Monday, you say?'

'Yes,' Harris nodded. 'On Monday. The night before last.'

'What time of day was that?'

'Late . . . dark had fallen. So it would be sometime after ten in the evening. We are near the solstice now, so very light nights, but strangely, I thought, there was no laughter or music.'

'Laughter or music,' Swannell queried, 'is that usual?'

'Yes, you see renters occasionally eat out, have a barbeque, and when they do there's laughter and music but not last Monday, just silence and the smell of coal smoke.'

'That's interesting,' Swannell commented.

'I thought they had gone on the Sunday,' Harris added. 'I drove past the cottage on Sunday afternoon and the blue van had gone but then I noticed that it had returned on the Monday when I got back from work.'

'That's also interesting,' Swannell said. 'Helps us to pin down their movements.'

'I assumed then that they had stayed on for an extra day,' Harris added.

'Did you see any of the renters?' Swannell asked hopefully.

'No,' Harris replied firmly, 'I didn't. Usually I do, but not this time. They kept themselves well out of sight during the day anyway. Came out for a bonfire on Monday night, though, didn't they?' he added with a smile.

'Do you think that your neighbours might have seen or heard anything?' Swannell glanced along the row of terraced houses.

'I really doubt it,' Harris replied. 'This is known locally as "death row". I am the youngest person in these houses. All my neighbours retire early each evening, and all have their provisions delivered, like old Eric, whom you have just met. Sorry if I have been of little help.'

'You have been of some help, Mr Harris. We didn't know when the fire was but now we do . . . the van leaving on Sunday but returning on Monday . . . and the renters keeping out of sight, it's all useful. Very useful. It's all very useful.'

Close at hand, but out of sight, a cuckoo sang.

SIX

The woman had a long, thin, drawn face, with sunken eyes and long, greasy, shoulder-length hair. She had long, bony fingers which she wrapped round the door as she peered out at Penny Yewdall and Tom Ainsclough through the narrow gap which she permitted between the door and the doorframe. She glanced wonderingly at the officers' identity cards and then gazed at Ainsclough and Yewdall in a seemingly confused and timid manner.

'Look,' Yewdall spoke calmly, 'we assure you that it would be a lot easier if you would let us in – much, much easier. You see we, my colleague and I, are from New Scotland Yard. We are members of the Murder and Serious Crime Squad and we are not at all interested in crimes that can be dealt with in a magistrate's court; anything lower than crown court material is of little concern to us. The crimes that we investigate get people put away for life, not fined twenty pounds and bound over to keep the peace.'

'We can smell the cannabis,' Tom Ainsclough added, with a serious tone in his voice, 'and we are not bothered about it, not in the slightest. All London smokes dope, we know that. Just don't smoke spliffs of blow in our presence. We just want some information, then we'll be on our way: we're not here to toss your drum.'

'Yeah . . .?' The woman suddenly sounded hopeful in a pathetic, almost childlike manner. 'So this is not a bust?'

'It's not a bust,' Yewdall assured her. 'Just keep it out of sight until we've gone.'

'All right . . . all right.' The woman opened the door and revealed that she was wearing a faded gold-coloured T-shirt emblazoned with the name 'Benidorm' and a short denim skirt. Her thin, almost emaciated legs stopped in a pair of ancient, much worn and torn sports shoes. Penny Yewdall thought the woman to be in her late thirties, possibly older.

She was, thought Yewdall, like so many people one meets in London, people who have immersed themselves in the 'hippy' lifestyle and are unwilling or unable to move on and take their place in the adult world of employment and civic duty and personal responsibility, like men in their sixties who keep their hair in ponytails, use expressions like 'far out' and keenly urge others 'to keep it together'.

'So what do you want?' the woman asked. 'What can I tell you?'

'We believe that Cherry Quoshie lived here?' Tom Ainsclough glanced up and down Tredegar Road, Tower Hamlets, London EH3 and saw unsurprisingly that the road had been largely redeveloped since the end of the Second World War, though a few of the flat-roofed, three-storey Victorian houses had escaped the wrecking ball, one such being situated near the junction with Ordell Road, and being the last known address of Cherry Quoshie. The remaining buildings in the area, he noted, were flats built in the sixties.

'Lived! Lived, you say?' the woman spluttered. 'She still does live here.' The emaciated woman spoke in a strong east London accent.

'No, she doesn't.' Penny Yewdall remained calm. Her voice remained warm. 'Can I ask if you are a relative?'

'No . . . no . . . not by blood, anyway, but you can see that,' the woman replied anxiously. 'I mean, last time I looked in the mirror I was a white bird. Cherry is a black chick and we are not related by marriage.'

'Yes . . . sorry . . . but we have to ask,' Yewdall explained calmly. 'In circumstances such as these we always have to be sure as to whom we are talking . . . it's essential.'

The woman seemed to the officers to become even paler, her sunken eyes widened, her narrow jaw slackened. 'What do you mean . . . in these cir-circumstances?' the woman stammered. 'And did Cherry Quoshie live here? Murder and Serious Crime Squad? Just what on earth has happened? What are you saying? What's going on . . .?'

Yewdall drew a deep breath and said, 'I'm very sorry but we believe Cherry Quoshie to have been murdered.'

The thin and wasted woman gasped loudly and then

staggered backwards with weakening knees into the hallway and sat heavily on an upright chair which stood beside and beneath a green payphone which was bolted to the wall. 'Oh . . .' she gasped again, equally loudly, 'oh . . . oh . . .' The woman buried her head in her hands and she too breathed deeply. 'I wondered where she had gone. I mean, I have not seen her for a few days right enough . . . but murdered . . . not Cherry . . . not her . . .'

'So when did you last see Cherry Quoshie?' Yewdall asked.

'Well, like I said, a few days ago.' The woman glanced at Yewdall. 'What's today, sweetheart?'

'Wednesday,' Ainsclough spoke with restrained impatience, 'today is Wednesday.'

'So . . . a few days ago, but you know that's Cherry, she comes and goes. She stays away for a day or two but she's never been away for as long as this. So if this is Wednesday,' the woman took her head from her hands and sat upright, 'a few days. She wasn't here last weekend so I reckon Thursday or Friday was the last time I saw her. I get lost with the days, you see . . . They all blend and merge with each other. But Thursday or Friday, that's a bit of a long time for Cherry to stay away. Oh . . . my . . . murdered. You read of such things but when it happens . . .'

'Does . . .' Yewdall paused. 'I mean, did Cherry have any particular friend or group of friends?'

'Only her mate, Anna.' The woman seemed to be staring into space. 'Just Anna . . . Anna was Cherry's only mate. If anyone knows anything about Cherry, it will be Anna.' Her voice developed a vacant tone, as though, Yewdall thought, her mind was wandering. 'Only Anna . . . Cherry and Anna . . . If anyone knows anything . . .'

'All right, all right,' Ainsclough spoke sharply, 'where do we find Anna?'

The woman shrugged her thin shoulders. 'Dunno . . .' she replied. 'Dunno where Anna lives; never did know where Anna lives.'

'Does Anna have a surname?' Yewdall pressed. She was also by then beginning to find the woman's fecklessness annoying.

'Day,' the woman continued to stare into space, 'she's called Anna Day . . . that's her handle . . . Anna Day . . . this is heavy . . . this is too heavy . . .'

'Age?' Ainsclough continued to press the woman for information. 'Do you know how old Anna Day is?'

'About Cherry's age, I reckon,' the woman replied, 'about that age.'

'So late thirties?' Yewdall clarified. 'Cherry Quoshie was thirty-seven. Anna Day is that sort of age?'

'I reckon,' the woman answered with another sullen shrug of her thin shoulders. 'Yes, I reckon so, a bit older than me but . . . neither of us will see twenty-five again, that's for sure. You know, I envy men. If I was a man I'd be halfway through by now, but that's life, sweetheart, men get out early, but women just go on and on. We don't get that sort of Donald Duck. I could live for another fifty years . . . imagine that, that's one heavy thought – fifty more years of this.'

'All right!' Ainsclough snapped. 'Enough . . . no more moping. Did Anna Day call on Cherry Quoshie at this address?'

'No,' the woman shook her head slowly, 'Cherry Quoshie was a bit of a lone bird, and she never got no callers. She always left her drum to go and call on people at their own drum or to meet up somewhere like some pub or other, but no one ever called on her here, not once in the two years I've been here.' The woman took a deep breath. 'I met Anna Day when I went for a drink with Cherry and Anna Day came with us. Cherry would tell me now and again that she'd been out with Anna but Anna Day never came here.'

'Which is Cherry's room?' Yewdall asked, sharply.

'Upstairs front . . . I mean top floor front.'

'We'll need to look inside,' Ainsclough insisted.

'Help yourself, mate.' The pale and wasted woman allowed a surly and cynical edge to enter her voice. 'I can't imagine Cherry will be bothered about the Bill going through her things, not now. I should think that she'll be past caring now. So on you go, darlin', red door at the top of the apples and pears. Red door.'

'That's a good way of looking at it,' Tom Ainsclough growled as he and Penny Yewdall walked in single file past the seated woman and began to climb the stairs. As they did so, they met the full damp-induced mustiness of the dark, old house, and found it difficult to draw breath.

Ainsclough and Yewdall discovered Cherry Quoshie's room to be disorganized. Clothing, they saw, lay strewn upon the floor and on the bed, which was unmade, with grimy-looking sheets which did not seem to the officers to have been changed for many weeks. Most worrying of all was the number of scorched pieces of tin foil and the large number of small hypodermic needles to be seen. Yewdall and Ainsclough cautiously and instinctively remained on the threshold of the room.

'I've never been in here before.' The thin, wasted woman who had opened the door to the officers by then stood behind and between them, having followed them up the stairs unseen, silent, creeping cat-like after them.

Tom Ainsclough turned. 'Don't enter this room,' he commanded. 'Apart from the fact that there are syringes every-where, it will have to be searched. I am surprised that the door has no lock.'

'None of the drums have locks, darlin',' the woman replied, continuing to peer curiously into Cherry Quoshie's room. 'We don't need them. None of us have anything worth stealing and we're all girls in here anyway . . . so what's the point of locks on the doors?'

'How many of you live here?' Yewdall asked.

'Three. Mind you, I dare say it's two now.' The woman continued to gaze at Cherry Quoshie's room. 'And I thought my old drum was untidy . . . love a duck. Mine's a palace compared to this. No wonder Cherry kept herself private.'

'Who is the third woman?' Penny Yewdall asked.

'Betsy,' the thin and wasted woman replied. 'It's Betsy. Betsy lives in the basement. She sleeps during the day and she walks about at night. She's a bit weird . . . she's been in the mad house but she takes her medication these days . . . that keeps her levelled . . . but she's still weird. Harmless but weird. She's a person of the night all right. She spends her summer nights sitting under a tree in Victoria Park. The park is fenced off but the night people always find a way in . . .

and sometimes she goes up to Stratford Marsh and sits by the river all night . . . but that's Betsy. Harmless. Like I said, weird but harmless.'

'So what was Cherry Quoshie like as a person?' Yewdall turned back to look at Cherry Quoshie's room. 'Apart from being private, that is?'

'She was a hard old cow, sweetheart,' the woman replied, also still looking at Cherry Quoshie's room. 'You can take it from me, darlin', Quoshie was a hard old cow . . . one hard old face. She really was. I wouldn't pick a fight with her, love a duck I wouldn't. I kept well out of her old way. Very well out of it. She'd come home, slam the door behind her, pound up the stairs then stay in her room until she left the house again, pounding down the apples and pears and then she'd slam the door hard behind her as she left the house. Don't know what she ate as she never used the kitchen we share – she must have eaten outside, in cafes or in mates' drums . . . but she was a big old girl. I mean, if we had ever got into a skirmish she would have flattened me no bother . . . but we never did 'cos I kept well out of her face. I kept well on my side of the river when it came to Cherry Quoshie – believe me, well on my side of the river. It's how you survive living in drums like this, keeping out of each other's way and by realizing who is the top dog.' The woman paused. 'I've seen her once getting into a skirmish with another girl in a pub . . . two black Amazons going at it like they were battling each other for their lives. It was easily, *easily* ten times worse than watching two men mixing it.'

'That I can well believe,' Yewdall murmured. 'If you were to give me the choice of fighting a man or a woman I'd take the man any day of the week. Women are unpredictable.'

'Well, these two Amazons wrecked the boozer and then they toed it down the road like two good mates when they realized the Old Bill was just around the corner and about to arrive any minute. I mean, trying to kill each other then running off into the night side by side . . . well, that's Tower Hamlets for you, isn't it? They well and truly wrecked the battle cruiser but the Old Bill didn't arrest them because no one saw nothing, did they?'

'Same old, same old,' Ainsclough growled. 'Then when you need the police we can't get there quick enough . . .'

'So . . .' Penny Yewdall smiled briefly at Tom Ainsclough but brought the conversation back into focus, 'what did Cherry Quoshie do for a living?'

'Cherry, what did she do for a living . . .?' The thin and much-wasted woman sounded genuinely surprised at the question. 'She was on the game, wasn't she?'

'We don't know,' Ainsclough replied icily. 'Was she?'

'Yes, she was,' the woman answered equally coldly, 'she was a sex worker. She worked King's Cross. The poor cow. She was a very low-end tart, really low end. She worked the street taking who and what she could and not charging much. She left at about six o'clock and got back making a lot of noise at midnight . . . about midnight . . . no . . . no . . . usually after midnight in point of fact . . . seven days a week, rain or shine. But she hardly made any money; it was not easy for her . . . it was hard for her . . . she was a big-boned black girl with a wide, flat nose and awful bad teeth and breath, trying to compete with thin fifteen-year-old white runaway girls. She had to work hard for very little, and that's the truth. That's the way of it on the street, but you'd know that, I suppose.'

'We do,' Yewdall replied. 'We know what it's like.'

'Well, sweetheart, Anna Day could tell you more . . . but I will tell you this for nothing and that is that she was a well-frightened girl all the last week that I saw her, really scared . . . Cherry, I mean, not Anna. Cherry was frightened and it takes a lot to frighten Cherry Quoshie . . . or it took a lot to frighten her.'

'Frightened?' Yewdall repeated.

'Yes . . . scared stiff, she was really edgy,' the woman vigorously scratched her side. 'I mean, in the middle of last week I saw her from the street, so I did. She was standing at the window of her drum and looking out like she was expecting someone . . . but you know she was not standing in clear view, she was well hidden by the curtain. I saw the curtain move, you see, and then Quoshie's face peered round it just for a second, looking out like she was looking for someone but it was like she didn't want no geezer to see her. That was obvious, because she went and hid herself again very quickly. She didn't want to be seen all right.'

'When was that?' Yewdall asked.

'Middle of last week, darlin',' the woman replied. 'The old days you know, they run into each other. Wednesday today, you said . . .'

'Yes, Wednesday,' Ainsclough growled, 'like yesterday was Tuesday and tomorrow is Thursday, so today is Wednesday.'

'Look, don't you get sarcastic, darlin', don't you get all high and mighty.' The thin woman turned on Ainsclough, 'It's all right for you, you've got a job, it gives your life structure, some reason to get out of bed each new day. Me . . . nothing happens in my life what didn't happen the day before and won't happen the day after . . . so I lose track of the days of the week. Except Sunday. You hear the church bells on Sunday, that's how I know when it's Sunday.'

Ainsclough did not reply and accepted her rebuke. He conceded that she was correct. If he lived her half-life existence then the days would eventually begin to blur into each other for him also.

Penny Yewdall asked, 'Do you do drugs?'

'Not if I can help it,' the woman replied. 'I avoid them if I can, and the heavy bevvy. Trying to avoid that poison as well. It's not easy but I'm winning more than losing.'

'Good for you.' Yewdall smiled approvingly. 'Do you work the streets?'

'Now and again . . . but . . . and it's happening more and more frequent . . . I'm losing that skirmish. I'm like Cherry was, I've got less to sell than a lot of the girls so I have to work harder . . . but I don't have to work as hard as she used to work . . . not yet anyway . . . But what's a chick like me to do if she wants to eat? Cherry said she'd take me down to King's Cross but I can still work Piccadilly. I've got the figure for Piccadilly still, so I go there. There's more men there who like their anorexics . . . seems that a living skeleton is a turn on for them . . . but I can see King's Cross on the horizon . . . Like I said, though, a girl's got to eat.' The woman shrugged. 'Even if the one meal of the day is beans on toast, a girl must still eat something, and fodder costs money, so it's the "Dilly Lady" for me more evenings than not.'

'Did Cherry ever say what she was frightened of?' Ainsclough asked.

'Or who?' Yewdall added. 'What or who was she frightened of?'

'No . . . well, she didn't hardly tell me nothing.' The wasted woman shook her head. 'We hardly ever spoke, but she may have said something to Anna Day; she only ever seemed to talk to Anna Day.'

'So . . .' Yewdall asked, 'you don't know where Anna Day lives?'

'No clue, darlin',' again the woman shook her head, 'but you do. I mean, she's well known to the Old Bill, so she is . . . you'll have an address on your files. She's got a few convictions and she was last up before the beaks just recent like, a couple of weeks ago, so her address will not have changed since then . . . it's not likely to have done anyway.' The woman paused. 'Well, it might have changed because Cherry told me once that Anna has a pimp who smacks her around so she moves address quite often to try and escape him, but he keeps tracking her down and when he finds her he gives her a hospital slap and then sends her out working again.'

'A hospital slap?' Yewdall queried, having never heard the expression.

'You know,' the woman explained patiently, 'a slap that will put you in hospital for a few weeks.'

Yewdall nodded. 'I was afraid that that was what you meant. A hospital slap,' she repeated with a deep sigh.

Tom Ainsclough took his mobile from his pocket, selected a pre-programmed number and pressed it. When his call was answered by the switchboard of New Scotland Yard, he identified himself and asked to be put through to the criminal records. 'Anna Day,' he said, once he had been connected to the right department, 'age mid to late thirties . . . address in the East End, possibly Tower Hamlets. Yes, confirm the address, please.' As he waited he heard the collator tapping a computer keyboard and then indicated to Yewdall to get her pen and notepad ready to take down details. He then said, '371 Vernon Road, Tower Hamlets,' and added, 'thank you,' as Penny Yewdall scribbled the address on her notepad.

'That's practically directly across the road from here,' the wasted woman gasped. 'I never knew that she was so close, I mean her not ever calling on Cherry . . . I thought that meant that she lived miles away, so I did, miles and miles away . . .'

'So what's your name, love,' Penny Yewdall asked with a warm smile. 'I mean, since I've got my notebook out . . . just for our records . . .'

'Lynne,' the thin woman replied, 'Lynne Bentley, twenty-nine old summers.'

'Oh . . .' Yewdall gasped, 'I thought . . .'

'Yeah, I know, I look a lot older, but alcohol . . . hard drugs . . . the street . . . I ran away from home in Wiltshire when I was fifteen, survived as best I could.'

'You don't sound as though you're from Wiltshire.'

'Oh, but I am, my dearie,' the woman replied in a thick Wiltshire accent. 'I picked up the East End accent so as to blend in, that's a way of surviving that I discovered very early on. I fetched up in this drum a couple of years ago and Cherry Quoshie started offering me loaded syringes and pulling me to King's Cross – she kept trying to, anyway. She wasn't doing me no favours there, just doing her best to drag me down to her level . . . but you see that's addicts the world over; an addict's take on the saying that "a trouble shared is a troubled halved" is to pull you into the same boat as they are in.'

'Cynical,' Yewdall said, 'but it's probably also very true. Anyway, this room is a potential crime scene and because we can't lock the door that means we have to secure the entire house. You'd better pack your bags; you'll be going away for a day or two.'

'So where do I go?' Lynne Bentley sounded alarmed. 'You want me to join Betsy under a tree in Victoria Park tonight?'

'The Town Hall,' Yewdall replied, 'go to the Town Hall, the Housing Department section. They'll have a Homeless Persons' Unit. You are not intentionally homeless so they'll fix you up with something . . . a shelter, a hostel . . . you'll be provided with something, and Betsy in the basement, she'll have to go there as well. The whole house has to be evacuated. So you pack up a change of clothes and we'll go and wake up Betsy, the night owl. She'll have to go to the unit with you.'

'She won't like that,' Lynne Bentley complained. 'That won't go down well with her.'

'Tough.' Ainsclough smiled. 'But it's going to happen. So go and pack a bag, enough clothing for two nights.'

'OK,' Lynne Bentley replied with reluctance, 'but I'll go to the Town Hall by myself; I don't want to go with her. She's weird. They might pair us up together.'

In the event Betsy Sullivan proved to be a meek and a compliant personality. Standing only about five feet tall, Yewdall guessed, she listened to Yewdall's explanation as to why she had to vacate her room and without complaint agreed to comply and turned away from Yewdall to begin packing a change of clothing into a bag. It was as if, Yewdall felt, she was pleased to have something to do, as if, as Lynne Bentley had suggested a few moments earlier, she was pleased to have some structure in her life.

When the house had been cleared of all occupants, Tom Ainsclough made a second phone call to New Scotland Yard and asked for a SOCO team to attend the house in Tredegar Road, Tower Hamlets, then he and Yewdall stood on the threshold of the property, enjoying the sun and the curious glances from the foot passengers who walked past the house, as they waited for the SOCOs to arrive. Upon their arrival, in the form of a three-man team, Tom Ainsclough showed them Cherry Quoshie's room. He drew the SOCOs' attention to the hypodermic syringes and then asked them to examine the entire house. 'Never know what you'll find,' he added with a grin. 'But be careful,' he added. 'As you can see, it's a druggies den.' He and Penny Yewdall then walked the short distance to the last known address of Anna Day, on Vernon Road.

'She's got her Giro,' the black woman told the officers by means of explanation. The woman was bedecked with cheap jewellery and gaily coloured plastic bangles and, unlike Lynne Bentley's manner of opening the front door to strangers, she stood square on the threshold of her house, having fully opened the door. She showed no fear of Yewdall and Ainsclough despite being much shorter than they were, and despite the fact that they were strangers.

'What on earth does that mean?' Yewdall asked, bemused. 'She's got her Giro? Is she at home or isn't she . . . it's a simple question, I would have thought. I mean "yes" or "no" will do . . . we don't know what "she's got her Giro" is supposed to mean.'

'It means she's not in.' The woman spoke with clear hostility. 'It means she's gone down the Lighterman, so "no", she's not here. She's in the boozer.'

'The Lighterman?' Ainsclough queried.

'Yeah, it's a boozer on Roman Road, the Thames Lighterman,' the woman pointed to the far end of Vernon Road and in the opposite direction from which Yewdall and Ainsclough had approached the house, 'left at the corner. You can't miss it,' she advised. 'You'll see it as you turn the corner.'

'When did she leave the house to go to the pub?' Yewdall asked.

'Half an hour ago, about that . . . she left as soon as today's post arrived. She'll call in at the post office, cash the Giro and be off down the Lighterman. She'll blow the whole Giro in a single day's boozing session.' The woman spoke matter of factly. 'That's Anna. If you get a wriggle on you'll likely catch her before she gets legless and might even get some sense out of her, but that's only if you catch her early enough . . . and that's a big "if" because once she starts drinking she doesn't waste time . . . neat double vodkas, that's her tipple.'

'What does she look like?' Yewdall asked. 'Who do we look for in the pub?'

'Black girl. Tall. Thin. She's wearing a black leather mini-skirt and a red leather bikers' jacket.' The woman paused. 'Careful she doesn't spit at you, careful of that . . .'

'Oh?' Yewdall queried. 'Why?'

'Because she's got AIDS, hasn't she, she's HIV positive.' The woman forced a smile. 'She's a walking, talking, drinking killing machine. Just like me. I'm HIV positive too. That's why you don't scare me none because if you tried anything, I'd spit in your mouth. It makes me very powerful. You two are the Old Bill, aren't you?'

'Yes,' Ainsclough replied warily, 'we are the police.'

'I can tell,' the woman said smugly, 'that's the reason I don't want to see no ID card because it's stamped on your foreheads as clear as day it is. Anyway, Anna's down the Lighterman getting well Brahms and Liszt, but like I said, you'll need to get a wriggle on if you are going to catch her before she's legless.'

The front door of the house was then shut firmly on Yewdall and Ainsclough.

'I'll let Harry know where we're going,' Tom Ainsclough fished his mobile from his pocket. 'Then we play this ultra-cautious.'

'Yes,' Yewdall replied as she and Ainsclough turned away from the door, 'as you say ultra, ultra-cautious. We'll have to be careful not to get her gander up. We must assume she's HIV positive and keep out of spitting distance. If we can,' she sighed. 'Not that I've ever heard of anyone contracting HIV through saliva, but still . . . There must be easier ways of making a living.'

Frankie Brunnie smiled broadly and nodded a welcome as Harry Vicary got out of his car and walked slowly towards Scythe Brook Cottage, followed by two scene of crime officers, both of whom wore bright yellow, high visibility vests.

'I can't let you have all the fun, Frankie,' Vicary said as he approached Brunnie, who stood on the grass beside the cottage.

'Of course not, sir.' Brunnie grinned. 'Of course not.'

'And it's such a lovely day for a drive out of London . . . and to such a beautiful part of England as well.' Vicary looked around him. 'So very pleasant.'

'Indeed, sir,' Brunnie replied. 'I would be content to live and work in these parts.'

'And so could I, Frankie, so could I, though I doubt my income would permit it. Bricks and mortar round here doesn't come cheap.' Vicary glanced at Scythe Brook Cottage. 'So, this is the address on the gas bill Cherry Quoshie had so courageously left for us to find?'

'It is indeed, sir,' Brunnie also looked at the building, 'and as you can see, it provides a very good place for criminal activity. A road runs at the front but is little used; the next

nearest buildings are the rooftops you can see over there
. . . the high hedge all round means that the lawn, at the
rear of the house where we found the remains of a fire, can't
be overlooked.'

'So I see,' Vicary replied. 'Have you found anything of
significance in the cottage?'

'No, sir,' Brunnie shook his head briefly, 'although we didn't
search it as such for fear of disturbing a crime scene, we just
did a superficial tour . . . but it has been thoroughly cleaned.'

'Unsurprisingly,' Vicary grumbled. 'Really, why am I not
surprised?'

'So as Victor and I agreed, boss,' Brunnie replied, 'we have
to hope that Cherry Quoshie and Gordon Cogan left us their
fingerprints or their DNA at some obscure location within the
cottage which escaped the cleaning. But outside . . . just over
there, as I have just said,' Brunnie pointed to the back lawn
of the cottage, 'is the remains of a small fire.'

'Ah . . .' Vicary responded with interest, 'that is significant.
Show me, please.'

'A coal fire,' Brunnie added, as he and Vicary walked to
the remains, 'going by the remnants either coal or coke . . .
it certainly wasn't a wood fire.'

'Really?' Vicary looked at the circle of stones as he
approached them. 'I didn't think that you could still buy coal.'

'It must be available at certain outlets, sir. Parts of the UK
still permit it as a domestic fuel and steam locomotive pres-
ervation societies must buy it by the tonne.'

'Fair enough.' Vicary looked at the rooftops in the distance.
'So coal or coke will heat metal to a higher temperature than
wood. A woman's scream will carry from here to those houses
. . . especially on a quiet night. So we can assume that if this
is where she was tortured she must have been gagged.'

'Yes,' Brunnie replied solemnly, 'the poor, wretched woman
. . . she had an awful life and she had an awful death.'

'No luck at all,' Vicary agreed, 'just no luck at all.' He
paused. 'OK, where is Victor?'

'He's up at those houses, sir,' Brunnie replied, 'seeking
witnesses.'

'All right. When he returns, you two get back to London.'

Vicary took a deep breath, '. . . I do so love country air . . . but you two get your tails back up to the Smoke and pay a call on Tony Smith.'

'"Pestilence"?' Brunnie replied. 'Tony "the Pestilence" Smith?'

'Yes,' Vicary confirmed. 'Him . . . the one and the same. He should be up and out of his pit by now. We both know how felons like to sleep until midday but he'll be up and about by now. Like I said earlier, just pay a social call, just to let him know we are sniffing about . . . and that we have found this cottage and are linking the murders of Cherry Quoshie and Gordon Cogan. You can tell him that. We don't know how they link . . . yet . . . but we'll get there, because we always do, and if we can link him to the murder of the man who abducted his daughter and took her to Ireland when she was still a schoolgirl . . . well, in that case, a room in one of Her Majesty's guesthouses awaits him.' Vicary spoke with a grin. 'He might even have a room of his own, as the longer staying guests tend to do.'

'And here am I just getting used to this lovely clean air,' Brunnie complained in a jocular manner. 'There's no justice . . . no rest for the wicked.'

'A policeman's lot,' Vicary replied with a broad smile. 'But it's back to the traffic fumes for you and Victor. I'll stay with the SOCOs and enjoy the countryside.'

Brunnie handed Vicary the keys to the cottage. 'The address to return the keys to is in the porch, sir,' he advised.

'Very good,' Vicary took the keys, 'I'll make sure they go back, and you and Victor make sure you give Tony Smith's cage a damn good rattle.'

SEVEN

'Quoshie?' Anna Day shrugged and took a sip of her drink. 'What can I say . . . what can I tell you about Cherry Quoshie?' Anna Day revealed herself to be as the woman at the door of her address had described: tall, slender, angular features and wearing a black leather skirt, although the red bikers' jacket was more of a tasteful, gentle maroon than the violent red Ainsclough and Yewdall had been expecting. Day wore cheap jewellery and plastic bangles in myriad colours. Yewdall thought Anna Day had a cold, hard look about her eyes and felt that the woman would not readily smile.

'She was treated like a dog all her life, was Cherry Quoshie, like a dog, so is there any wonder she used to bite and snarl the way she did?'

'You seem to know she's dead,' Yewdall commented. 'Do you . . . do you know that she is dead?'

'Just a guess,' Anna Day told Yewdall with a cold stare. 'She's not been seen round here for the last few days. She's got nowhere else to go but her drum on Tredegar Road and those streets and this battle cruiser, and now the Bill coming asking about her. So is she brown bread? Oh . . . and she was edgy, I can tell you that . . . At the end of last week she was worried, well worried about something.'

'Yes,' Ainsclough answered. He, like Yewdall, sat at greater than usual distance from Anna Day, 'but we can't say much more than that. So . . . what can you tell us about her?'

'Double straight vodka,' Anna Day replied. 'Ice . . . a couple of slices of lemon, tell the guv'nor it's for me . . . he knows how I take my printer's ink . . .'

Tom Ainsclough stood and went to the bar. Anna Day watched him walk across the carpet and remarked, 'Blimey, even the plain-clothed Bill look like children these days. Reckon I'm now a lot nearer the end than the beginning. A lot nearer. But, you know, I keep telling myself it's better than the alternative. I always say that you can grow old or you can die young.'

'That's a good way of looking at it,' Yewdall replied. 'It's a fair point of view. Quite frankly I feel the same.'

'Don't push me too hard, darlin',' Anna Day continued to look at Yewdall in a cold manner. 'I mean, when the quiz session starts, don't lean on me too hard. I might spit at you, you and your mate both.'

'Yes. We know. Your housemate told us – she said that you were HIV positive. She said that she was also HIV positive.'

'We're carriers,' Anna Day explained, 'so was Quoshie . . . all three of us were HIV positive, two of us still are, the two that are left, but we haven't "turned" or "converted" or whatever the term is. We haven't developed the symptoms but we can "convert" any time, and when that happens our bodies will start to fall apart.'

'I'm sorry,' Yewdall forced a smile, 'it can't be easy to live like that.'

'One day at a time, sweetheart, it's one old day at a time.' Anna Day took another sip of her drink. 'But so long as you know and so long as you know that I'm accurate. I can spit into a wine glass from two feet . . . and if you keep your mouth shut, or keep your mouth covered, I can still aim at your eye.'

'My eye?' Yewdall asked, with some degree of alarm.

'Your eye, lovey, you can transfer bodily fluid by spitting into someone's eye . . . in the tear ducts . . . in the inside corner.' Anna Day put her long middle finger to her left eye, close to the bridge of her nose. 'It'll do the trick just as well as spitting into some old geezer's north and south. I mean, if a punter gets rough and keeps his mouth shut you can still spit in his eye. All right, all right so you'll get a right good slap but he'll get AIDS . . . that's what I call a good trade, especially if you don't tell him and especially if he's married and goes home to his trouble and strife.'

'You're still working!' Yewdall gasped.

'I've got to – a girl's got to eat but the punters know the risks and they all want protected. I mean, they take a look at yours truly and what do they see? They see an old black street worker and all they want is protected, they don't even offer more for unprotected . . . not with me anyway . . . not anymore . . . but if it gets rough I can spit at them but I don't tell them . . . I like it that they find out the hard way.' Anna Day winked at Yewdall.

'You can get five years in prison for that,' Yewdall spoke calmly, 'deliberate transmission of sexually transmitted diseases.'

'Hey, girl,' Anna Day leaned forwards and placed her drink on the table top, 'have you seen Cherry Quoshie's drum?'

'Yes,' Yewdall replied, 'we've just come from there.'

'Well, I only went in once and believe me it's a palace – a real palace compared to mine. So right now five years in Holloway is very inviting – a cot for five years and all the food I can eat and lots and lots of little girls to play with because I swing both ways . . . I like the girls as much as I like the boys. So when the screws turn out the lights, well, then that's when the fun begins. If they're not HIV positive when they go in, they will be when they come out. Imagine a young girl getting sent to Holloway for a month for shoplifting and coming out with AIDS because she cuddled up to me one night when she was upset because she felt she'd let her family down and I kissed her on the mouth, or because I spat at her in a recreation room skirmish,' Anna Day smirked. 'Now that's getting a life sentence with no parole for stealing a pair of jeans. Five years in the slammer sounds like my idea of heaven right now. So don't annoy me . . . and if I don't do it to you then I'll do it to some poor little creature who's in prison for the first time.'

'Don't threaten me in any way,' Yewdall spoke sternly, 'and you have to remember you don't get that in prison.' She pointed to Anna Day's vodka.

'I can live without it if I have to.' Anna Day shrugged. 'I've been inside a few times. You ache for a drink for the first week; after that it doesn't bother you and you sleep better and have really interesting dreams if you don't drink. Since the only time a prisoner is free is when they're asleep, well, that's a fair exchange. And don't kid yourself anyway, darlin', pretty well anything can be smuggled in if you've got the right contacts. And I've got the right contacts.'

'So I hear, so I believe,' Yewdall replied dryly, 'but never-theless, try to keep your threats to yourself, especially since we're on the same side.'

'You reckon?' Anna Day sneered. 'Since like when has the Old Bill been on my side? Since when?'

'We're on the same side this time.' Penny Yewdall glanced round the interior of the Thames Lighterman. It was, she saw, wholly in keeping with the sixties redevelopment of Tower Hamlets. She found it superficial and cheap, and even on a hot day like today, she felt cold within the pub. She thought the tables were too small, and the chairs round them also too small. The faded brown carpet was matted with spilled beer which had been trampled into the pile and was clearly long overdue for replacing. The bar was a single long bar behind which the Afro-Caribbean publican was serving Ainsclough and doing so with evident distaste. Prints of old London Town hung on the walls of the pub but did nothing to provide any sense of depth or history. The Thames Lighterman was not a pub Penny Yewdall would want to spend an evening in, no matter how convivial the company. 'Yes,' she said again, 'if Cherry Quoshie was a friend of yours, then we are on the same side, at least on this occasion.'

Anna Day nodded, picked up her drink and sipped it. 'All right,' she said quietly, '. . . so long as you know that it's only on this one occasion, just this once that we're on the same side. I can't be seen as being a friend of the Filth. Not in this boozer. So why are you and me on the same side apart from me being a mate of Quoshie's? There has to be more than that – there's more going down than that otherwise you wouldn't want me on your side.'

'There is,' Yewdall said flatly, 'you're very clever . . . it's because she was tortured before she was murdered.'

Anna Day gasped, 'Tortured!'

'Yes. Tortured.' Penny Yewdall spoke softly and matter-of-factly. 'There was a massive circular burn on the inside of her left leg, just above the ankle. It is believed to have been caused by something metal being heated until it was red-hot then pressed against her flesh. That sort of treatment can get a lot of information from anybody.'

'Dare say it would.' Anna Day's jaw sagged. 'It would get a lot of information from me, that I can tell you for nothing. It would get a whole shedload of information.'

Tom Ainsclough returned from the bar carrying three drinks on a tin tray. He placed the requested double vodka in front of Anna Day and a fruit juice in front of Penny Yewdall. He also bought a fruit juice for himself. He put the tray on a vacant seat and sat down at the table.

'Thanks, darlin'.' Anna Day swallowed the vodka she was drinking then exchanged her empty glass for the full one Ainsclough had bought for her. 'I've just told your good mate here not to annoy me because if you do I'll spit at you.'

'Yes,' Ainsclough sat down, 'we know. Your housemate warned us.'

'I also told her, your mate here, that I am an accurate spitter, and she told me I could get five years inside for deliberately transmitting sexually carried diseases. Just to fill you in on what we've been nattering about when you were at the bar.'

'Yes,' Ainsclough smiled, 'that's true. You could also get life.'

'I didn't know that.' Anna Day looked worried. 'I thought five years, out in three . . . that's a holiday . . . but life . . . I never knew that.'

'Life if you persist,' Ainsclough explained. 'First offence you'll collect five years, second offence you go down for life. You're a persistent danger to public safety, you see.'

'Oh . . .' Anna Day gasped.

'So . . . Cherry Quoshie,' Penny Yewdall refocused the conversation, 'we understand that she was frightened of something or someone when she disappeared just before last weekend? Did you see her after Friday last?'

'Yes, she was frightened . . . and no, I last saw her on the Wednesday, the day we both get our Giros. We had a printers ink in here. She was edgy . . . constantly looking over her shoulder.' Day sipped her drink.

'Do you know what she was frightened of?' Yewdall asked. 'Or who?'

'No . . . but I definitely think it was more of a "who" not a "what",' Day explained. 'She was frightened of some heavy face but I don't know which one. But I will tell you this, Quoshie was full of guilt, I mean, really full . . . brimful.'

'Oh?' Ainsclough sat back in his chair. 'That sounds interesting. Did she say why she felt guilty?'

'Yes, she said that she had once helped put a good man, an innocent face, away for life. She said the poor guy was set-up.'

'Did she mention his name?' Yewdall pressed.

'She might have . . . I can't remember it, though.' Day shook her head. 'Sorry.'

'Cogan,' Ainsclough suggested, 'could it have been Gordon Cogan? We believe that Cherry Quoshie's murder is linked in some way to the murder of a man called Gordon Cogan who was sent down for life, but we are unsure as to how they are linked.'

'Gordon,' Anna Day nodded, 'that name . . . that name rings a bell . . . yes . . . yes I think she did say that his name was Gordon.'

Yewdall turned to Ainsclough. 'That's how they link,' she said. 'That's the link we have been looking for.'

'Has to be,' Ainsclough replied, 'has to be.' He turned to Anna Day and asked, 'Did Cherry Quoshie give any details of what she did to help him get sent down for life?'

'She didn't tell me all the details, but guilt was really eating into her in a big way.' Anna Day took a deep breath. 'Quoshie, she was a hard case . . . but even hard cases can feel guilty and Quoshie was carrying an awful lot of it, a real boatload of guilt and she had plenty to spare.' Anna Day paused, took a sip of her drink and then said, 'I suppose I'd better tell you this . . . Quoshie told me recently that this geezer, Gordon Cogan had contacted her and that he only wanted her to go to the Filth with him. I mean, that wasn't going to happen but she did say that she told him she'd help all she could. She said that she didn't know that she was helping to fit him up. She remembers being strung out . . . her supplier was holding back on her horse . . . she didn't get any for two days, no H for forty-eight hours. For two days she was climbing the walls and in that state she would have done anything for a fix . . . and I mean anything. I've been there, I know how it can get you.'

'You're a smack head?' Yewdall asked.

'I was.' Anna Day spoke calmly. 'I was, darlin'. It's behind me now, I kicked it. I went into rehab. I'm one of their success stories. Most smack heads do rehab then return to being a user, that's because after rehab they go back to the same streets where they're known as users . . . the pushers give them freebies . . . and before they know it they're hooked again. It's a merry-go-round that isn't so merry.'

'But not you?' Yewdall smiled.

'No, darlin'. I knew the dangers of going back to where I was known as a smack head, so when I left rehab and I came to live in Tower Hamlets where I wasn't known . . . but I was where Quoshie was that time, you live your old life from fix to fix; heroin, crack . . . whatever the addiction is it's always the same, you live from fix to fix. You get to the state where you start to chew your finger ends off if you don't get a fix. Like I said, I was there . . . you'll do anything for a fix.'

'So, is that how you got AIDS,' Yewdall asked, 'from using dirty needles?'

'No . . . I was infected; I was deliberately infected by a geezer who was out for revenge. He offered well over the odds for some unprotected. I was younger then and I was short of cash, and I mean well short, and so I agreed. I even felt a bit complimented, to tell you the truth. A white geezer asking a black girl for some unprotected . . . it made me feel good about myself. Anyway he put himself together again, and as he walked away he then turned round and said, "That's what you get for being promiscuous". So I wondered what he meant but it began to worry at me and so three or four days later I went to the clinic and had myself checked out and there I was: HIV positive. So that's how it happened to me . . . it was then I began to learn how to spit accurately. Dead accurate. If you get my meaning.'

'We get your meaning,' Yewdall replied. 'It's not lost on us.'

'So I might look healthy, but like I said, I could convert at any time. I can take anyone down with me if I want . . . you two, some frightened little chick in Holloway, in for a month for shoplifting . . . there's justice for you but that guy, I made well sure he didn't do it to no other girl.'

'He won't?' Yewdall asked. 'You reported him?'

'No, I murdered him, darlin',' Day replied calmly. 'I chilled him. I iced him.'

A pause descended around the table. It was broken by Tom Ainsclough who said, 'You'd better be careful what you say to us, Anna.'

'Oh, yes?' Anna Day took another sip of her drink and grinned broadly. 'Am I really going to sign a statement or make a taped confession in a police interview room . . . I don't think so. No, it won't happen so I can talk free. I knew the geezer, you see, knew who he was . . . I knew where he lived. So I waited outside his drum one dark and lonely night. I was all in black. I am black. I wore black sports shoes. I was as silent as a mouse – he didn't see me until the last minute and the chiv was in his stomach, right up to the hilt, before he knew what had happened. I saw the look in his eyes and he knew it was me. Then the blade went in again and again. Then I took an old woollen sock from my shoulder bag . . . it had a rock inside. I bounced that off his head a few times. He didn't get up. He was well still. Next day the newspapers, they were full of his murder . . . police appealing for witnesses . . . all that number, all that old malarkey . . . witnesses, some hope. I made well sure there'd be no witnesses.'

'Where was that?' Tom Ainsclough asked. 'And when?'

'Why? Are you going to look the murder up,' Anna Day looked at Ainsclough, 'so you can close a cold case?'

'Possibly,' Ainsclough replied cautiously. 'Possibly.'

'Well, it wasn't in the Smoke, darlin'. I wasn't even in old England.'

'Scotland? Wales? Ireland?' Tom Ainsclough pressed. 'Abroad even?'

'Possibly. Possibly. Possibly.' Anna Day wasn't giving anything away. 'And as to the when . . . well, sometime in the last fifteen years. That's when. And that's all I'm going to say. But the point is . . . the old point is . . . I've got a victim. I can take another. So don't you two annoy me.'

'Point taken,' Yewdall replied coldly. 'So, Cherry Quoshie?'

'Yes, like I said, I don't know no details but she told me she wiped her hands all over a dead girl.' Anna Day continued to speak in a calm, matter-of-fact manner.

'She did what?' Yewdall queried. 'Wiped her hands all over a dead girl, did you say?'

'Yes, so she told me,' Anna Day continued. 'She said that the girl was brown bread. I believed her. It was the way she spoke, like she was getting something off her chest so I was listening, wasn't I? Real intently like. She told me she'd wiped her hands all over this boy Gordon's chest and then wiped them all over a dead girl . . . and then put her hands all over the girl's room and in her drawers and cupboards. Then she took a pair of the dead girl's knickers and dropped them in the boy's room.'

'Why did she do that?' Ainsclough asked.

'To get a fix,' Anna Day replied, as if irritated by the question. 'I told you . . . she was strung out. She was crawling up the walls.'

'Yes, but what was the reason she was told to do that?' Ainsclough clarified. 'That's what I mean.'

'Beats me, squire, beats me,' Anna Day shrugged. 'Don't think Quoshie knew either. Tell you the truth, I don't think she much cared either.'

'Where was Gordon Cogan?' Yewdall asked.

'In his room, next room to the girl's room, so Quoshie told me.' Anna Day glanced round the interior of the Thames Lighterman. A few elderly isolated daytime drinkers had entered the pub and were keeping themselves to themselves. 'He'd demolished a bottle of this stuff,' Anna Day tapped the side of her glass of vodka. 'He was half cut so Quoshie told me . . . in and out of consciousness. Quoshie said that she wiped her hands all over his body then wiped them on the dead girl, especially round the dead chick's neck. It was a hot day . . . weather like this,' she pointed to the windows of the pub. 'The boy was sweating cobs and Quoshie's hands were covered in his sweat and she smeared his sweat all over the dead girl and all round her room. Quoshie told me she could see no harm in it, not at the time. The girl was brown bread, well chilled, and like I said, she was well strung out, so she did it and she was given a wrap. She went straight up to her room in the attic and shot up. She was still out of it when the police came sometime later and bundled the boy into the back of a van. She was of no interest to the Filth. All they saw was a black heroin addict, in a daze, in an upstairs room well away from the action.'

'So what happened after that?' Yewdall asked, feeling a strong sense of dismay.

'Nothing. In a word, nothing,' Anna Day spoke calmly, 'nothing at all. Life went on. The Filth took statements from everyone who lived in that house . . . in Acton it was, Acton Town, so Quoshie told me but she didn't tell them nothing, the Old Bill just put her down as a spaced out, brain-dead, black as the Ace of Spades heroin addict who lived in the attic. There was nothing they could see linking her to the murder of the girl. She wore gloves, you know, washing up gloves, when she was putting the boy's sweat all over the dead girl, so her DNA wasn't mixed up with the boy's and so the case against Gordon Cogan was solid. Quoshie said he protested his innocence, but she wasn't about to speak up.'

'But he was convicted for it anyway.' Penny Yewdall sighed and then took a sip of her orange juice. 'Yes, we know what happened to Gordon Cogan. So tell us what happened to Cherry Quoshie.'

'Life went on, like I said. She kept on working as best she could. She carried on shooting up. She moved out of that house in old Acton Town and got herself another drum.'

'Did you know her at the time?' Ainsclough asked.

'Yes . . . yes I did.' Anna Day glanced to her left and nodded at someone she recognized who had just entered the pub. 'Yes, I knew her at the time, we go back a long way do me and Cherry but it was only a week or so ago that she told me what had gone down at the house in Acton Town all those years back. That was all news to me, darlin', all news to yours truly.'

'All right,' Yewdall replied, 'so do you know what, if anything, happened to make Cherry Quoshie want to tell you what she did?'

'Gordon Cogan only found her, didn't he?' Anna Day responded in a matter-of-fact manner. 'Like I said . . . he found her and asked her to go to the Filth with him.'

'He did?' Ainsclough commented. 'That's interesting.'

'Yes, he did, he was a determined little weasel, I'll give him that. Once he set his sights on something he went after

it with all he's got.' Anna Day raised her eyebrows. 'His
memory of that night after being out of it on alcohol must
have returned, and he went all over London looking for her.
When Quoshie heard that Cogan was looking for her she got
scared. Like her old past was catching up with her.'

'But he found her . . .?' Ainsclough sipped his drink.

'Yes, it wasn't difficult really. I mean, ten million people
live in this city, probably more, but if you want to find someone
you use this, don't you?' Anna Day pointed to the side of her
head. 'If you know a little bit about someone, then there's
only a few places you need to search. I mean, use your old
loaf. You go where they go, don't you? I mean, if you're
looking for a bus driver you don't go to the sort of wine bars
that merchant bankers use, do you?'

'Understood.' Yewdall nodded.

Anna Day continued, 'Quoshie was an old black street
worker so he knew to look for her down the King's Cross
meat rack. You don't look for lions where the penguins live,
do you? So Cogan trawls King's Cross and he asked the girls
for Quoshie by name. The girls were well wary at first because
he said he needed her help, but eventually they believed him
and believed he wasn't going to harm her. They put her in
touch with him and after a while they met up with each other.'

'Where?' Ainsclough asked.

'That table over there,' Anna Day pointed to a table at the
far end of the lounge of the Thames Lighterman. 'Quoshie
wanted me with her as a kind of insurance, and he wasn't going
to try anything because we let him know just how good we
both were at spitting. It was like . . . don't try anything little
man or your body will begin to fall apart and you'll be getting
it from two directions at once. You just won't get out alive. He
was well worried and I reckon by then he was more frightened
of Quoshie than she was of him. So we came into the Lighterman,
they sat over there and I sat here in case I was needed. I didn't
hear anything that was said and I don't lip-read so I can't tell
you what was said, but he got up after a while and he went
away looking happy . . . Well, he was definitely looking happier
than when he arrived.' Anna Day took another sip of her vodka.
'Any old way, Cherry Quoshie came over to me and said, "He

only wants me to go to the Old Bill with him, doesn't he".
That's what he wanted. So I said, "Some hope!" and knock me
down with a feather because Cherry Quoshie only says, "Dunno,
Anna . . . I might". She said she asked him if she could think
about it, and he agreed to let her have some time. So I ask why
does he want you to go to the Old Bill and she says he wants
her to help him clear his name, so she says, "Yes, I remember
what I did . . . but it means I'll go down for conspiracy to
murder" and she said she needed time to think about it. So I
said, "You're serious?" and Quoshie says she is. She was
suddenly coming over all Gandhi, you see, banging on about
doing some good in her life for once and she says, "What have
I got to lose? I mean, look at me. I've got nothing and no one
to be on the outside for . . . I've got nothing. I'm the lowest of
the low, not good looking, HIV positive, black street worker,
forty years old soon. I'll make a confession. I'll get five years,
out in three. I'll have company, decent food, but I've got to
grass up Pestilence . . . that's the only thing stopping me. I've
got to grass up Pestilence Smith".'

'Wait!' Ainsclough held up his finger. 'Are you saying Tony
"the Pestilence" Smith was involved in the murder of Janet
Frost?'

'Well, that's what Quoshie told me and she's well frightened of him. From what I have heard about the geezer she's
right to be scared of him. He's seriously bad news is
Pestilence.'

'How was he involved,' Yewdall pressed, 'do you know?'

'Well,' Day explained, 'Quoshie told me that Pestilence was
her supplier; he was holding back her supply. Like I told you,
he had her well strung out, and it was Pestilence who told her
to put some washing-up gloves on and then rub Gordon
Cogan's sweat all over the dead chick's body.'

Yewdall and Ainsclough sat back in their chairs and looked
at each other. 'Well, well, well,' Ainsclough said, to which
Yewdall echoed in reply, 'Well, well, well.'

'Is that important?' Anna Day asked.

'It's a link,' Yewdall replied, 'and it's a stronger link than
the fact that they were living in the same house at the time
that Janet Frost was murdered.'

'Well, it was fear of Pestilence that was stopping her going with Gordon Cogan to the Old Bill. Pestilence can get at you anywhere, so people say, even if you're on the inside. He can still get at you. Anyway, they said they'd meet up later and that's how they left it. Then she vanishes and her body is found in Wimbledon, of all places,' Anna Day sighed, 'Wimbledon.'

'You read the newspapers?' Yewdall asked. 'That's how you know where her body was found?'

Anna Day shook her head. 'I'm a lazy girl, I saw it on there.' She pointed to a plasma screen which was attached to the adjacent wall showing the Test Match from Trent Bridge. 'This is my seat, at this time of day anyway. I get the news here each day. So poor old Cherry Quoshie ends her days in Wimbledon . . . leafy, posh old Wimbledon. Who'd have thought it? Proper funny . . . she had to die to go up in the world.'

'These are the Filth.' The man sneered at Brunnie and Swannell. 'You'll learn to hate them. You will really learn to hate them.' He clasped his hand on the younger man's shoulder. 'They're not called the Filth for nothing.'

'Yes, Grandad.' The youth stood beside the older man and also viewed Swannell and Brunnie with hostility, 'but what's all this "I'll learn"? I hate them already, Grandad. I really hate the Filth. I have nothing to learn in that respect.'

'You're a good boy, Pancras, a very good boy. A real scout.' The older man turned and beamed at the younger man.

'Ah . . .' Frankie Brunnie nodded to the younger man, 'so you'll be Pancras Reiss. We were told you'd pass for a nineteen- or twenty-year-old. Our colleague was correct . . . I wouldn't have guessed that you're still shy of your sixteenth birthday.'

'Yes, he's a big lad,' Tony "the Pestilence" Smith said proudly. 'He's a Smith, different surname but he's a Smith and that's what matters. In his blood he's a Smith.'

'Yes,' Swannell observed, 'I can see the family resemblance . . . he definitely takes after you, Tony.'

'Yes, he does,' Tony once again patted Pancras Reiss on the shoulder, 'and being big helps a lot in our line of work . . .'

'And what, may I enquire,' Brunnie asked, 'would be your line of work?'

'Whatever comes along,' 'the Pestilence' replied. 'We don't have a particular speciality. Whatever we can make a profit out of. If it earns, we'll do it. If it's not an earner we won't do it.'

The four men stood in the living room of Tony Smith's house in Southgate. Swannell and Brunnie stood side by side, facing Tony "the Pestilence" Smith and Pancras Reiss who also stood shoulder to shoulder. Victor Swannell read the room in a single sweep of his eyes and thought there to be little depth to Smith's house, in terms of the decoration and the taste in furnishings. It was, he felt, clearly the home of a very materialistic home-owner. The brightly coloured wall-to-wall carpeting, the designer chairs and settee, the huge, flat-screen television mounted on the wall, shiny metal objects in a glass display case, the glass-topped coffee table, and all with an everything-in-its-place neatness. There were no comforting shelves of books or prints of famous paintings, no human touch of any kind that Victor Swannell could detect, like a loosely folded-up newspaper resting on the coffee table or an open magazine resting on the arm of a chair. The house had been found to occupy a corner plot on the junction of Maxim Drive and Vera Road, and appeared to exhibit the same square inch by inch perfection on the outside that the officers found within the house. The house had clearly been built in the thirties. It was detached, and an extension had been built on in the form of a double garage with living space above. There was seen to be a balcony above the main door with access clearly only from the master bedroom. A tall chimney rose from the side of the house, on to which had been bolted a satellite dish. Unlike any of his neighbours, Tony 'the Pestilence' Smith was not at all concerned about advertising to the world that he had nothing better to do with his time than to soak up twenty-four hour television. The garden surrounding the house had a similar appearance, with not a blade of grass, not a flower out of place, again totally in keeping with the interior of the house.

'So what brings the Old Bill here anyway?' Tony Smith asked, his hand still resting proudly on his grandson's shoulder.

'Mind you, we are always happy to cooperate with the boys in blue, aren't we, Pancras?'

'Certainly are, Grandad,' Pancras Reiss smiled an insincere smile, 'we most certainly are. Anything you think we can help the police with, just ask.'

'Anything to be public spirited,' Tony Smith added. 'We all have to support our wonderful police force.'

'You've certainly amassed a lot of police interest for someone who is keen to help the police,' Swannell observed.

Tony Smith let his hand fall from his grandson's shoulder and opened both palms towards the officers. 'I mean, be fair guv'nor, what can I say?' He smiled but did so with a menacing attitude. 'But no convictions . . . no serious convictions anyway . . . I'm Mr Clean. I'm as clean as clean can be.'

'So what about you, Pancras,' Brunnie asked, 'you've got convictions already . . . and now you are suddenly very keen to help the police?'

'I turned the corner, didn't I?' Pancras Reiss smiled. 'It's all behind me now.'

'That's good to hear, Pancras,' Brunnie replied, 'very good to hear.'

'So what can I do for you gentlemen?' Tony Smith asked. 'You'll note I have let you into my house quite willingly. I didn't ask for a warrant. I am giving total cooperation, even though you are still the Filth, even though I hate the ground you stand on. You've been trying to pin something on me for years.'

'Even though we're standing in your living room,' Swannell asked, 'do you still hate the ground we stand on?'

'I can always have the carpet cleaned,' Smith snarled his reply. He had a large, round face, wore his hair in a ponytail and had a ring in his ear. 'It's no big deal, is it, Pancras? No big deal at all.' He smelled strongly of aftershave.

'No big deal at all,' Pancras Reiss parroted.

'It's good when Pancras visits me,' Tony Smith smiled, 'it gets him off the estate he lives on . . . away from trouble and it lets him see this house where his mother grew up. You see, by visiting me, his old grandad, he sees that an honest pound goes further. Only honest pennies bought this drum. So his mother, my only child, she only gets herself arrested for shop-lifting and what does she get to live in? A cheap little council flat that's no place to bring up a boy like Pancras; it sets him off down the wrong road. So he comes here and gets some good advice and guidance from his grandad. He sees the lifestyle he could have if he keeps his nose clean. We have a chat about this and that and then we go down the pub for a beer.'

'He's underage,' Brunnie growled, 'that's an offence right there, Mr Clean, buying alcohol for a minor.'

'Look at him,' Tony 'the Pestilence' Smith protested, '. . . what, a boy of sixteen . . . he's no minor . . . not in any real sense.'

'Fifteen,' Brunnie corrected Smith. 'He's still of school age. Right now he should be at school, and you're taking him to the pub and buying him beer.'

'So are you going to stay here all day? Are you going to hang around and make sure we don't go to the boozer? I don't think so. Not New Scotland Yard. The officers from the local station maybe but not you guys,' Smith sneered. 'So, I'll ask you again . . . what can I do for you?'

'Gordon Cogan,' Brunnie spoke softly.

'Him!' Tony Smith snarled. 'That little toe-rag!'

'Yes, him,' Swannell added, 'that man.'

'Hardly a man,' Smith hissed. 'Do you know what he did to my daughter, Pancras's mother? He only kidnapped her and took her to Ireland. She was only fifteen at the time.'

'Yes, we know,' Brunnie smiled, 'more or less the same age as Pancras is now, whom you plan to take to the pub for a beer.'

'That's different . . . it's a different level of offending. Not in the same league,' Smith protested, 'and he only got six months for that . . . kidnap and rape . . . and he gets six months. There's no justice in that . . . there's no justice at all. But then he messed up, he messed up big time. As soon as he got out he messed up and then he went down for life for murder.'

'Yes, we know that as well,' Brunnie replied flatly.

'So why bring his name into this house?' Smith demanded. 'I don't like his name being mentioned in this house.'

'Because he was murdered a few days ago.' Swannell took another look around the superficial, lifeless, soulless room.

Tony 'the Pestilence' Smith smiled. 'Well, isn't that a turn up for the old books – so there might be justice after all. I always said that someone would have it in for him one day. I always said that.'

'But of course you wouldn't know who'd want to murder him?' Swannell asked. 'Or would you?'

'Me?' Smith pointed a fleshy finger to his chest and smiled. He wore a blue T-shirt, white slacks and white sports shoes. 'Why should I know who'd want to ice the little toe-rag?'

'Well, he did what he did to your daughter,' Brunnie explained. 'It gives both you and Pancras a powerful motive. People have been murdered for less of a reason than that. We know that Pancras knows what happened to his mother when she was fifteen.'

'Yes, I told him,' Smith replied defensively. 'Kids, they grow up quickly today. He's old enough to know. I told him because his mother wouldn't but the boy had the right to know so I told him. The boy knows. There's no secrets in this family.'

'Fair enough,' Brunnie replied, 'so long as we can speak freely in front of him.'

'Yes, you can,' Smith smiled, 'as freely as you please.'

'Good,' Brunnie smiled. 'We'll take you up on that, Tony. So, Cherry Quoshie, tell us about her.'

'Who?' Tony Smith looked surprised.

'Cherry Quoshie.' Brunnie repeated the name.

'Yes, I heard the name, but who is she?' Smith asked.

'She is . . . she was an Afro-Caribbean sex worker,' Swannell explained.

'And . . .?' Smith began to sound nervous.

'Well,' Brunnie continued, 'she too has been murdered.'

'And so . . .?' Smith replied aggressively.

'Well . . .' Brunnie explained, 'you see, Tony, we would not normally associate the murder of Cherry Quoshie with the murder of Gordon Cogan, had it not been for the fact that both bodies were left in exactly the same place with a twenty-four hour time gap between the dumping of each body . . . the same place almost to an inch. Twenty-four hours apart, exactly.'

Tony 'the Pestilence' Smith's face paled.

'That means that the murders are definitely linked,' Swannell explained. 'If the bodies had been dumped, separated from each other by many miles, then in that case we would not have linked them. But both bodies dumped in the same place in the same street in Wimbledon where neither person had any connection . . . then the stolen cars which we assume were used to carry the bodies were burned out also in more or less the same place . . . they have to be linked. The two murders have got to be linked. You see our thinking, Tony?'

Swannell enjoyed the look of anger that began to well up in Tony Smith's eyes.

'So then we also discover that the two people were murdered in the same way, battered on the head with a linear object . . . same MO . . . dumped in the same place . . . carried to where their bodies were dumped in stolen cars which were abandoned and torched in the same street . . . that means intrigue, that means New Scotland Yard Murder and Serious Crime Squad,' Swannell added.

'That's us,' Brunnie smiled, 'and we know that you have a great dislike for Gordon Cogan.'

'Had,' Smith replied quickly, defensively, 'had. I had a great dislike for him but he went down for murder. I moved on in life, like you have got to do. I don't see any debt outstanding.'

'Yet you just described him as . . . what did you call him . . . "that little toe-rag"? Sounds like there's still a lot of hate in you, Tony,' Brunnie observed.

'So why link me? Where do I fit in?' Smith appealed.

'We don't know yet . . .' Brunnie replied. 'Not yet.'

'Yet?' Tony Smith echoed. 'What do you mean "yet"?'

'We mean yet . . .' Swannell repeated. 'You knew Gordon Cogan; you have a motive for wanting to harm him. If we can find a link between you and Janet Frost, and you and Cherry Quoshie, like supplying heroin to Janet Frost . . .'

'You can't prove that,' Tony Smith growled.

'We can't prove anything at the moment, Tony, but you are in the mix somewhere . . . and we are under no time pressure. We've got all the time in the world, and it's only a matter of time before we find out where, and how, you fit in.'

Tony Smith remained stone-faced but both officers saw the look of worry in his eyes.

'So,' Brunnie said, 'do you know what we will find in Scythe Brook Cottage, down in Hampshire? We're going over the building now – well, not us personally, of course, but our scene of crime officers are. And they are very efficient.'

A look of fear flashed across Tony Smith's eyes. Swannell saw the look and thought *Gotcha, Tony*, but he said, 'We came from Scythe Brook Cottage today – quite a nice little retreat. Rented, we have found, so it can't be linked to you; we assume that you paid hard cash to the rental agency using an assumed name, but we'll check anyway. We saw the burn on Cherry Quoshie's leg, that was really quite horrible, and the remains of the coal fire in the garden, the fire you had on Monday evening, as if you were trying to make Cherry Quoshie tell you something by burning her leg. Somebody smelled the coal smoke, you see; it has a distinct smell, that's how we know when the fire was burning, the night before Cherry Quoshie's body was found in Wimbledon.'

Tony Smith remained silent. His face was set hard. Pancras Reiss stood motionless. He also had paled and looked worried.

'Bet you'd like to know who's been talking, wouldn't you, Tony?' Brunnie smiled. 'But sorry, we can't name our sources . . . I dare say you had the cottage cleaned, all surfaces wiped of fingerprints . . . but you know Cherry Quoshie, she was a very clever girl, she obviously wasn't supervised all the time and she left us a present. And if she left us another present in the form of her fingerprints in an obscure place . . . such as inside a drawer, underneath a table . . . a place like that which would not be wiped down and if she got Gordon Cogan to do the same, that will place them both at the cottage at the same time, and if we can find some link with you and Cherry Quoshie and Gordon Cogan and the cottage, then we'll be back and we'll have a warrant for your arrest, Tony. Imagine swapping this house for a cell in Wormwood Scrubs.'

'You might have just gone and tripped yourself up at last,' Swannell said, 'but, like I said, this is really just a social call. We'll see ourselves out.'

Swannell and Brunnie turned away from Tony 'the Pestilence' Smith and Pancras Reiss and walked to the front door of the house, leaving grandfather and grandson both looking very pale.

'We palled up in Wormwood Scrubs, me and Gordon . . .' Philip Dawson sat in the armchair of his flat in Pennyfields, Poplar, crossed his legs and smoothed down his three-quarter length skirt. Tom Ainsclough sat opposite him in the second armchair whilst Penny Yewdall sat on the settee. The flat, she noted, was a sixties development and was on the first level above a parade of shops. 'We were both graduates, both of us had fallen from grace and we very quickly found each other among all those really awful rough boys. You know how it is, like always finds like. Gordon was in for life for murder and I was serving seven years for the manufacture of ecstasy tablets. He was classed as being IDOM at the time but I was with him, I mean that I was present, the instant he changed his mind. I was still a boy then.'

'And now?' Penny Yewdall asked warmly.

'Pre-op transgender, pet,' Philip Dawson replied. 'I have been on hormone therapy for some years, oestrogen supplements and testosterone suppressants. All my male bits have shrunk to next to nothing and my female bits have budded and developed nicely. I am due for SRS in the winter, just before Christmas. It will be a lovely Christmas gift for me.'

'SRS?' Ainsclough asked. He felt fearful and fascinated at the same time.

'Sexual reassignment surgery, pet,' Dawson explained, 'the awesome point of no return.'

'Are you nervous?' Penny Yewdall asked.

'Yes . . . a bit, but I'm going to go through with it. No turning back now, darling. I spent my life since I was about seven or eight waking up each morning and feeling as though I was in the wrong body. I used to try on my elder sister's clothes and play with her toys.'

'That must have been difficult,' Yewdall commented.

'It was hell, believe me. I went through the usual stage of denying it and taking macho jobs: night watchman, digging holes in the roads over the years, that sort of thing. I accumulated a lovely wardrobe of skirts and dresses and heels and wigs and dressed at home, then I threw them all away in an attempt to accept my male body and instantly regretted doing so. Then I decided I couldn't be a man if I wasn't a man . . . so I applied for surgery . . . it takes a long time. A lot of men with inadequate personalities apply for SRS because they think all they need do is to become a girl and then find a nice boy to look after them and that will be the end of their troubles, but those sort get weeded out very early on. Then you have to live as a woman for two years, and I mean be fully accepted as one . . . at home, in the community, in the workplace. It used to be one year that you had to live as a woman but they extended it to two; they are really testing your resolve, you see . . . and the nurses at the clinic can be real cows, no acceptance from them at all. No sympathy. No welcome to the woman's world. No warm welcome into the universal sisterhood. It's all part of the test. Anyway, I have won through and I have an operation date now.' Philip Dawson smiled contentedly. 'Been there, done that and all but got the T-shirt.'

'Are you employed?' Yewdall asked.

'I help out in a charity shop to fill in the time, but I work as a woman though technically I'm on the dole, pet.'

'How do your family feel about all this?' Ainsclough grew more and more curious as he crossed his legs tightly.

'Oh, I'm *persona non grata*, pet. They're all up in Newcastle so there's a nice and comfortable distance between us. It was all really unfortunate, they were so proud of me, the first of our family to get to university . . . then I did what I did – I committed an act of betrayal. I used my gift to do ill and I also betrayed my family because none of them had ever been in trouble with the police. I nose-dived. No recovery. I graduated in chemistry and got a job in a pharmaceutical company and used, or misused, my knowledge to make ecstasy tablets, initially on the side, then I gave up my job and started producing ecstasy tablets full-time. The money was the lure, you see. Me and a couple of other guys were based in a little house which we rented in Wales. A remote little farmhouse, very remote, and that was our mistake. You've heard the old English saying "the fields have eyes and the woods have ears"?'

'Oh, yes.' Ainsclough nodded. 'I have heard that expression.'

'Well, that was our undoing. We were engaged in an unlawful activity but we were not criminals, if you see what I mean. We were just not savvy enough. We were not clued up. We had no street wisdom. We should have stayed in the city and benefitted from the anonymity a city offers.' Philip Dawson shook his head. 'We were stupid. I mean, were we stupid or were we stupid? The local people noticed strangers in the midst, as they would do, three men in a little house, lights burning all night, and they saw all the comings and goings. So they tipped off the local police and the police put us under observation but we just kept working thinking no one was noticing us because we stayed in all the time apart from going out to buy our food. We said we'd quit when we had made a million pounds each.'

'That's seriously big money.' Ainsclough sat back in the armchair.

'Oh, yes, big enough,' Dawson replied. 'We were coining it in, and that helped us to be blind as to what was happening. So then, one fateful day, we got raided at seven a.m. and the jig was up. We got seven years each and all our money was confiscated under the proceeds of crime legislation.'

'Yes, it would have been,' Yewdall commented dryly. 'All of it.'

'So now I live on hormones and a little food and help out in a charity shop.' Philip Dawson forced a smile. 'Some success story.' He had a thin body, a larger man's face and wide, male hands; his voice was deep throated and would require work to develop it to enable it to pass as a woman's voice, but Yewdall had to concede that already he would make an acceptable woman. She certainly thought that he suited the blue dress he wore. 'So I'll soon be Lydia Dawson. I really can't wait. It's been a long journey but at least it's my choice.'

'Isn't it always?' Yewdall asked.

'No . . . it's a horrible story . . . this is a horrible story . . . you ought to know about it but I don't think you can do anything.'

'Oh?' Ainsclough replied. 'Something the police should know about?'

'Yes . . . but what can be done?' Dawson opened his palms.

'Tell us anyway,' Yewdall prompted. 'Then we'll tell you if anything can be done.'

'Well, there's a girl at the clinic . . . if we see each other there we go for a coffee and a natter . . . two girls together. Her story . . . she ran away from home in Scotland when she was fourteen so she told me and then lived as a rent boy in London for two years and eventually found a "guardian".'

'A "guardian"?' Yewdall asked.

'It's a term,' Dawson explained. 'When a boy or a girl, usually a runaway who has nowhere else to go, teams up with an older man who offers them a home he's known as their "guardian".'

'I see,' Yewdall commented.

'So, she lived with her guardian as his boy for a while and then one day he took her to Germany. She remembers a large house and a German man in his fifties. She went to sleep. She woke up a day or two later and she'd had the operation . . . the whole lot . . . male bits removed, artificial female bits created.'

'God in heaven!' Ainsclough gasped. 'You're right that is something we ought to know about.'

'I told her to go to the police but she says she has no information about the German geezer . . . but thinks he is a surgeon with his own private operating theatre in his basement . . . she didn't know where in Germany . . . and any crime took place in Germany, so it's a matter for the German police, not the British police.'

'Dunno . . .' Yewdall said coldly, 'we'd still like to chat to this so-called "guardian" if she'd identify him . . . we can liaise with the German police, put them in the picture.'

'I can ask her but she says she's not too unhappy because she's a tiny little thing, so delicate, a real waif. As a man she would have had a hard life: no qualifications, no skills. She says forty per cent of her misses being a boy but sixty per cent is pleased that she's a girl now. Anyway, when she returned to the UK she walked out on her guardian and went to the clinic and said, "Look at what they did to me, you have to let me have hormones", so they did, they had to. So it's not always your decision . . . if you fall into the wrong hands and that's one story of that being done, there'll be others.'

'Yes.' Ainsclough looked at the flat, the flowers in a vase, the bowl of scented leaves, copies of *Elle* and *Cosmopolitan* on the coffee table. It was, he had to concede, a very cosy woman's home. 'Yes, that is true, but she can help others by coming forward. We would like to take a statement from her. It's the sort of thing we need to know about and, as Penny has just said, we'll share it with the German police.'

'All I can do is ask her next time I see her,' Philip Dawson agreed. 'I will volunteer to accompany her if she wishes me to do so.'

'We'll leave that to you.' Ainsclough uncrossed his legs and sat forward. 'So, Gordon Cogan . . . we are really here about him.'

'Yes, enough about me – it's Gordon that you are interested in, of course it is.'

'It's quite interesting, though.' Penny Yewdall smiled. 'It's really quite illuminating. I didn't know SRS was so complex and so long drawn out.'

'It's never-ending, pet. After the operation I'll still need hormones until I draw my last breath . . . otherwise I'll grow facial hair and chest hair to go with the girlie bits,' Philip Dawson explained. 'But Gordon . . . with Gordon it all started in the TV room in the "scrubs". Usually all the lags wanted to watch those empty-headed comedy shows with that canned laughter but one geezer saw that there was a documentary being shown about DNA, and all the rough boys wanted to watch it – it was of real interest to them, you see, so we watched it and it was all about how flawed DNA is when used to prosecute. The study of DNA is still so new that, apparently, if what is known about DNA is represented as a golf ball, then what is likely to be still out there waiting to be discovered about it might, on the same scale, be represented as a basketball. Scientists have found out, for example, that the insect, the common name of which is the water boatman, you know, that beetle-like creature which sits on the surface tension of ponds . . .'

'Yes,' Penny Yewdall replied, 'I know what you mean.'

'Well, it is apparently the case that that creature has a more complex DNA structure than a human being,' Dawson advised.

'That I didn't know,' Yewdall said patiently.

'Well, yes . . .' Philip Dawson continued, 'it's because of that discovery and other similar breakthroughs that DNA evidence alone is not sufficient to ensure a conviction in UK courts. In the UK, courts need DNA plus an additional strand of evidence to ensure a safe conviction.'

'Yes,' Ainsclough nodded, 'that is true, though I didn't know the reason, but yes, it is indeed the case that these days DNA alone is insufficient to secure a conviction.'

'DNA really comes into its own as a tool of elimination,' Dawson explained. 'It's flawed, deeply so, when used as a prosecution tool, so I have read.'

'And so we have heard. All right,' Yewdall held eye contact with Dawson, 'so where is this leading?'

'Well, where it is leading,' Dawson explained, 'is that the scientist who was being interviewed for the television documentary said to the interviewer, "I've got your DNA on my hands. I will now leave your DNA on everything I touch until I wash my hands".' Dawson paused. 'Anyway, when he heard that Gordon's head sagged forward. He didn't say anything at the time but the following day he said, "That's how they did it" and "That's how they got my DNA all over Janet Frost's body, and all over her room and inside her cupboards and drawers". He said they must have known how easy it was to transfer someone's DNA to a crime scene . . . and remember, Gordon was convicted before the change in the law. He was convicted when DNA was thought irrefutable and deemed sufficient in itself to secure a safe conviction. He also says that he had recovered the hazy memory of a black sex worker who lived in the house wiping her hands all over his body, gathering up his DNA from his sweat. He was half naked at the time, it being a hot day, and he was sleepy with alcohol excess, but he remembers enough. At the time of his trial he had no memory of it. Only in later years did patchy bits of memory emerge. He also told me that he'd spoken to her before, so he knew her name . . . it sounded like a soft drink

. . . like Cherry Squash . . . not orange or lemon squash but Cherry Squash . . . something like that. I can't be sure. Sorry.'

'Cherry Quoshie?' Yewdall said. 'Yes, we know about her living in the house at the time of the murder. Did Gordon tell you who he believed had stitched him up?'

'A geezer called Smith. Sorry, can't be of much help to you there, given the number of geezers called Smith in London,' Dawson looked apologetic. 'But he reckoned this guy Smith had it in for him because of what Gordon had done to his daughter. He had taken her to Ireland when she was underage or something. So this geezer called Smith fitted Gordon up with something to make sure he went away for a long time for taking his daughter to Ireland. Me,' Dawson smiled, 'I could well cope with a nice geezer like Gordon taking me on holiday to Ireland, but Mr Smith didn't like it.'

'It's a bit more complicated than that,' Yewdall smiled, 'but we know Mr Smith and what you have said makes sense.'

'Makes all the sense in the world,' Ainsclough sighed. 'I can see that happening.'

'So can I,' Yewdall replied, 'so can I.' She turned to Dawson. 'So what did Gordon Cogan do then?'

'Changed his plea . . . he dropped the IDOM stance, admitted that he was guilty and began to work for his parole. It took him five years . . . I was out by then, pursuing my own agenda. I got paroled after five years. All that testosterone made me convinced that I was a girl, probably just the push I needed, but Gordon's plan was half-baked, totally half-baked.' Dawson shook his head.

'What was his plan?' Yewdall asked.

'To get out, he told me, track down the girl, Quoshie, and ask her to go to the police with him and make a statement about what she had done.'

'Yes,' Ainsclough replied, 'a bit half-baked, as you say.'

'Well, that was Gordon,' Philip Dawson shrugged, 'not really on this planet of ours . . . head in the air. Even fifteen years in top security couldn't mature him. He had this air of naivety about him even after being banged up for all that time amongst the hardest cons in London. I tried to tell him it wouldn't be that easy. OK, he might get his conviction overturned but she'll get a long sentence for conspiracy to murder. What is the likelihood of her, of anyone, doing that? But he was determined. He was like an overgrown schoolboy. It was like he'd get the girl Quoshie to do that and then spend the rest of the day trainspotting.'

'If he had only gone to a solicitor,' Ainsclough sighed, 'and done it through legal channels – asked his solicitor to raise an action to have his conviction overturned. He didn't need Cherry Quoshie . . .'

'It might have . . . would have saved his life,' Yewdall agreed. 'A conviction based on DNA evidence alone can now be overturned.'

'I think it was more than that,' Dawson explained. 'If you'll pardon me, he didn't merely want his conviction to be deemed unsafe. With that the question of his guilt still hangs in the air. He wanted complete acquittal. He wanted his innocence to be a matter of record. For that he needed the woman, Cherry Quoshie, to come forward and make a statement, admitting her part in the whole thing.'

Ainsclough stood. 'Well, thank you for your information, Mr Dawson . . . it has been illuminating.'

'And thank you for visiting me. I appreciate it greatly.' Philip Dawson also stood, as did Penny Yewdall. 'I know that I have my operation date, but I still didn't want to go into a police station in my summer dress and heels and say "Excuse me, my name is Philip Dawson . . ."'

Back in the car, Yewdall turned to Ainsclough. 'If Cherry came forward, that would implicate Tony Smith in the murder of Janet Frost,' she suggested, 'which Smith could not allow to happen. So he had them both killed, but not until after he had tortured Quoshie to determine what she had said and to whom.'

'Seems so.' Ainsclough met Penny's gaze. 'Now all we have to do is prove it.'

Penny Yewdall stopped to re-tie her shoelace. It was mid-evening, the heat had largely subsided and she knew she had time to reach Greenwich Park before the gates were locked for the day. She had dressed in a blue T-shirt and baggy blue jogging bottoms, matching blue sports shoes with loud red laces, and left her small terraced house in Tusker Street. She ran along fume-filled Trafalgar Road and entered Greenwich Park at the Park Row entrance. She ran in front of the Maritime Museum and then put herself at the path which led up Observatory Hill to Flamsteed House. At the top of the hill she paused and turned to look at the vista of buildings that was the Square Mile of the City of London and identified the Gherkin, pondering that earlier that week she had viewed its eastern aspect from Whitechapel Road after she and Tom Ainsclough had left the Blind Beggar pub upon talking with great interest to Gordon Cogan's brother, Derek.

She had turned south again and jogged past Flamsteed House where she saw the usual sight of tourists photographing each other, standing astride the Prime Meridian Marker. She mused that being photographed walking across Abbey Road where the Beatles had once walked and being photographed standing astride the Prime Meridian Marker were probably the two essential photographs for any tourist visiting London to take or have taken. Yewdall ran down the straight-as-a-die stretch of road that was Blackheath Avenue, suitably tree-lined as any thoroughfare called 'avenue' ought to be, with a flat green sward extending at either side beyond the trees. At the bottom of the avenue she turned left by the park keeper's house and jogged steadily beside the tall brick wall which formed the park boundary and went the length of Charlton Way. At the first junction she turned left and ran down Maze Hill, keeping up a steady pace but finding the going easier now the incline of the hill was in her favour. She eventually entered an area of prestigious suburban development to her right, while the red brick wall that formed the perimeter of Greenwich Park remained to her left. Beyond the junction with Westcombe Park, Maze Hill steepened sharply and Yewdall began, as most often when she ran this route, to find her pace increasing. The increased pace caused the lace on her left shoe to work loose and so she stopped and knelt down to re-tie it. She reached for the lace ends, lowered her head forward and then stood bolt upright in a spontaneous movement. 'There's more,' she spoke aloud. 'She didn't tell me everything . . . there's much, much more.'

Thursday

EIGHT

Harry Vicary pyramided his hands under his chin with his elbows resting on his desktop. 'Are you sure you're better alone? You're taking quite a chance. The investigation is reaching a critical stage and if Pestilence Smith is silencing people . . . well then, you could be putting yourself at considerable risk.'

'I think I'll be safe, sir.' Penny Yewdall sat back in the chair in front of Vicary's desk. 'I sensed that she and I developed a rapport, and I feel that two officers might be a trifle intimidating for her and counter-productive. If we need to take a statement we can always do that at a later date.'

'Very well.' Vicary nodded and then rested his palms on his desktop. 'But you know the rule, Penny – let me know where you are at all times.'

'Of course, sir,' Yewdall stood, 'of course.'

Just an hour later Penny Yewdall was sitting in Lysandra Smith's council flat. 'You can call it feminine intuition,' she said. 'It came to me yesterday evening; it was early doors . . . I was out jogging, I leaned forward to tie a shoelace and I suddenly realized it, what I felt was as certain as a religious conviction.'

'Yes, I have heard of that.' Lysandra Smith calmly rolled a cigarette. 'I have heard how it can be the case that the act of leaning forward, as when you are bending down to pick something up, or in your case, tying a shoelace, can make you realize something which is totally unconnected with whatever it is that you are doing. I can't say that I have experienced it myself but I have heard more than once that that can indeed be the case.' She lit the cigarette with her yellow disposable lighter and once again cupped her hand round the end of the cigarette, as if protecting it from a breeze. 'So what is it that you have realized? It has to be important otherwise you would not be here.'

'I have realized that you did not tell me everything,' Penny Yewdall replied. 'I have realized that there is a lot more to your story.'

'You think so?' Lysandra Smith smiled briefly. She then inhaled and exhaled slowly through her nostrils. 'That's quite a safe thing to say . . . not committing yourself . . . very cautious of you. It's like you are tiptoeing through a minefield.'

'I cannot lead you . . .' Penny Yewdall cast her eyes round the flat and found it as she remembered from her previous visit. 'I can't put words into your mouth.' She paused and then pointed to the ceiling. 'Is Pancras at home?'

'No.' Lysandra Smith shook her head. 'He went out early, about ten o'clock which is quite early for him, very early; in fact, unusually early. He wouldn't tell me where he was going or what he was going to do though I doubt that he will be helping an old lady across the road and he certainly was not going to go to school.'

'Worrying . . .?' Yewdall commented.

'I've got past the worrying stage,' Lysandra Smith sighed, 'long past it. He'll be out crooking somewhere or planning a job with his cronies. He's anxious to build up his street cred. He's fifteen and all he wants to do is be a career criminal like his father and his grandfather.' Lysandra Smith took another deep drag on the cigarette.

'It must upset you?' Yewdall observed.

'Worry . . . upset . . . it does both . . . but by the Ancient of Days what can I do?' Lysandra Smith looked at the carpet at her feet. 'You have seen for yourself how big he is. I can hardly pinch him by the earlobe and lead him to school when he can walk into a pub and get served beer. He can walk twenty miles without getting tired . . . I can't reason with him . . . no chance of me ever doing that.' She scratched her head. 'I mean, you know, to be fair on him, I can see his point in a way . . . look at this, a cramped little council high-rise flat and then he compares this to my father's mansion up in Southgate and he thinks "who says crime doesn't pay"? But no . . . he's not in the house, there's just you and me . . . just the two of us.'

Penny Yewdall smiled. 'So we can talk, you and me, woman to woman?'

'Yes,' Lysandra Smith nodded but persistently avoided eye contact, 'we can talk woman to woman.'

'Good . . . because you see, Lysandra,' Yewdall explained, 'that what I realized the instant that I leaned forward to tie my shoelace yesterday evening is that a fifteen-year-old girl does not run away with her French teacher . . . or with any teacher really. I mean, she might carry on a secret liaison with one of her teachers and that happens all too often and is usually kept discreet but it takes more than that, much more, to make her run away with one of her school teachers if it is kept secret. So, one woman to another, am I correct? You were not going somewhere with Gordon Cogan. It is more the case that you were going away from . . . running away from . . . something. Was it the case that he was in fact rescuing you . . .?'

Silence. A car's horn was heard from the street below. An aircraft flew low overhead on its final approach to Heathrow Airport. Lysandra Smith breathed deeply and continued to avoid eye contact with Penny Yewdall. Yewdall thought she looked uncomfortable and knew then that she had touched a raw nerve.

'Yes . . .?' Penny Yewdall pressed. 'Look, Lysandra, I have been a police officer long enough to say that I am very angry with myself, furious in fact, for not seeing it in you sooner . . . the unfulfilled potential . . . the lack of self-worth, the petty crime . . . the inappropriate partner . . . the plunge from grace. So am I right that you were running away from something horrible at home in your father's house in Southgate?'

'Yes . . . yes . . . yes . . .' Lysandra Smith hissed her reply but still avoided eye contact. 'Yes, you are right, Penny. How right you are . . . all right, you are correct, Gordon was taking me from something but he didn't know it, I never told him. He was in love with me . . . but I allowed him to take me away. I was willing to go with him in order to escape.'

'That's interesting,' Penny Yewdall replied softly, 'that is a point that I was unsure of. I didn't know whether or not he was motivated by the need to rescue you or whether he was motivated by passion alone.'

'Passion alone,' Lysandra Smith confirmed. 'As I said, I told him nothing. It was passion for me as well but with escape thrown into the pot.'

'From?' Yewdall asked quietly.

'Sexual abuse . . . what else? You hear about it all the time these days but back then it was unheard of – it was especially unheard of in posh areas like Southgate and it didn't happen to posh girls who go to expensive schools, and good girls don't rat on their fathers, do they?'

'Are you prepared to make a statement?' Yewdall asked. 'We can still prefer charges despite the time lapse.'

'No!' Lysandra Smith shook her head vigorously. 'Believe me . . . look around me . . . what I have isn't much, but I'm not ready for clay, not just yet. I want to live a bit longer yet, if that's all right with you.'

'You're saying that your father, Tony Smith, will murder you if you talk?' Penny Yewdall gasped. 'Surely not . . . you're his daughter.'

'I know he will . . . believe me. If he thinks that anyone is going to give evidence that will put him behind bars he'll murder them, I know him . . . and that includes me . . . if . . . if . . . he's feeling lenient, and it's a huge if . . . if he's feeling lenient he'll give me a slap, as a warning . . . as a shot across my bows.'

'You mean the sort of slap that will have you in hospital for a few weeks with your arms and legs in plaster?' Yewdall replied. 'That sort of slap?'

'Yes . . . that sort of slap and not just my arms and legs in plaster but my ribcage as well, that's the sort of monster he is. He's just not a human being. But most likely he'll have me iced.' Lysandra Smith dogged her cigarette in the Bass Charrington ashtray. 'I can tell you what happened but I won't be making or signing any statement. Not ever.'

'Understood.' Penny Yewdall nodded in agreement. 'So what happened?'

'Where to start . . .' Lysandra Smith reached for her pouch of tobacco and began to roll another cigarette. 'It started when I was about eight years old . . .'

'Oh . . .' Penny Yewdall groaned, 'that's young.'

'Young enough but at first it was just photographs, like I was his wood nymph . . . little naked elf-like me in the woods during summertime, usually the summer, but he was also fond of a winter backdrop. That didn't do me any harm . . . not physical harm, anyway. I would jump out of my clothes and then jump back into them again thirty seconds later.'

'Did your mother know about it?' Yewdall asked.

'Oh, yes, but she was terrified of him; she couldn't stand up to him and protect me.' Lysandra Smith lit her roll-up cigarette. 'I don't blame her. I don't blame her at all.'

'I see,' Yewdall replied.

'And she's dead now . . . she's been gone a good few years . . . cancer took her, but she didn't fight it; in fact, she ignored the symptoms until it was too late. I think that she had just lost the will to live. That's what I feel, looking back.' Lysandra Smith shrugged her shoulders.

'I have come across that attitude . . . I mean, losing the will to live,' Penny Yewdall replied.

'In your own family?' Lysandra Smith made sudden eye contact with Yewdall.

'No . . . my parents are both alive, retired to the coast but both still with us . . . thankfully . . . both still going strong.'

'What is your accent, Penny?' Lysandra Smith asked. 'I can't place it.'

'Staffordshire . . . I grew up in the potteries.' Yewdall smiled. 'My accent and the Birmingham accent were once voted the least pleasant accents in the UK.'

'The potteries?' Smith smiled. 'The five towns?'

'There are six actually but yes, that is the potteries . . . the belief that there are five towns comes from the novel *Anna of the Five Towns* by Arnold Bennett.'

'I'll remember that. But me,' Lysandra Smith forced a smile, 'I've never been north of London . . . mind you, I got to Ireland once.'

Yewdall smiled broadly. She enjoyed Lysandra Smith's dry humour. 'Yes,' she said, 'so I believe . . . all the way to Galway, in fact.'

'Yeah . . . next step America . . . if you can discount the Aran Islands.' She took a deep breath. 'So anyway, it escalated . . . what my father did to me, I mean . . . that escalated, as it would do, from photographing me naked indoors and out of doors, to touching, to highly inappropriate touching. He touched me and he made me touch him. He taught me how to touch him. It got to be a way of life and I grew up thinking it was normal and that it was happening to all the other girls at our school. When I saw girls get into their father's car at the end of the school day and be driven away I thought where are you going to stop for half an hour on your way home? Where's your daddy's favourite parking place?'

'Your father had one?' Yewdall asked.

'A supermarket car park,' Smith replied.

'A public car park?' Yewdall commented.

'It was a huge car park and he parked at the far side, well away from the supermarket and under some trees. No one else parked there unless it was mega busy and at four p.m. on a weekday the car park was always practically empty,' Lysandra Smith explained. 'To an onlooker he looked like a geezer sitting alone in the car in the driver's seat . . . like he was waiting for his wife to push the shopping trolley to the car.'

'But in fact?' Yewdall asked.

'But in fact,' Lysandra Smith drew heavily on the cigarette, 'I was kneeling between his legs in the footwell pleasuring him with my hand or my mouth depending on how the fancy took him.'

'And your mother knew all this?'

'Oh, I reckon so, she wasn't naïve . . . she certainly knew the gist if not the details and the extent. She held my hand when my father took my virginity.'

'Oh . . .' Yewdall groaned, 'I am so sorry.'

Lysandra Smith shrugged her shoulders. 'That was my mother, it is just the way she was. She was also Irish, you see, like my father. They're both from Connemara. In rural Ireland it used to be the way of it that the youngest girl would take her mother's place in the marriage bed. It kept the man at home and that kept the money coming in. It happens less now . . . much less because children are learning to speak out and television dramas and films are exposing the practice. People are learning that it's wrong . . . but . . . well . . . when money's tight and I go on the street I get to talking to the Irish girls and they tell me it still happens . . . and not just in Ireland, but in rural communities all over the UK. But because of her background my mother never questioned it when it happened in suburban Southgate and I never knew any difference. I sensed rather than knew it wasn't right but there seemed no escape.'

'Again,' Yewdall said softly, 'I am so very sorry.'

'So that was what I was running from, and when you leaned forward to tie your shoelace your sudden rush of woman's intuition was spot on.' Lysandra Smith once again looked down at the carpet as she spoke. 'So that was what I was experiencing, a neat, well-scrubbed schoolgirl, smart in her school uniform, doing my homework and then servicing my father when he came into my room at night. If I didn't do it on the way home then I'd do it at home. So when Gordon offered me emotionally driven sex . . . as an expression of mutual love . . . and he offered companionship and a way out of London, well, then of course I accepted. That's why I ran away with him, and you see, Penny, that explains my father's anger towards Gordon. It wasn't the anger of a father towards the man that abducted and raped his daughter; it was the anger of one man towards another man who had stolen his sexual plaything. Nobody steals from Tony "the Pestilence" Smith. So when I returned home, after my parents had convinced the authorities that I'd be safe, my father said . . . "we'd better give you something to make sure you don't run away again", and that was Pancras.'

'Oh . . .' Yewdall groaned, 'this just keeps getting worse . . . you mean that Pancras . . .'

'Yes. Pancras is my son,' Lysandra Smith spoke firmly and clearly, 'and he's also my brother. My father is Pancras's grandfather, and he's also Pancras's father.'

'Does Pancras know?' Yewdall asked.

'No.' Smith shook her head. 'No . . . and he must never, ever find out.'

'The birth certificate,' Yewdall queried, 'what does it say on the birth certificate?'

'Father unknown.' Lysandra Smith inhaled and then exhaled as she spoke. 'He'll find out that Elliot Reiss is not his real father soon enough but he must never know who is actually his blood father . . . never. It will destroy him. He'll ask me and I don't know what I am going to tell him.'

'I see,' Yewdall replied calmly. 'Well, we won't tell him.'

'Thanks.' Smith forced a smile.

'But it might come out,' Yewdall advised, 'you have to be prepared for that.'

'I know,' Smith replied. 'I'm so dreading that it might happen. The resemblance between them is very strong, they do look like father and son . . . but my father always says it's the family genes, it's because he's Pancras's grandfather and so far Pancras has believed that to be the case,' Smith glanced up at the ceiling, 'but . . . what's that saying? "The truth will out". I am so dreading the truth coming out, so, so dreading it.'

'Do you know what happened between Gordon Cogan and the girl he was convicted of murdering?' Yewdall asked.

'No . . . sorry . . .' Lysandra Smith once again looked at the carpet, 'I don't. Like I said, Gordon decided that we had no future as a couple once he'd lost everything and I never saw him again after that . . . but Gordon strangle someone . . .? No . . . never, not Gordon, not ever, ever, ever . . . not in a million years, even when he was in the drink. When he was half cut he just got more affable, not violent. I don't have any proof but I just know whoever it was that strangled that poor girl wasn't Gordon Cogan. What was her name?'

'Janet Frost,' Penny Yewdall said. 'Her name was Janet Frost.'

'Yes,' Lysandra Smith smiled, 'yes, that's it. But I tell you; whoever it was that strangled her, it wasn't Gordon Cogan.'

'What was your father's reaction to Gordon Cogan's conviction for Janet Frost's murder?' Yewdall asked. 'Do you recall?'

'I recall it very well. Like it was yesterday.' Lysandra Smith flicked the ash from her roll-up cigarette into the ashtray. 'He was well pleased. He was very well pleased; he said, "At least he's going down for a decent old time now, the little toe-rag . . . no Father Christmas for a judge this time, not for him".'

'Do you know if your father had any involvement with the murder of Janet Frost?' Yewdall asked. 'I am just fishing, you understand.'

Lysandra Smith glanced at Penny Yewdall and as she did so her face paled. 'I never knew of any involvement but I was kept well out of the loop,' she replied softly. 'Why? Do you think . . . he might have had some part in it? Frankly I wouldn't put it past him.'

'As I say,' Yewdall said, 'just curious.'

'I see. Well, as I said, he seemed pleased when Gordon was sent down but he is capable of fitting someone up, well capable . . . But after the trial he just seemed to go about running his empire and he never mentioned Gordon again,' Lysandra Smith explained. 'He lost all interest in me as soon as I fell pregnant with Pancras but he kept me in the house until it was too late for me to have a termination . . . he did that.'

'What about your sisters?' Yewdall asked. 'What was your father's attitude to them?'

'What sisters?' Lysandra Smith shot an alarmed glance at Yewdall. 'I don't have any sisters . . . none that I know of, anyway.'

'Oh . . .' Yewdall expressed surprise. 'At Gordon's trial . . . Gordon's brother, Derek, told us that your family, your father, mother and your brothers and sisters and cousins all sat in the public gallery. Derek Cogan described them as a really heavy crew . . . your sisters were hard-faced, cold-eyed women, he said, and your brothers . . .'

'Hey!' Lysandra Smith held up her hand. 'I have no brothers or sisters.'

'You don't?' Penny Yewdall couldn't contain her surprise. 'But . . .'

'No . . .' Lysandra Smith smiled, 'there was only me and my father and mother. Those people in the public gallery at Gordon's trial were street girls hired by my father to look the part, and all the men were thugs in my dad's firm . . . he probably wanted to intimidate the judge into passing a heavy sentence. He didn't get what he wanted there . . .'

'I see,' Penny Yewdall said. 'I see.'

'Well, I'm glad you see,' Lysandra Smith replied with an angry tone of voice, 'because quite frankly I don't see. I don't see Gordon murdering that girl, Janet Frost. I don't see Gordon getting any justice at all, but what I do see is my father getting away with everything . . . like he always does.'

'Well . . . if you feel like that you could always change your mind about keeping Pancras in the dark,' Yewdall suggested. 'We could bring a solid case against your father for raping you. We can prove your age and Pancras's age and show that you were still just fifteen when your father impregnated you . . . his DNA will confirm him as being the biological father of Pancras . . . that could, in fact it would, put your father away for a very long time.'

'No . . .' Lysandra Smith shook her head, 'I can't ever let Pancras know who his father is . . . and also my father has a tendency to murder anyone who is planning to give evidence against him . . . so I believe . . . he'll stop at nothing to ensure he keeps his liberty . . . and I mean nothing, even if it means his only daughter goes missing, permanently so . . . if he thinks I am about to give evidence, I will vanish . . . maybe even Pancras too.'

'Bad situation.' Yewdall sighed.

'Couldn't be much worse; it's a real mess,' Lysandra Smith forced a smile, 'but I can at least thank my father for a classy name and a fine, handsome son.'

Again, Yewdall enjoyed Lysandra Smith's dry humour. 'Will you tell Pancras what your father did to you?'

'Yes, I'll do that,' Lysandra Smith sighed and then nodded. 'In fact, I'll do that later on today when he returns home from wherever he is. Pancras is always asking me the reason why I don't visit my father, why I refuse to go near that house in Southgate. He's wise beyond his fifteen years and he's old enough to understand, so yes, I'll tell him, but I'll stop short of telling him who his father is. I can't ever tell him that.'

*   *   *

The two uniformed police officers approached the door in the high-rise tower block with extreme caution. They instantly saw that it had been kicked off its hinges.

'Heavy crew,' the first officer commented.

'Seems so,' the second officer replied. 'They certainly know how to kick a door in.'

'Police!' The first officer called out as he entered the flat, followed by the second officer. 'Police! Is anyone here . . .?'

The two officers noted signs of violence; upturned and smashed furniture, broken mirrors and panes of glass.

'Police!' The first officer called out again. 'Police!'

The officers found the young woman in the bedroom. She was on the floor beside the bed, dressed in a man's shirt, frozen with fear.

'All right, love.' The first officer switched on his radio. He spoke into it. 'Hello . . . control . . . we're here now . . . one female victim. Can you send an ambulance, please? No other victim found yet, but we'll make a thorough search. There are signs of extreme violence . . . it's a crime scene all right. Yes, sir . . . no obvious injuries but in a state of shock. Very good, sir.' The officer replaced the handset. He turned to his colleague and said, 'The ambulance is on its way. We are to search the flat for any other victims and await CID and the SOCO team.'

'You'll be all right now, pet.' The second officer addressed the woman though he doubted she heard him. 'We'll soon have you in hospital, get you looked at.'

Four hours later the woman who had been found in a shocked and dazed state on the floor of her bedroom was sitting, fully clothed, sipping sweetened hot tea in an interview suite in New Scotland Yard. She had been prescribed a mild sedative but she proved able and willing to talk to Harry Vicary and Penny Yewdall.

'So why the VIP treatment?' the woman asked.

'You are Bernadette Bailey?' Vicary asked.

'Yes, that's me.' Bernadette Bailey was a tall woman with a thin figure and long black hair.

'You were flagged up as being of interest to us,' Vicary replied.

'Well, your old wires are crossed, my old china, 'cos this filly has not done nothing the police would be interested in, especially not New Scotland Yard.'

'No crossing of wires,' Harry Vicary replied calmly, 'our computer made an interesting sound when your local nick placed a notification on the system that they had responded to a three-nines call from a member of the public reporting your front door had been kicked in . . . and you are of interest because you are on record as being the partner of Davy "the Cobbler" Bootmaker. We're looking for him, you see . . . he's not in his drum and we want a chat with him.'

'No, he moved into mine a few weeks ago. So what do you want him for?'

Penny Yewdall noted a lack of concern on Bernadette Bailey's face about Davy Bootmaker.

'Well,' Vicary replied, 'let's just say he left his fingerprints in a cottage in Hampshire.'

'So that's what happened.' Bernadette Bailey continued to show no concern for Bootmaker. 'I did wonder what they meant. He messed up somehow but I don't know how. I don't know the details. He works for Pestilence Smith . . . and this morning my door got kicked in by a team of Pestilence Smith's soldiers. They said to him, "Pestilence wants you . . . and he's not a happy man. He wants you because you messed up, Davy". He put up a real fight but they carried him away anyway. I kept out of it. As they were leaving one of the soldiers turned to me and said "You're a sensible girl, you know the rule". Then he put his finger to his lips and drew it across his throat. So I nodded. So I saw nothing, I will say nothing.'

'But you're here,' Vicary smiled, 'and you've just told us what happened. You are saying something.'

'Yes, but I won't be signing no statements. I won't be standing up in no court. I won't be giving no evidence.' Bernadette spoke firmly. 'I won't be skipping that old rope. But Pestilence has him.'

'You're not frightened for his safety?' Yewdall asked. 'You don't seem to be very concerned about him?'

'That's because I am not concerned.' Bernadette Bailey sipped the tea. 'Davy Bootmaker is a low-life villain. I'm still in my twenties and I want out of his world and this is the "out" I've been waiting for.'

'You reckon?' Vicary asked.

'Definitely.' Bernadette Bailey held eye contact with Vicary. 'Definitely. Definitely. Definitely. Even if Pestilence lets him live he won't ever walk properly again . . . it all depends on how badly he messed up. So one way or the other I'm out of it. No more Davy Bootmaker for this filly. Not ever . . . I'm a free filly now.'

'Do you know where Pestilence's soldiers took Davy?' Vicary asked.

'No. It won't be to his house, though,' Bailey replied, offhandedly, 'I can tell you that for nothing.'

'We assumed that,' Harry Vicary replied dryly.

'Pestilence,' Bernadette Bailey put the plastic cup down on the low table which stood in front of the chair in which she sat, 'has got buildings all over the place which he uses to store stuff . . . but you know, there is one Davy told me about.' Bailey raised a long, bony finger. 'It's one he keeps clear of stuff so he can use it to give someone a slap. It's in the East End.'

'That's helpful,' Vicary sighed, 'the East End is a big place. Do you know where?'

'Well, it's all I know, innit?' Bailey protested. 'I'm trying to help all I can. Can I have a fag? I need a smoke. Have you got a fag?'

'No,' Vicary replied firmly, 'and you can't smoke in public buildings anymore. It's been like that for a few years.' Vicary paused and then he asked, 'Do you know any of the men who work for Pestilence Smith?'

'Some . . . mostly by sight,' Bailey replied sullenly.

'We're also looking for a man called Larry Ryecroft,' Vicary said.

'Now him I do know.' Again Bernadette Bailey raised a long, bony finger. 'Him and Davy get teamed up from time to time. In fact, Davy and Larry did the job together, last weekend . . . the one that Davy messed up.'

'So has Larry Ryecroft been taken to the lock-up as well,' Vicary asked, 'because he's not at home either?'

'No,' Bailey shook her head, 'don't think so.'

'Why not?' Vicary asked.

''Cos he toed it, didn't he,' Bailey replied. 'Scarpered . . . done a runner . . . hopped it . . . cleared the pitch . . .'

'And how do you know that?' Vicary pressed.

''Cos one of the heavy geezers, one of Pestilence's soldiers asked Davy where Larry Ryecroft was because they'd called on him and he'd fled.' Bernadette Bailey picked up the cup of tea from the table top. 'So they gave Davy a good kicking to make him tell them where Larry Ryecroft was . . . but eventually they gave up when it was clear he didn't know and then they took him away all bloody and pleading for his life. I reckon someone must have tipped Ryecroft off, but Davy, his mobile was switched off, wasn't it, so no one could tip him off.'

'That has probably cost him his life,' Yewdall observed.

'Probably . . . but do I care? Like I said, I'm out of it now.' Bernadette Bailey shrugged her shoulders. 'I'm not going to be no bottom of the ladder villain's chick no more, I've seen how they end up . . . no money . . . making a pair of tights last two weeks . . . visiting their men in prison. Na, me, I'm leaving the lifestyle, and I'm leaving the manor. I'm going where I'm not known and I'll start looking for an honest geezer who can hold down a job and bring in steady money. I'm making a fresh start.'

'Well, good for you,' Vicary replied, 'but right now we need your help, and Larry Ryecroft needs your help. You'll be saving his life. That's something you could do before starting your new life.'

'Oh . . . oh . . . no . . .' Bernadette Bailey put her hand on her head. 'Oh no . . .'

'You've realized something.' Harry Vicary asked, 'What is it?'

'They'll be looking for Rita as well,' Bernadette Bailey panted.

'Rita?' Vicary asked.

'Rita Hibbert . . . I like her.'

'Who is she?' Yewdall asked.

'Larry Ryecroft's chick,' Bailey advised. 'You see if Davy

and Larry messed up, Rita will have messed up as well because she went on that job with them . . . whatever it was . . . Larry, Rita and Davy, the three of them. Oh, no . . . oh, no . . . Pestilence will destroy her face and she's a looker . . . he'll burn it with acid. That's what he does to chicks who cross him or who mess up. The boys, he'll likely kill them but he'll burn a chick's face off . . . like he'll let her live but wishing she was dead. One girl once skimmed fifty sovs . . . that's all she did, helped herself to fifty quid . . . but Pestilence found out and had her face burned off in front of the other runners.'

'Runners?' Yewdall asked.

'Women who work for Pestilence carrying money and stuff across London. They attract less suspicion than men so they say, or sometimes delivering it to places outside London. I used to be one of them. He gathered all the runners together in a field one night up in Hertfordshire and made them watch as his soldiers poured acid on her face. God . . . the screams . . . then they left her there, crawling about the grass while we got back into the cars and drove back to London. Pestilence doesn't like things being taken from him. Any other villain would have told the other girls to give that girl a slap or he would have told the girl to give him twice the money back, but not Pestilence . . . a runner took something from him so he destroyed her face. She was a looker too.'

'So where has she gone?' Harry Vicary asked calmly. 'I mean, Rita Hibbert. When we called at Ryecroft's drum this morning there was no one at home.'

'If we find her she lives,' Penny Yewdall added, 'even if you don't care about Davy Bootmaker or Larry Ryecroft, you obviously care about pretty Rita Hibbert.'

'This didn't come from me . . . I'll never be able to hide from Pestilence.' Bailey's voice shook with fear.

'Agreed.' Vicary nodded. 'It didn't come from you.'

'Just tell us,' Penny Yewdall pleaded. 'We're under real time pressure if we're going to save her and Larry Ryecroft. Just tell us!'

'Rita has a sister,' Bailey replied quickly. 'I don't think Pestilence Smith knows about her. In fact, I'm sure he doesn't know about her. She's got a council flat in Hampstead, just down the hill from the Royal Free Hospital. I have the address in my address book,' she turned and opened her handbag, 'but I didn't tell you . . .'

Harry Vicary thought the flat was a little cramped but also quite cosy, and he assumed that the flats must be sought after because they offered affordable accommodation in a fashionable part of London. The building which contained the flat, and the other flats like it, was a medium-rise inter-war development in red brick, with one of the suburban railway lines carrying traffic in and out of central London running behind it. To the front of the block of flats were delicatessens, fashionable pubs and a bus terminus. Inside the flat Larry Ryecroft and Rita Hibbert, both in their twenties, sat side by side on the two-person sofa clutching each other and shaking with evident fear. The tenant of the flat, Joyce Hibbert, sat in a posture of despair and indignation and annoyance at the table in the window, refusing to look at her sister. Brunnie and Vicary stood in the centre of the room.

'I tried to warn Davy,' Ryecroft stammered, 'but the idiot had left his mobile switched off and Bernadette Bailey hasn't got a landline. She didn't pay her telephone bill so they cut her off.'

'So who warned you?' Vicary asked.

'Anonymous text,' Ryecroft's voice shook with fear, 'but I think I know who it might have been. One of Pestilence's crew owes me a favour, reckon he was paying it back. All it said was "get out . . . both of you . . . you've less than ten minutes" but that was all the warning we needed. We both know what Pestilence Smith can do and we didn't need to be told twice. I grabbed her and we toed it . . . out the back, over the fence, down the alley, along the street to the Tube station. Once we're in the Underground system we reckoned that we were safe for the time being . . .'

'When I first started working for Pestilence Smith,' Rita Hibbert spoke with a shaking voice, 'I was told to keep a bolthole in case he turns on you but I wasn't to tell anyone about it. It had to be a well-kept secret.'

'Well, you told someone!' Joyce Hibbert turned to her sister and shouted angrily. 'Thanks. So now I'm going to have half the gangsters in London at my door now, looking for you and him.'

'We won't be staying,' Rita Hibbert attempted to placate her sister. 'We'll be away soon.'

'Damn right you won't be staying, but if they can find you here,' Joyce Hibbert pointed to Brunnie and Vicary, 'if they can find you here, so can this Pestilence geezer. It stands to reason.'

'So how did you find us?' Ryecroft asked meekly.

'I can't tell you, but this lady's right,' Vicary replied. 'If we can find you then so can Pestilence Smith and his soldiers. If you want us to help you, you have to help us.' He paused. 'So, Davy "the Cobbler" Bootmaker – where have they taken him?'

'The lock-up,' Ryecroft replied in a defeated tone of voice, 'it's the only place they would take him.'

'Address?' Vicary snapped. 'Where is it . . . this lock-up?'

'Copenhagen Street,' Ryecroft replied.

'By King's Cross Station?' Vicary asked. 'That Copenhagen Street?'

Ryecroft shook his head. 'No . . . another street called Copenhagen Street. It's in the East End, off the Mile End Road . . . but he'll be brown bread by now.'

'Not unless he's got information which Pestilence wants . . . like your whereabouts . . . and if we get a wriggle on we can save his hide.'

'OK . . . lock-up . . . white painted door,' Ryecroft advised, 'black letters on it saying "Beresford Removals and House Clearances".'

'That's just a front?' Vicary clarified. 'I assume it is?'

'Yes, the name was already on the door when Pestilence took over the lease. He kept the sign up.' Ryecroft nodded slightly. 'But, like you say, governor, it's just a front. It's just to make it look kosher.' Ryecroft glanced out of the window at the blue, near cloudless sky over Hampstead, 'I mean, he can hardly put "Pestilence Smith's Torture and Execution

Chamber" on the door, can he? But that's what it is and that's where Davy Bootmaker will be.'

Frankie Brunnie took his mobile from his jacket pocket, turned and left the sitting room and stood in the short narrow hallway to make a phone call. He returned a few moments later and said, 'They're on their way, boss.'

'Thanks,' Vicary replied, 'hope we are in time.' He then turned to the trembling Larry Ryecroft and said, 'So what happened?'

'It was Pestilence Smith, wasn't it; he'd got wind of it that a teacher geezer had got out after fifteen years of bird and was asking for a black street worker called Quoshie. Pestilence had it in for the teacher geezer . . . and so he had a young chick who lived in a rented house over in Acton strangled, the same house that the teacher geezer was living in at the same time.'

'Who told you that Pestilence Smith had strangled the girl?' Vicary asked. 'Or did you witness it?'

'Dunno . . . and no, I didn't see it. I wasn't one of his soldiers then . . . all Pestilence's crew knew it was him – two of them were there, they saw it go down . . . but Quoshie was strung out, they said, desperate for a fix and Pestilence was her supplier. He made her put on a pair of gloves, rubber washing-up gloves, and take the sweat from the teacher's body . . . he was half undressed 'cos it was a hot day . . . and then wipe her hands all over the dead girl and especially round her neck, and then all over the room. They said that Pestilence had found out that someone's sweat will have their DNA in it and back then DNA was all that was needed for a conviction, so the teacher geezer was well fitted up.'

'All right,' Vicary growled. 'Then what . . .?'

'So Pestilence heard that the teacher geezer was looking for Quoshie to get her to turn Queen's evidence against Pestilence. Like she was going to do that, some hope, you would think . . . I mean . . . this teacher was just not on this planet but Pestilence heard about it, and he also heard that Quoshie was actually thinking of doing what the teacher wanted her to do. She was feeling all guilty, you see, so

Pestilence wasn't taking no chances. He had them both snatched and taken to the lock-up on Copenhagen Street, then sent for me and her and Davy Bootmaker.' Ryecroft once again looked longingly at the blue sky as if he was wishing himself to be somewhere else, somewhere a long way away.

'Just carry on,' Vicary prompted.

'Well, me and her and Davy Bootmaker got to the lock-up and those two, Quoshie and the teacher geezer, were well trussed up in the back of a van and we were given directions to a cottage in Hampshire. Pestilence rents it now and again . . . assumed name and hard cash. It's fairly remote. Sometimes Pestilence likes jobs done well out of London.'

'We know,' Vicary remarked. 'We have been there.'

'How did you find it?' Ryecroft asked. 'We cleaned up. Well . . .' he turned to Rita Hibbert, 'she cleaned up.'

'Not as well as she might have done,' Vicary remarked, 'and you didn't keep Cherry Quoshie and Gordon Cogan very well supervised. You must have left them alone for a bit . . . even a short time. I dare say that it will all come out in the trial but let's just say for now that Cherry Quoshie left us a present where she knew we'd find it and where you wouldn't think to look, and that led us to the cottage where we found Cherry Quoshie's fingerprints and Gordon Cogan's fingerprints on the underside of a table . . . and also on the inside of a drawer.'

'I cleaned all the surfaces,' Rita Hibbert protested, 'like you told me to do. I never thought about the underside of the table or the inside of a drawer.'

'You read the *Daily Mail* when you were at the cottage?' Vicary confirmed.

'Yes.' Ryecroft nodded. 'Davy Bootmaker likes it for the sports reports. So do I.'

'We know.' Vicary smiled. 'We found both your fingerprints on the sports section.'

'I told you to get rid of that paper!' Ryecroft turned angrily to Rita Hibbert. 'I told you to burn it.'

'I did,' Rita Hibbert protested, 'I took it outside and burned it on the fire on the back lawn.'

'Not all of it, you didn't.' Vicary spoke calmly. 'Cherry

Quoshie must have seen you reading the sports pages and when you had finished and she was alone she must have taken out a page from the sports section and put it in a drawer underneath an older sheet of newsprint used to line the drawer hoping, even knowing we'd find it and hoping, even knowing that you would not check the newspaper to see whether or not all the pages were there. But we found it and we found Bootmaker's dabs and your dabs on it.' Vicary addressed Ryecroft. 'And we found Cherry Quoshie's prints and Gordon Cogan's prints on the same page . . . and the date of the paper puts all four of you there at the same time.'

'Can you put me at the cottage?' Rita Hibbert asked.

'Not forensically but the keyholder, the lady in the village, she will be able to identify you as being the person to whom she gave the key for the weekend in question,' Vicary advised. 'She remembers you well, Rita. All dolled up like you were going out to a night club, instead of hiking boots and a green jacket which is what all other people who rent the cottage wear for a few days of birdwatching. She remembers you well. She gave a good description of you, in fact.'

Rita Hibbert looked crestfallen. Her sister glared at her and mouthed, 'Half-wit'.

'It's enough to put all three of you away for murder, if Bootmaker is still alive, that is, and that remains to be seen. Murder times two, in fact.' Vicary emphasized the point. 'So it's really time to start working for yourself, both of you.' Vicary paused. 'The burn on Cherry Quoshie's leg; who did that?'

'Davy Bootmaker.' Ryecroft hung his head.

'With you holding her down?' Vicary suggested. 'She would not have just lain there.'

'Yes . . . outside . . . with a gag in her mouth.'

'Then you both did it,' Vicary advised, 'in the eyes of the law you both caused the injury. What caused it?'

'A long metal bar with a sort of circular metal bit welded to the end. Pestilence had it made up. He called it his 'persuader'. He told us to use it to get information from Quoshie about who she had said what to. She claimed she hadn't told no one nothing, even when we threatened to burn her again . . . so we believed her.'

'Brave girl,' Brunnie commented. 'Brave, brave girl.'

'Yes,' Vicary nodded in agreement, 'it makes Anna Day an exceedingly lucky woman, a very exceedingly lucky woman indeed.'

'Who's Anna Day?' Ryecroft asked. 'Who's she?'

'A friend of Cherry Quoshie's. Cherry Quoshie told her the gist of what had gone down fifteen years ago in the house in Acton and when Anna Day finds out that Cherry Quoshie didn't give in to torture so as to keep her name from reaching the eager ears of Pestilence Smith then she might be very willing to make a statement, out of a sense of gratitude if nothing else,' Vicary explained. 'I know I certainly would.'

'And me,' Brunnie added. 'And me.'

'So the case against you is building quite nicely,' Vicary smiled. 'From our point of view, that is, not very nicely from your point of view.'

'I have to ask you,' Brunnie said, 'where did you get the coal from . . . to build the fire?'

'Pestilence got hold of it from somewhere, don't know where,' Ryecroft replied. 'When me and her and Davy Bootmaker got to the lock-up on Copenhagen Street, the coal was already in the back of the van, plus the kindling, plus the branding iron thing, plus a golf club, plus Quoshie and the teacher geezer.'

'So at the end of it all the golf club was the murder weapon?' Vicary confirmed.

'Yes,' Ryecroft confessed, 'but Davy Bootmaker did them both . . . I swear.'

'Doesn't matter,' Vicary said, 'you're all as guilty as each other . . . all three of you.'

'Including me?' Rita Hibbert protested.

'Including you, pet,' Vicary smiled. 'You're fully part of it.'

'What will we get?' She hung her head.

'Life,' Vicary replied, 'but . . . full confession, give evidence against Pestilence Smith, who is the person we really want, not his foot soldiers. With good behaviour you could be out inside ten years, still young enough to build a life.' He paused.

'OK . . . on your feet. Lawrence Ryecroft, I am arresting you for the murder of Cherry Quoshie. It may harm your defence if you do not mention, when questioned, anything you later rely on in court.' He paused. 'All right, that will do for now.' He put a pair of handcuffs on Ryecroft. 'Tell me something, Larry,' he said, 'why did you dump the two bodies in Wimbledon?'

'No CCTV,' Ryecroft replied. 'Simple as that.'

'Yes, we thought that was the reason,' Vicary replied. 'Then you joined the commuters later in the morning?'

'Yes, we spent the night in someone's overgrown front garden in the next street then left when folk started walking past on their way to work,' Ryecroft explained. 'We joined them ten minutes apart. Davy left first.'

'But why dump them both in the same place?' Vicary asked. 'Why did you do that?'

'Got away with it once . . . why not again?' Ryecroft said. 'It seemed like a good idea. Davy suggested it. So I said "why not"?'

'But that made us realize there was a link between Gordon Cogan and Cherry Quoshie, so we looked for it . . . and here we are,' Vicary spoke calmly. 'If you had dumped the bodies twenty miles apart we would not have linked them and there would not have been this investigation, and you would most likely have got clean away with it.'

'You idiot!' Rita Hibbert leapt up at Ryecroft and clawed his face. 'You idiot! You idiot!' She screamed until she was restrained by her sister and Frankie Brunnie who put his handcuffs on her and arrested her, also for the murder of Cherry Quoshie, saying, 'There will be more charges, but as Mr Vicary has just said, that will do for now.'

Tom Ainsclough met Harry Vicary as Vicary brought his car to a halt outside Beresford Removals and House Clearances on Copenhagen Street, Whitechapel. 'Whatever happened in there,' Ainsclough said, 'well . . . it wasn't pleasant, sir, not pleasant at all.'

Harry Vicary nodded, got out of his car and walked into the gloom of the lock-up. Tom Ainsclough followed Vicary as he walked through a small open door which was set in a larger door. Within, the lock-up was dimly but sufficiently illuminated by two low-powered bulbs. 'It seems so,' Vicary mumbled. 'Seems so.'

'A SOCO team is on its way, sir,' Ainsclough advised, 'but the dark staining on the concrete . . . that will be blood . . . two teeth beside the blood . . .'

'Yes, I see them,' Vicary replied, 'clearly human, even to my untrained eye. They'll have once belonged to Davy Bootmaker . . . and the blood will be his . . . and the rest of him . . . who knows?'

'Shallow grave in Epping Forest?' Ainsclough suggested. 'Or waiting to be put in the river after dusk has fallen?'

'Probably either, the river or the forest, they are where the bodies of all felons who vanish tend to be found. If they are found at all.' Vicary glanced round the lock-up. 'No windows,' he observed, 'no one to look in when whatever happens in here is happening. He'd be alive if he had kept his mobile phone on. Part of me feels sorry for him despite what he did to Cherry Quoshie and Gordon Cogan.'

'Do you think it's time we paid a second call on Tony "Pestilence" Smith,' Ainsclough asked, 'with a warrant this time?'

Vicary smiled. 'Yes, yes I do. Larry Ryecroft and Rita Hibbert are talking to us; they've already got both eyes on reduced charges and early parole. That's sufficient for a warrant for his arrest and if this lock-up is leased in his name . . . then . . . well, then that's more than sufficient.'

The front door of Tony 'Pestilence' Smith's house in Southgate was found to be open when Harry Vicary, Tom Ainsclough and six constables arrived to execute the arrest warrant. Vicary stood on the threshold and called out 'Police!' There was no response from within the house. He called again. He heard his voice echo strongly within the building but there was no answering call. Vicary entered the house, followed by Ainsclough and the constables, then 'proceeded with caution' as Vicary would later write in his report, calling out as they did so. Eventually they found Tony Smith in the lounge of his home.

He was sitting on the settee. Arms by his sides.

His head was slumped forward.

He was dead.

The police officers stood in a silent semicircle looking at the body. The bloody knee caps, the small, bloody hole in the throat just below the Adam's apple. They saw an empty wallet on the carpet at his feet.

'Robbery gone wrong?' Ainsclough suggested, breaking the silence.

'No . . .' Vicary replied, 'there is no sign of a forced entry. He knew his killer and let him . . . or her into his house. The killer then did the business, helped himself or herself to the contents of his wallet and walked out leaving the door open. Job done.'

'Her?' Ainsclough queried. 'You think a female did this, sir?'

'Small-calibre bullet holes,' Vicary observed. 'A .22, that's a woman's gun. A man's preference would be for a .38. Minimum.'

'A contract killing perhaps?' Ainsclough suggested. 'They like .22's, they're quieter and neater. If you can get close enough to the victim a .22 is the preferred weapon of a contract killer, so I understand anyway.'

'Still don't think so,' Vicary replied. 'Like I said, he knew his killer. And a contract killer wouldn't drill the kneecaps like that. This is personal. Somebody hated him and wanted him to know his time had come, and they disabled him so as to be able to take their time. No, this is very personal . . . and there's an awful lot of hate here. An awful lot of hate.' He paused. 'All right, this is a crime scene; secure it at the front door, please. Whistle up a SOCO team and a pathologist. You know the procedure.'

The pub was called the Empress of India and he chose it because the name appealed to him. He walked into the saloon and saw, as he had expected, that it was occupied by only about half-a-dozen people enjoying an early evening beer. He took the gun from his jacket pocket and shot it into the ceiling, then he shot at the bottles of spirits behind the bar which, as he had hoped, sent the customers rushing for the door and to the safety of the street. It also, as he had also hoped, sent the barmaid running to the back office to make an emergency call whilst the publican, neatly dressed in a blue shirt, dark trousers and a gold watch stood quite courageously, thought the man, at the bar looking at him.

The man walked up to the bar and asked for three pints of strong lager: 'The strongest you've got.' He laid the gun on the top of the bar. 'Don't touch it,' he said in a warm manner. 'It's loaded . . . and you don't want your old dabs on it.'

'Don't worry, mate, I won't.' The publican, a large, clean-shaven man, pulled the first pint and stood it on the bar.

The man picked up the drink and downed it in one go. He put his hand in his pocket and pulled out a wad of ten-pound notes. 'That's for the drink and the damage,' he said. 'He never carried less than one hundred and fifty sovs . . . so that should be enough. Put it out of sight before the cozzers get here; they'll only want to keep it as evidence.'

'I think you're right.' The publican swept up the money and pocketed it. He put two more pints of lager on the bar top. 'You know how the Bill work all right.'

'The armed cozzers have a twelve-minute response time in central London.' The man picked up the second pint. 'Do you think I've got time?'

'Three pints in twelve minutes . . .? A young bloke like you . . .?' The publican nodded. 'Yes, it can be done.'

The young man carried the two pints of lager to the nearest table and sat at it. 'I'm on my way now,' he announced proudly. 'You need some prison time under your belt – you don't get nowhere without prison time. I mean real prison, not youth custody, but real prison . . . like my old man . . . he's in Parkhurst doing a long stretch for armed robbery.'

'Is that right?' The publican rested his two meaty hands on the bar and leaned forward. He no longer felt frightened of the youth.

'It's right.' The youth gulped the beer. 'I've just blown away my grandad. I thought he was all right, all this time I thought he was all right, then my mum, she told me this afternoon . . . she told me why she would never visit him. She told me what he used to do to her when she was a girl . . . I mean, still at school.'

'Oh, yes . . .?' the publican replied calmly.

'Yes, so I got my shooter from where I keep it and I visited him. He let me in, all welcoming like.' Pancras Reiss gulped down more beer as the two-tone police klaxons were heard. 'Reckon that's my transport.' He drained the second glass.

'Reckon it is, reckon you've still got time to do it . . . get three down you,' the publican spoke encouragingly. 'Go on, son . . . go for it.'

'Yes. So I waited until he was sat down then I popped his kneecaps so he knew I was the business, then I told him what I was going to do and why. I never thought I'd see Pestilence so frightened.'

'He's your grandfather? "Pestilence" Smith? The publican spoke as if impressed. '"*The* Pestilence" Smith?'

'Yes.' Pancras Reiss picked up the third pint. 'Do you know him?'

'I pay protection money to him. So, yes, I know him.'

'Not anymore you don't.' Pancras Reiss drank more beer as the klaxons reached the street outside the pub. 'Not anymore you don't pay no protection money, you don't pay it anymore.' He drank more beer. 'Then I popped him in the throat . . . just the once but I knew it would be enough . . . I stood over him until he stopped making gurgling and wheezing sounds . . . but I'll be all right inside, no one is going to carve me up in the showers for icing the man who raped my mother . . . and that is real street cred.'

The two armed officers burst through the door. The publican held up one hand in a gesture of calm. He pointed to the gun on top of the bar as Pancras Reiss stood some ten feet away and finished the third pint.

'There you go,' the publican smiled, 'I told you you could do it.'

The dart thudded into the board. John Shaftoe looked pleased as he strode forward to remove it from the double thirteen slot.

'Good arrow, mate,' his partner said. 'That's the game.' Shaftoe glanced at his wife who sat with other women in the corner in front of a schooner of sherry. She smiled at him and gave him the thumbs-up sign. They were in the tap room of the Noah's Ark on the Old Kent Road in Deptford. They were among their own kind, 'touching base' as they had promised they would.

Friday

G eoff 'the milk' Driscoll turned his float into Lingfield Road and drove past the place where he had found two bodies within twenty-four hours of each other. His eye was drawn to that stretch of pavement with horrific fascination and each time he had past it he could not stop himself from looking at it. He reached the end of Lingfield Road, efficiently placing milk on appropriate steps as he did so. It was Friday, collection day, but at 5.30 a.m. it was still too early to start knocking on doors. From Lingfield Road he turned into Southside Road, and then he saw the body.

It was a youth. A young man lying face up on the pavement, the knife still sticking out of his chest.

Driscoll wondered whether it had been a good move after all? On the sink estate, the Clifton Towers round, he had to deal with folk who didn't pay their milk bill, folk who stole milk from his float when his back was turned. He often came across signs of violence, smashed windows, burnt-out cars, but he had never come across a dead body. But here, in leafy, civilized Wimbledon, he'd found not one, not two, but three.

All in the space of five days.